homebound

homebound

A NOVEL

puja changoiwala

HarperCollins *Publishers* India

First published in India by
HarperCollins *Publishers* 2021
A-75, Sector 57, Noida, Uttar Pradesh 201301, India
www.harpercollins.co.in

2 4 6 8 10 9 7 5 3 1

P-ISBN: 978-93-5489-055-0
E-ISBN: 978-93-5489-063-5

Typeset in 11/14.7 Adobe Caslon Pro at
Manipal Technologies Limited, Manipal

Printed and bound at
Replika Press Pvt. Ltd.

MIX
Paper from responsible sources
FSC® C016779

This book is produced from independently certified FSC® paper to ensure responsible forest management.

For the dreamers,
the seekers,
the fighters,
the survivors,
whom we failed.

'There shine the eyes that only see
  The good I've tried to do;
They think me what I'd like to be;
  They know that I am true.
And whether I have lost my fight
  Or whether I have won,
I find a faith that I've been right
  As soon as day is done.'

—Edgar Albert Guest in his poem, 'Home'

Contents

1

Food, Clothing, Shelter, Internet

16 April 2020
Dear Ms Farah,

It was a fairy dressed in white, the tear-gas bomb. She descended upon the earth with a golden explosion and serenaded it with her confetti—little diamond-like droplets that smelt like spices and burnt like the earth's core.

I watched from inside a sewer, as the beneficiaries of her spell, migrant men, women and children like me, rushed to escape her, the darkness she thrust in their eyes and the fire she lit on their skins. Then, still resolute to enchant, she unleashed her little elves—police officers with wooden batons for magic wands—and the elves did what elves do. They fettered the migrants' wrists with steel bows and ribbons, packed them up in their iron-walled sleigh, and prepared to deliver them to a lower world. The fairy, meanwhile, disappeared, after whitening the air and darkening the ether.

I'm not naïve, Madam Journalist. Even as a fifteen-year-old, I understand that humans of a certain stature must expect a degree of bombing and beating from uniformed goblins. All of us in Mumbai's hundred-square-foot homes know that. That's why, when the cops pounded my father's spine with those blunt blows two days ago, he did not kick up a fuss. When Ma nursed those scarlet contusions with ice, she did not cringe; and when Happy, my little brother, and I saw his haemorrhaged skin turn into a velvety violet, we did not look away. It was predictable, mundane, almost boring.

Unexpected was my father's resolve after the assault: Home. We must return home.

'So when does our charter flight arrive?' mocked Ma. 'National lockdown for the coronavirus, Your Majesty. No trains, buses or cars.'

'We'll walk,' said Baba.

'Do you know how far it is?'

'Nearly nine hundred kilometres. Precisely eight hundred and eighty one.'

'It's dangerous,' argued Ma. 'Heavy police deployment everywhere, day and night. Many have died on the road already.'

'Many haven't. And once we finish this journey, we'll be home.'

'But this *is* home,' I registered my protest.

'No,' asserted my father, too curt for his make. 'This is its mirage.'

Baba is full of mirage analogies. It's because we belong to a small village in the Great Indian Desert of Rajasthan, where the devious sun often sketches mirages, and foolish feet often beg for futile chases. They call it Balhaar, our village, meaning: surrounded by strength, an eponym for the belt of dunes around it. Mounds of sand worthy of every being's indulgence—sculpted by the wind, glommed together by gravity, majestic and sterile, divine and godless.

I'm certain you're fond of the dunes too, ma'am. They're a megahit with tourists, especially the namaste-iterating, nuts-about-the-sun foreigners. Did you know the goras pay up to ₹300 for an hour of camel safari on the dunes? ₹300! At ₹2 a poop, that's 150 or four–

five months of defecation in our slum's communal toilet, or thirty train rides to the city's famous Gateway of India, or a lifetime supply of high-quality, non-dust erasers, or most of my Class Ten textbooks, or all of my father's daily earnings, or all of... You get it.

Ma, Happy and I moved to Mumbai four years ago, three summers after Baba settled here. Today, we're walking back to Rajasthan, looking for the home we once fled, feeding the behemoth of full circles. Although Baba appears foolish for having led us on this expedition of perils through a locked-down state, you must know he's a first-class father. A man with the usual human burdens but the tensile strength of tungsten, who lost his hinges only recently. Let me tell you about that manic moment, ma'am, the one that stole my father's bearings and went on to introduce us to the smoky fairy.

It was a bright, hot morning two days ago, and social distancing had slipped away. I was seated in my home in Dharavi, one of the world's largest slums, when our neighbours started pouring in, at least two dozen of them—mostly daily-wage labourers, who had refused television to save on rent, and families that had their electricity connections severed, as they could not pay the landlords this month. 14 April marked three weeks of the first Covid-19 lockdown in India. Over a billion people sat captive in their homes to dodge an obscure enemy. However, in Dharavi, where India goes to hell, a different, invisible antihero had taken centre stage: fright.

To accommodate the assembly, Baba lifted the children to our two-foot-tall loft, while grown-ups crowded the room. As the kids squeezed and pushed, wrestling for the best view of the television, Father intervened. 'Feet to the wall, heads out of the loft,' he instructed. The children obeyed, now morphed into live shrimps, their bellies pressed on the concrete and chins pushed high. The mystery of space was solved, but with time, the floating heads resumed their pinching and tussling. It was the heat, sweat and some whacked-out stroke of evolution, which was turning the crustaceans into jumpy frogs. Soon, as the clock struck ten, the hullabaloo evanesced. A sudden death.

'And now, we bring to you live, Prime Minister Narendra Modi,' announced the newscaster on the television show *Khabar Garmagaram* (Very Hot News).

With the news anchor's announcement, a tide of excitement hit the frogs. The Prime Minister's recent speeches had brought much joy to the children, comparable with the mirth of summer holidays. The leader, during his first live address about the coronavirus on 19 March, had requested all Indians to clap hands, and clang pots and pans, for five minutes on the upcoming Sunday. The purpose was to express gratitude to our country's virus warriors—the doctors and police officials, the healthcare volunteers and civic staff, the sweepers and sewer divers. On the day of the national chore, Dharavi's children, even the elders, went bonkers banging. Some ran through the streets, the Indian tricolour flying tall in their hands, disturbing the drying laundry. It was as if India had just won a cricket match, and not just any other match, one against Pakistan.

Some ballbusters on TV called the festivity an empty gesture, pointing to the shortage of protective gear for frontline workers and instances of assault on Covid-19 soldiers. However, the majority of India, like Dharavi's narrow alleyways, rejoiced. We banged and we clanged, and we spared no flat surface—pots, pans, dishes, pressure cookers, rolling boards, buckets, walls and bare palms. We played the drums, and we blew whistles and conch shells. We danced, sang Bollywood's top patriotic songs, and blasted speakers at maxed-out decibels. The babies and oldsters were a little annoyed, so were a few birds, but the noise was important.

Two weeks after our stupendous performance, the Prime Minister announced new national homework. 'Listen carefully,' he said. 'On the fifth of April, at nine p.m., turn off all the lights in your homes, stand at your doors or in your balconies, and light candles or diyas, torches or mobile flashlights for nine minutes. I repeat, light candles or diyas, torches or mobile flashlights for nine minutes at nine p.m. on the fifth of April.'

Come assessment day, our locked-down shantytown erupted into a carnival, with warm, golden lights and loud, dazzling fireworks. We burnt diyas with as much oil as we could afford, we lit candles until their wicks burnt out, and we flashed phone lights until the batteries died. It was a spectacle, a Diwali before Diwali, and, as we learnt soon, a divine solution for the ungodly virus.

Television news anchors were also in a festive mood, reporting how India's gentry and glitterati, too, were participating in the coronavirus carnival, lighting gold diyas and scented candles on their private, moon-drenched terraces. There were some other reports too, mostly banter about a possible power outage in the country if all of India shut its lights out at once. However, as many esteemed journalists reported, the experts were exaggerating. The party poopers had overlooked the greater purpose behind the national errand—Sir Prime Minister was activating cosmic energies to defeat the virus. Of course, he was activating. WhatsApp forwards told us that. Wait; let me share one of the top viral messages with you:

The Honourable PM's brilliant numerology:

- *Modiji addressed the nation today, April 5 or 04/05. 4 +5 = 9*
- *The current lockdown ends on April 14. Exactly 9 days to go.*
- *Honourable PM's national address started at 9 am today.*
- *It lasted for 9 minutes.*
- *He asked us to light diyas on April 9 for 9 minutes at 9 pm. So, 9, 9, 9 and 9 x 3 = 27. And 2 + 7 = NINE!!!*

Number 9 stands for Mars, and Mars = light and fire. The Honourable PM is activating energy of the red, angry planet to save us. With a focus on number nine, He is also pleasing all

> *the nine planets and now the whole universe will fight corona. Game over, you yellow virus.*

Eight planets now, I wanted to tell the sender, but I got lost in that rainstorm of instant messages. One text explained how the nationwide luminosities would join forces to become a single beam, which would strike straight at the heart of the coronavirus, thereby murdering it. Another offered that the heat generated from candles and diyas would allow cosmic waves to enter our bodies, thereby creating antibodies against the pathogen. Yet another stated that since the light of candles travels faster than the sound of pots and pans, this time, the round, ugly virus was certain to collapse to its chubby knees. 'Go Corona, Corona Go,' went the triumphant, virtual chants.

Celestial insight aside, some messages enlightened with science and reason. Exhibit A:

> *Coronaviruses cannot survive hot temperatures, as per research by NASA. If 130 candles are lit together, the temperature will rise by nine degrees. Therefore, the corona will die at 9.09 pm on April 5. Masterstroke by Honourable PM!*

I wondered why NASA, a space agency, was researching an epidemiological issue. Perhaps a lot of free time during the lockdown. Or wait, is the virus an alien? I'll have to wait for WhatsApp forwards to confirm.

While the world is grappling with the novel pathogen, Ms Farah, I'm happy to report that India is winning the battle already. After all, we are not just fighting the virus with science, but also on cosmic, religious and mythical planes. Best of all, we have godmen and politicians performing mass prayers for it. Do you remember that guru from Delhi, ma'am? The sadhu with the flex banner, with the image of a rakshasa, and the word 'Corona' stamped across the demon's chest. Dressed in saffron robes, the garlanded godman sprinkled generous amounts of gaumutra or cow urine on the demon's face, chanting, *'Corona, shant ho jaao. Shant ho jaao, corona.'* (Corona, calm down. Calm down, corona.)

Later in the ritual, he offered rice pudding and deep-fried bread to the coronavirus, ordering it to abandon its airs of uppity, as devotees savoured earthen cups filled with cow urine. Then, the sadhu addressed the press: 'I'm toh saying, we must serve gaumutra to every Covid-19 patient, one 240 ml cup per person. Forget corona, cow urine can cure cancer. We're also sending some to President Trump.' I wondered where all the American cows were. I assumed British ones took generous leaks.

To my life, the guru would have remained a televised sample of smelly humour, had he not inspired Ma. Now, she's hard at work to score some cow excrement, especially after a legislator proclaimed that cow pee and potty can boost immunity, even cure the Covid-19 disease. I mean, I understand cows are sacred, ma'am, that some Indian states charge a cow tax, that we have self-appointed cow police, and that beef is banned in our country. The cud-chewing gods are important; the bovine faeces are divine. I understand, yes. I also appreciate that they have a long cultural history, their waste historically used for therapeutic, medicinal and religious purposes, even in cosmetics. I get it all, thank you very much. Still, madam, I cannot eat shit, even if it belongs to a cow. No, no. Holy cow, no.

After the Prime Minister's two enchanting tasks, the children in our home were looking forward to the next one. They wondered which of the coronavirus's five senses they would now annihilate, after we'd destroyed its hearing through the banging and its vision through the lighting. Perhaps, touch—we could rub each other's bodies with coloured powder, as during the festival of Holi, and the virus would die from the sacred, synthetic scrubbing. Or its sense of smell—we could burn effigies of the pathogen, as we do of cricketers when they lose matches, and the powerful pong of burning plastic would neutralize its nose. Or maybe, its sense of taste—we could dive into bacteria-rich rivers, as we do in Mother Ganges, and the contagion would die of the microplastics it swallows.

The Prime Minister, however, disappointed. He gave out no national assignment this time. He did, however, toss a bomb—the lockdown has been extended for another three weeks until 3 May. And that, Madam Journalist, was the moment when my father jumped proper to loony.

As soon as Baba turned the TV off, the crowd inside our home erupted into a clamour. The minors were only dispirited; the seniors, frightened. They listed their many angsts, looking for answers that seemed more elusive than shadows. Some elders were afraid of death. 'Social distancing is an oxymoron in this slum,' said one uncle. 'The virus can catch us at any moment.' 'Yes,' agreed another, 'five dead in Dharavi already, forty-seven others have tested positive.' 'Forget corona,' added a third, 'hunger will beat it in killing us.'

Other grown-ups feared living—'No work, nor money. Our landlord can kick us out any time now'; 'I went to buy rice for my hungry children, and the cops made me do sit-ups'; 'They let you off easy. I was beaten.'

As the fears thickened the air in our home, my dementing father stayed quiet. He left us after a few minutes and returned several hours later. Bruised. Altered.

Minutes after the Prime Minister's new national address, WhatsApp messages started pouring in again. Not those riveting opinions on reality that I mentioned before, but ones that conspire to alter reality, warp lives. Like those recent murders that you reported on, ma'am, only a few hundred kilometres away from Mumbai. Social media messages about prowling child-kidnappers were doing the rounds across the country, but in a small village in Maharashtra, those texts murdered five men. The victims, all wanderers, had offered a cookie to a young girl, so the villagers dragged them for a kilometre, beating them with sticks, stones, bricks and shoes.

I sat before the television, stunned at the power of digital falsities, as a police officer spoke to you and other journalists. 'The mob had swelled to three thousand people,' he had said. 'The crowd was so incensed that it would not let our staff take over the corpses. They wanted to burn the bodies. The mob, as in other such murders in the country, assumed the victims were kidnappers.'

The village's name was Rainpada, but I knew it could easily have been Balhaar. Yet, I assumed that my family and I would never fall for such falsehoods. We were city folks now, I told myself, far from the eccentricities of rural illiteracy. We knew better now, I told myself, but that was soon to change. Minutes after the lockdown's extension, Baba's phone beeped, announcing the arrival of a WhatsApp message, one with a sharply targeted audience—migrant workers in cities, desperate to return to their villages.

> *Just nOw, govt announce spcl trains 4 migrants. Trains n seats limitd. Go 2 ur nearst railway statn & get ur tickets NoW.*

In response, thousands of migrant workers, including Baba, gathered outside railway stations in major metropolises across the country. Their faces covered with handkerchiefs, they balanced their scanty worlds, fitted in two bags, on their heads and shoulders. They rushed to the empty ticket counters, and on to the vacant platforms. They demanded to be ferried home, their strained, raspy voices muddled into a chorus, vocalizing their fear, anguish and despair. Loud, so loud. Unheard.

Nearer home, in Mumbai, the men were beaten. Baba was one of those men. Ma, Happy and I watched the caning live on TV. Uniformed in khaki, the cops wielded the colonial lathi and charged at men with the zest of imperial vainglory. They jumped and squealed, these men, as the sanitized wooden batons landed on their chests, limbs and buttocks. They wailed and pleaded, these men, as the weapon of the Crown gloated over its longevity. They ran and never stopped, these men, as the dance of collective disorder reigned.

Certain that the shower of thumps and thwacks had also drenched our father, Happy almost leapt off the loft, looking for Baba's face in the throng. He could not find him. Worried, he kept calling our father. No answer. The television commentary, meanwhile, ran unabated: 'The situation has been tense for the past two hours. The Mumbai police have had to resort to a lathi-charge, and politicians are appealing to the crowd for peace. Investigators are baffled over the enormous assembly, probing how hundreds of workers managed to gather at one spot. But sources point to a habitual felon: fake news on the internet.'

As I waited for my father to return, I kept thinking about the madness in our digital world, and how it often spills over to our physical life, even overpowers it. I mean, it was a three-sentence message that drove thousands across India to railway stations, crammed together, unmoving, unheeding, blind to the virus, and deaf to their own cries. How does a lie wield that kind of power? As I sat wondering, I remembered an axiom that our computer teacher had shared with us: 'The internet is a lot like our universe,' he had said, 'and like the universe, most of it brims with a dark energy.'

I recollected the teacher's analogy, and his postulate seemed sound: The universe and the internet, both are vast, amorphous and eternally young, with pasts that do not go on forever, but futures that might. The internet functions through a worldwide network of billions of computers, and the universe, a cosmic web of billions of galaxies. The universe has the airless, black blanket of outer space, while the internet has cyberspace, also a province of all civilization, beyond sovereign claims and national appropriations. Nothing can travel faster in the universe than the speed of light, and the web, the information superhighway, has the astonishing speed of data travel. The universe and the internet, both are expanding at spectacular speeds. A dark energy is accelerating the universe's expansion, but we do not know what constitutes that mysterious enigma. A dark energy is also accelerating the internet's growth, and we do know what makes up this black force. It's lies, the internet's dark energy, and what's the internet? A web of lies.

As I sat mulling over the bloody faculties of the internet, I remembered more instances like Rainpada, where the dark energy had evoked the animal in men, making predators out of some and prey out of others. The recollection brought a lump to my throat and I grew afraid for my father. Squeezing my eyes shut, I prayed for his return.

'Let his bones be broken,' I indulged in a rare bargain with God. 'We'll manage. Just send him back, please. I promise I'll deposit ten rupees in your temple every week. I promise I'll bow to every cow and never talk back to my mother again. I promise I'll be a good girl.'

Looking at me kneeling on the floor, my palms joined in prayer, Ma sat beside me. 'Don't worry,' she said, running her fingers through my hair. 'Your father always lives to tell the tale, and he tells it over and over again.'

Ma was right. Baba was a survivor, a talkative one at that. It's just that Mumbai enjoys flirting with death, and as a resident of the city, you, too, make many casual acquaintances with Yamraj, the fire-eyed CEO of Hindu Hell. The city has pushed Baba close to his end many a time, and each time, he emerged in one piece, cheating the god of death and justice, his noose, his mace and even his water buffalo.

For instance, when Baba had just moved to Mumbai, he was staying inside a garment factory that recycled cloth. A short circuit in the meter room led to a fire. Baba and his cohabitants smelt it in time, rushed out of the factory, and escaped the flames that went on to engulf 150 shanties. The raging blaze consumed men, women and children. It ate up homes, businesses and dreams. Baba lived, and he told the tale.

Another time, an LPG cylinder exploded in the bar-and-restaurant where he works as a waiter. The impact of the blast was such that it blew a chef's limbs to smithereens, killing him in an instant. It also led to a fire, causing critical burn injuries to three others. Baba crawled on his belly like a commando, rolling on the floor to smother the flames on his back. Upon reaching a window of the first-floor establishment, he jumped off its ledge. He landed on the ground with a few fractures and burns, and he told the tale.

Minutes turned into hours as we waited for our father, but Ma had managed to keep Happy and me from imagining the worst. She pointed out that news reports did not mention casualties. A storm of blows, a run for one's life, a stampede, yes—but no Yamraj. I felt better. It was no light at the end of the tunnel, just a tunnel-shaped life, but it seemed workable.

After a few more 1000-minute hours, Baba returned. His face was grimy, shirt torn, body bruised, and his tale-telling will lost.

'Why did you go there?' Ma asked him. 'Do you know how worried we were?'

'Give me some water.' Father looked away. 'And turn that TV off.'

After three hours of sleep, Baba woke up with a jolt, now sitting bolt upright, as if right after a nightmare. From his quickened breathing and sweating face, I could tell it was the same dream again. I'd heard him tell Ma about it once. He'd said that he finds himself standing atop a sand-walled void, an enormous emptiness that whirls and whistles like a tornado. He tries to hold on to the breeze, but the very air pushes him into the blank. His body then jerks him awake, saving him from dissolving into that infinite hole.

Fright grips his bones thereafter, and the void continues to dance before his open eyes. Like a wanderer, he keeps peeking into the golden-walled, dark vacuum. Minutes pass before his heart stops with its furious thumping, his pulse slower, and his mind, once again, is able to separate the real from phantasms.

Ma told Baba to inform her when the nightmare revisited, and after a few months, our resident psychoanalyst had a diagnosis: 'You twitch yourself awake when you're stressed or afraid,' deduced Ma. 'It happened when your father started losing his vision to cataracts, and we did not have the money to fix his eyes. It happened when Happy fractured his leg after that crazy goat in Balhaar knocked him down. It kept happening when I wasn't able to find work in our initial days here, and it stopped after your boss employed me as a cook.'

The nightmare had not tormented Baba in a long time, but lately, the abyss had started stirring his dreams again. This evening, however, he did not bother with its aftermath nor waited for his heart to stop quivering. He patted his eyes and pushed the vacuity aside. Paying no heed to the swollen bruises on his spine, he jumped to his feet, wore his shirt, and left home. About an hour later, he returned with Proton Uncle and his family.

Side note: Proton Uncle is Baba's childhood friend from Balhaar, and the two moved to the city together. While his parents named him Jairaj, I call him Proton Uncle because, like protons, the positively charged particles found in atoms, he is too optimistic all the time. Like when Happy slipped and fell face-first on a pile of fresh camel poop. The little boy emerged disgruntled, struggling to get rid of the dung in his mouth. Proton Uncle slapped his back in commendation, saying that camel crap brought luck. I was furious, ma'am, so tempted to make him taste some of that fortune too. While Proton Uncle is this utopian nut, his wife, Bindiya Aunty, is his antonym. A non-stop moaner, she whines and bleats wherever she goes, finding faults in everything, including babies, flowers and freedom. She, hence, is Electron Aunty. Their son, Sameer, meanwhile, is as old as I am, scores the same grades as me, but thinks he's much smarter than me. He's Neutron Sameer. He has no electric charge and is capable of nothing.

'We must leave for Balhaar,' Baba announced upon returning, with Uncle nodding in agreement—brisk nods, urgent.

'Why do you keep disappearing without a word?' Ma was annoyed.

'I was figuring a few things out,' he answered. 'Now start packing.'

'But why?'

'It's not just us, Bela,' said Baba, calling Ma by her name, as opposed to the usual 'Happy *ki amma*' (Happy's mother). The address was to accentuate the gravity of his words. 'Four out of five people in this slum haven't received their March wages. Our boss has not answered his phone in ten days. I'm sure he does not intend to pay us, and with these lockdowns, I do not know when we'll start working again. Meanwhile, we're losing five grand on rent every month.'

'But we'd worked during the first three weeks of March. He should clear those dues,' said Ma.

'He won't. They announced the lockdown in the last week of March, at a four-hour notice. Many of these employers have gotten away without paying their staff for that month.'

Soon after the state announced the first national lockdown, Baba called the bar owner, who informed that the establishment, too, would remain shut. He promised to pay our parents once the tavern reopened. My father, like tens of thousands of workers in Dharavi, was hoping to resume work after the restrictions eased. The lockdown, however, stretched, turning into the void in Father's nightmares—bleak, boundless and ominous.

'I spoke to our landlord,' said Proton Uncle. 'He promised to return our refundable deposits of five thousand rupees if we leave tomorrow. He'll deduct half the amount towards the rent for this month, but we'll still have twenty-five hundred per family.'

'Excellent,' Baba exclaimed. 'Get the deposit from him first thing tomorrow, and I'll see if I can find our boss's home.'

He then turned to our mother. 'Have you cached any cash?'

Baba knew that Ma, an illicit hoarder, would have some notes tucked away somewhere. Back in 2016, a few months after we moved to Mumbai, the government announced demonetization, suddenly retiring currency notes of ₹500 and ₹1000, issuing new ones. The motive was to take counterfeit notes off the Indian bazaars and neutralize the country's shadow economy, but the greatest triumph of the intervention was observed in our home. That morning, Ma had been badgering Baba for not handing her enough cash to run the household, how she always fell short when buying essentials. Come evening, after the epoch-making announcement, Mother dug into a few pillowcases and returned with three ₹500 notes.

'Get these exchanged for new ones,' she told Baba. 'And don't ask questions.'

Father laughed. He knew she wasn't the only one. As reported in the news, the government's move had busted the underground economies of many Indian homes, compelling homemakers to divulge their black money—the cash they secretly set aside from their monthly household budgets. I do not know if demonetization fixed our economy, ma'am, but it did expose Ma and her criminal liquidity.

'Are you sure this is all?' Baba asked Ma after she handed him ₹900 in cash. 'We have to go all the way to Balhaar. If you're hoarding any more cash, my blossom, please surrender.'

'Okay,' Ma gave in, and returned with a few more notes, taking her tainted wealth–count to ₹1300.

Proton Uncle made the same enquiry with Electron Aunty, and was happy to learn that she, too, had swindled 'around eleven hundred, give or take'. The men made their calculations and announced their final numbers: ₹6400 with Baba, ₹6900 with Proton Uncle, including our refundable deposits of ₹2500 each.

'Now, we can either use this money to stay in Mumbai for another month, or we can use it to go back home,' said Baba. 'If we stay, we face four threats—we'll soon run out of cash as we have no income, and we'll be thrown to the street when we miss rent. We'll die starving on that street, and if life still remains in us, the virus will devour it. That's unemployment, homelessness, starvation and death. Balhaar, meanwhile, poses only one danger for now: loss of work.'

'And even if we manage cash by borrowing it from lenders, we cannot leave home to buy essentials,' said Proton Uncle. 'The cops have been reckless with the lathi lately, especially with the mounting infections in Dharavi. One lawmaker also suggested that officers must "shoot the traitors" who violate the lockdown. A cash reward for every bullet.'

'How much cash?' asked Sameer, the simpleton.

'How does that matter?' I answered.

'Fifty-one hundred rupees per bullet,' said Baba. 'But that's not the point here. The point is that borrowing money isn't an option either. I asked already. With so many people in need, the lenders have tripled the interest rates. A bloody debt-trap.'

'What about the children's school?' asked Ma, voicing my greatest worry. 'Meher and Sameer have to appear for their geography exam soon. They've written all their Class Ten papers, only one remains.'

'Yes, please, this is the most important year of my academic life,' I pleaded with my father. 'They've postponed our geography paper because of the pandemic, but they will conduct the examination soon, and I must be here to appear for it. If not, the past ten years of my life will turn to waste.'

As you might know, ma'am, these state-level examinations determine the course of all student careers in our country, whether they empty into the gutter, or join forces with the sea, become the ocean. These Class Ten examinations were a privilege I'd earned through our passage to Mumbai. Back in Balhaar, my school was a semi-concrete structure with seven rooms for seven grades. The government-run school in Mumbai, meanwhile, is a four-storey building. Its classrooms have desks, benches and walls enlivened with charts and diagrams. Of course, the building is ancient, and rainwater seeps into our classrooms through its cracked ceilings. It also floods the playground. However, unlike Balhaar, this school is cattle-free, there are as many girls in my class as boys, and teachers show up every day.

When we moved to Mumbai, I knew that schooling was the greatest boon of our shift to this city, one that established me as the most educated person at home. I wanted to write my last paper, go to college and become the first graduate in my family. I wanted to be the first one to learn English and computers, and the first to triumph over this intergenerational legacy of rancid scarcity.

'Education can wait, Meher,' said Baba, addressing me by my official name instead of the usual Gudiya or doll. The same purpose, accentuating the gravity of our patriarch's words. 'We do not know when schools will reopen. Meanwhile, many, many people here are dying from the new disease. Staying in Dharavi would be like seeking shelter in a lion's den, drinking from the oasis in a mirage.'

'But Balhaar has no schooling beyond Grade Seven and the nearest college is several hours away,' I persisted. 'Leaving Mumbai would mean quitting education.'

'It won't,' Baba asserted with a finality, avoiding my gaze.

'Plus, our parents are back home,' Proton Uncle bolstered my father's madness. 'The virus hasn't reached Balhaar yet. When it does, we must be there to take care of them.'

As the men counted more reasons to justify our illegal escape from Mumbai, Electron Aunty weighed in with negatives. 'We will always be outsiders in this city,' she droned. 'For people in this jungle, families like ours are good enough to build their subways and skyscrapers, but not good enough to deserve decent homes, paid leaves, even pending wages. You're right. We must leave. But what if we die on the road?'

'We won't,' said Baba. 'Aren't you watching the news? Millions are walking home already. They are saying that the Covid-19 exodus in India could be bigger than the one after our country's violent partition in 1947. At the time, migrant caravans were crossing the new boundaries between India and Pakistan, and over ten million were displaced.'

'Yes, and the same news reports have also confirmed that death, too, is walking with the migrants,' countered Electron Aunty.

Responding to our pensive silence, she turned her eyes to the ceiling: 'Oh dear Lord, why have you landed us between these two fires, this chasm where the earth and sky are closing in? What did we do to deserve this? What did we do wrong?'

Proton Uncle swooped in, now speaking for the ceiling. 'Many like us, who've fled the cities in the past few weeks, have reached home,' he said. 'A few died, but we must remain positive, focus on numbers that serve us.'

As the elders spoke, I had an idea—Twitter Uncle. For a non-refundable fee of ₹300 per post, Twitter Uncle puts up people's grievances on the micro-blogging site, tagging relevant authorities, egalitarian elites and armchair revolutionaries. Six out of ten times, he gets the job done. His modus operandi is simple: post the problem with pictures; the good, angry folks on social media will share and reshare it, and authorities will be compelled to act. The man has had police complaints registered this way, got potholes fixed, and even had civic officials demolish a shaky building once. Indian authorities, he says, respond either to hard cash, or to harsh online criticism, and with his Twitter enterprise, he is cashing in on the whole Digital India fracas—no food but broadband, no shelter but mobile phones, no clothing but 4G internet.

'Your Twitter Uncle is useless,' Baba rejected my idea as soon as he heard it. 'Many migrants have paid him already; he got no response. And his pandemic rate is five hundred per post.'

With no further objections to their plan, Baba and Proton Uncle discussed the means of our journey to Balhaar. Trains, buses and cars were unavailable during the lockdown, so Uncle suggested that we use second-hand bicycles. 'It's fifteen hundred rupees per bike,' he said. 'The shopkeeper will part with six cycles for about seven to eight thousand. We can ride one each, and Happy can go pillion.'

'Oye,' said Electron Aunty, 'I don't know how to ride a bicycle-vicycle.'

'Even I don't, but we can learn,' offered Ma.

'There's no time for that,' said Baba. 'And it won't be safe on the highway.'

'What about freight trucks?' Proton Uncle had a new idea. 'Even during the lockdown, they've been carting agro and food products to Mumbai from Rajasthan. They're returning empty, and their drivers charge three thousand rupees for every person crammed in their cargo space.'

'That's four times our regular train fare and twenty-one grand for the seven of us.' Baba was quick to calculate. 'No, we cannot afford trucks.'

'So we walk,' concluded Uncle.

'We walk,' agreed Father. 'We'll start the day after tomorrow. Let's stay tomorrow to pack our things, get our deposits from the landlord, and look for our boss. We should also rest before we start walking.'

'Let's only leave when it's dark, okay?' added Electron Aunty. 'I don't want to face the cops.'

After the family of atomic elements left, Ma continued to voice her concerns, and my father, like a legit lunatic, kept defending his insanity. If Happy got tired walking, Baba would carry him on his shoulders. If the sun showed no mercy, we would find a big tree with ample shade. No, the cops will not apprehend us, as we would walk through the by-lanes and arterial roads. No, we will not go hungry, as bananas—the bread of Indian penury—are available everywhere. I'm so tired of bananas, Ms Farah. My father is the universal brand ambassador of the fruit, and he makes us have two every day, reiterating its digestive, nutritious and cardiac benefits.

Daddy Bananas thinks we're stupid, that we don't know that the monkey-treat, both cheap and filling, is the star food of breadline residents.

When we appeared unconvinced with Baba's logics and logistics, he continued, 'See, we don't have to walk all the way. We can hitchhike, or hire one of those freight trucks. They won't ask for as much money once we're out of this extortionate city. And even if we do have to walk, at just sixty kilometres over twelve hours each day, we'll cover nine hundred in fifteen days. So fast, so easy.'

'Okay.' Ma gave in, closed her eyes, murmured a prayer, and enlisted a new set of demands for the Almighty. 'Okay.'

Although Ma was convinced, I wasn't ready for this anticlimactic end to my alliance with Mumbai. This city was a land that no one had promised us, ma'am. Yet, ever since we moved here, everything in my life has been happy, lucky, hunky and dory, until the unannounced arrival of this novel coronavirus. Now, like the migrant workers in your news reports, we too are walking up the spine of India, looking for our home. I'm writing this letter, hoping that you would report on our expedition as well. It will keep this journey from robbing us of its destination, and it will ensure we remain safe on this road infested with armed elves and ash-white fairies.

Sincerely yours,
Meher Gopal Balhaari
Waiting near the exit to Mumbai

2

Slumgods

16 April 2020
Dear Ms Farah,

As we left Dharavi at 3.30 a.m. this morning, my grandma's words rang in my ears: No good happens after midnight. It's the hour of the dead, when angels sleep in their white robes and demons in black capes take over the world. The secret to the universe, says Dadi, lies in those colours—black and white. She did not engineer the philosophy, of course not. That glory rests with the millennia of human civilization, moving indomitably through time and space, shaping the world with their evolutionary wisdom—white is pure and black, occult.

Dadi, so you're warned, is the doyen of killjoys, but she insists that she's the enlightened one, a domesticator of the esoteric, whose 'state-of-the-art life skills' have revealed the world's greatest secret to her. Our astute ancestors and contemporary sapiens know something, she believes, the reason why they've demonized black and sanctified white. For instance, black is the colour of death, worn by mourners at funerals in many cultures, while priests perform their prayers in white. Black amulets are so malicious that they can stave off the evilest of evils, and the sacred thread that men wear around their torsos, white. It's doom if a black cat crosses one's path, while a white dove symbolizes peace. People get blacklisted and end up in black books if they blunder, and white lies are polite. The black market is illicit, while white-collar represents the respected suit-and-tie workers. There are black sheep of the world, and their saviours, white knights.

'It's an age-old world order, evident across realms—life and death, religion and sorcery, vocation and emotion, virtues and vices, and animals and humans,' explained Dadi. 'That's why the whites are still the overlords of the world, much after the British ruled us for two hundred years. The darker-skinned, meanwhile, still find themselves at a disadvantage. Go on now; put some of that turmeric paste on your face. White skin also begets richer in-laws.'

See, I told you, d-o-y-e-n of killjoys.

The British rule in India ended over seven decades ago, and yet, it often crops up in conversations, still immortalized in popular culture. I've inferred it's because the past never passes, that we study history only because we cannot bear to wipe the slate clean, and that historians are gatekeepers of nostalgia, helping us cage our bygones. As we left Dharavi today, I too attempted to abduct our past, clicking pictures of our empty home, trying to hold it hostage in Baba's phone. I also likened our long march to a historic walk from India's yore: Mahatma Gandhi's Salt March, exactly ninety years ago.

It was March 1930. Clad in a homespun white shawl and dhoti, armed with a walking stick, the Mahatma set out for the 386-kilometre walk from his religious retreat in Gujarat. His purpose: a non-violent protest against the East India Company's lucrative monopoly on salt.

The British Raj's Salt Act, which criminalized salt production and sale, burdened every Indian, compelling them to buy the imported mineral at exorbitant, heavily taxed prices.

Even before the Salt March commenced, thousands thronged Gandhiji's ashram in anticipation of the dramatic events that lay ahead. When protestors reached the Arabian Sea in a coastal town twenty-four days later, the group had swelled to 50,000. Then, as the world watched, the Mahatma committed his symbolic crime—he lifted a lump of salt-rich mud from the beach and held it aloft in triumph. The gesture signified that he had breached the salt law, defied the Crown.

'With this,' the Great Soul announced, 'I am shaking the foundations of the British Empire.'

Pompous, no? It worked! I studied it two years ago; Class Eight history. There was something peculiar about the image of the old, underweight Mahatma that stirred my imagination, and evidently, that of the entire planet. Millions around the world watched the black-and-white reels, as they broadcasted the nationalist leading his three kilometre–long trail of protesters. Mass civil disobedience swept the country, government officials resigned from their posts, and aroused Indians went about violating the Salt Act. 60,000 were thrown behind bars, including the Father of the Nation.

'It was one of the greatest walks in world history. It rattled our rulers, drew massive international interest, and *Time* magazine named Gandhiji as Man of the Year,' our history teacher proclaimed as we wondered about the significance of the foreign publication. 'The walk also inspired the likes of Martin Luther King Jr during America's civil rights movement in the sixties.'

When Baba locked the door of our Mumbai home, I thought about Gandhiji and the fears that might have plagued his mind, as he left his ashram for the celebrated walk. There were many terrible possibilities—cops could tan his hide, hunger could kill him on the way, the summer sun could beat his spirit, fatigue could defeat his body, and/or he could end up in prison. These were the exact fears that also tormented my being, only three differences:

1. We had a bonus adversary: the virus.
2. Our destination was almost thrice as far as Bapu's.
3. The Mahatma wanted to attract attention; we intended to avoid it.

'Shhh,' said Baba, as Proton Uncle and his family walked out of their shanty. 'Shhhhh.'

'Relax,' said Uncle. 'Even the strays are snoring.'

'I don't have a good feeling about this,' Electron Aunty started. 'How much food do you have? Ours won't last beyond three meals.'

'Shhh,' said Happy. 'You can have my bananas.'

The no-noise rule, along with our masks, made me feel like a thief. Baba's friend, a tailor in our slum, had given us the masks without charge. The man, who used to sew cloth bags, had turned into a business mogul overnight. With mask sales running into the thousands, his home-based industrial unit runs round the clock. He also employs neighbouring aunties, outsourcing the stitching for ₹2 apiece. Some complain that the micro-entrepreneur's product is substandard. They say his sewing machines aren't disinfected, that he follows no sterilization protocols and that his home is unhygienic. I say shut up. Do you know how much masks cost, ma'am? ₹30, ₹50, ₹70, ₹150, even ₹400. Tailor Uncle, meanwhile, parts with one for ₹15. If you purchase in bulk, anything upward of 2000 pieces, he slashes his price down to ₹8. So what if his masks don't meet the basic safety standards? They're washable, and more efficient than the alternatives other skint Indians are using—leaves fastened around their mouths and noses, loose ends of saris, and tattered scarves and towels.

As if leaving on an undercover mission, Baba discreetly turned on the torchlight of his cell phone. The glare helped us overleap the occasional rodent and many broken tiles on the floor, as we walked through Dharavi's alleyways, one elongated dungeon making way for another. The previous night, the men had drawn out our escape strategy—we would walk through the maze of our ghetto, avoiding patrolling officers on the road, until we reach the furthest end of the slum. There on, we would take the highway, and in just 900 kilometres, we would be home.

As plotted, our group of seven was travelling light: clothes, food, water and documents. I managed to smuggle some notebooks and my favourite gel pen too. We had a mini, second-hand refrigerator that Baba sold to a family for ₹1000 before we left, taking our wealth up to ₹7400. Father did not tell the buyer of our secret journey, just that he needed money. Our remaining world was too cheap for sale, so we abandoned it. It included my old schoolbooks, my drawings, a few storybooks, some gifts, my school uniforms, even my art—lentil necklaces, embroidered pillow covers and a photo frame embellished with chickpeas.

'This isn't fair,' I told Baba. 'These things are important to me.'

'Gudiya, how will you make room for the new if you don't get rid of the old?' answered Baba, throwing one of his homespun dictums at me. 'It's baggage from your past, beta, it'll weigh you down.'

'I'm fifteen, Baba. I like my past. And I'm not throwing these things. I'll store them with a friend.'

'You cannot tell your friends that we're leaving. No one can know.'

'So... I don't get to say goodbye?' I asked, thinking of my best friend, Ira.

I knew she would be pissed if I left without seeing her. Ira and I, we share a school, a classroom and a slum. We share our notes, our clothes and our dreams. Our favourite subject is the same: science, because it comes closest to magic and because it's the only antidote to magic. Our favourite teacher is the same, our science instructor, Ms Vaz, and so is our favourite scientist, Missile Man, A.P.J. Abdul Kalam. We wear matching earrings that we bought on a local train, make greeting cards for each other's birthdays, and we don't let one evening pass without strolling by the Mithi River near our slum.

'What good are goodbyes anyway?' Baba responded. 'Unhappy endings keep the hearts hooked.'

'Enough with those one-liners,' Ma intervened. 'A little stress and you start talking like those doped-out grandpas in our village square. Now, tell me, do you want me to pack these boots?'

'No,' said Baba, hugging the pair before letting them go.

Baba bought those shoes just before he moved to Mumbai. He used them for six years, sewing and resewing the torn parts. He was proud of the damages. They reminded him of where he came from, especially now that he was happy as a pup with two tails, having won over Mumbai. His unyielding farmland in Balhaar was no more a concern, the agricultural distress that once tore him was history, and so were his thoughts of suicide. He was a winner now, a smiler now, and those shoes, those resilient shoes had walked with him as he crossed over. The boots, however, lost their will to resurrect last year, and although father bought a new pair, he refused to get rid of this old one. He said he would revisit it when he achieved his biggest dream—a Chinese food stall in the Dharavi market; perhaps, even momos, who knows? Despite their intimate relationship, I was surprised that Baba was letting the shoes go. He seemed to *believe* that Mumbai was baggage.

'What about the gods?' asked Ma, pointing to the five bronze figurines sitting atop a plastic stool, her makeshift shrine. 'Do you want me to abandon the gods too?'

'Take any two,' said Baba. 'They're heavy.'

Ma murmured under her breath, inaudible but unmistakably vexed. She wasn't happy about renouncing her material past either, especially the curtain she sewed for our home, her cutlery, her boxes and containers, her bedsheets, and the sartorial emancipation she found in this city—her jeans, trousers, tops and tunics. Happy, meanwhile, was happy to be indifferent.

'Just keep a knife and a few forks handy,' added father. 'In case there's trouble.'

We walked in a single line through Dharavi's sinuous lanes, and I tried to memorize the place. I realized I had developed a slow, stable friendship with our shantytown. When I first walked in, I was unimpressed by its little homes and little lives. There were no warm fuzzies, not one. Mumbai's celebrated skyscrapers had disappeared as soon as we entered the ghetto, giving way to an endless warren of tiny alleyways. Cramped, boxlike homes sat on top of each other, some with concrete roofs, and others with blue tarpaulin. The fuggy homes were abuzz with shrieking television sets, and the air tasted metallic with fumes from nearby factories. The sky, meanwhile, sagged under the weight of entangled wires, many transporting stolen electricity from the street pylon. At that first glance, our favela had looked like a many-hued maze to me, a specimen of disturbing resilience.

Over four years, however, Dharavi and I grew close. The slum is not a conventional beauty, the world knows that, but what it does not know is that everyone here speaks the same language. Not Hindi, Marathi, Tamil or Telugu, but the language of people who know what it's like to leave their homes, falter, mend, learn, experience and evolve. Now that we are returning to Balhaar, Ms Farah, I think I will feel lost in my village, more than I ever did in this alien ghetto.

Hordes of narrow lanes later, our group approached an exit to the slum, where we encountered our first hurdle: a police officer seated on a step stool. He seemed to be looking away from us, towards the road.

As soon as he spotted the cop, Baba, who was leading our party, froze, and a sleepy Happy bumped into his back. Father turned around, and made a circle with his forefinger, indicating that we too must turn.

'Pandu,' he whispered the derogatory slang for cops. 'Light steps, light breaths.'

Goggle-eyed and tongue-tied, Baba kept pounding his lips with his forefinger, reiterating his call for silence. Even the slightest sound could attract the cop's attention. Nights in Dharavi are quieter than the rest of the world, perhaps because of its robust orchestra during the day—the crackling of fried food, the whirring of sewing machines, the cacophony of recycling units, the clucking of chickens, the quibbles and squabbles of children, the tinkering of pots, and the bargaining with street vendors. Languages blend into each other, and as you cross lanes, you feel like you're moving across a multiverse.

Baba was afraid because if the cop spotted us, he would send us back to our hovel. Worse, there would be a beating. As our party inched away from the exit to find another one, we heard a snore. It was the policeman, asleep. Our group turned around and started walking towards the officer. Once we were close enough, I saw that his large, protruding belly heaved in perfect rhythm with his snores, moving up and down, and down and up, like a planet waiting to break free from his stretched shirt. Although he had covered his mouth with a mask, I could see his lips quiver with his wheezes. Mosquitoes played on his nose, and even in that deep sleep, he struggled to balance his ample posterior on that tiny, backless stool.

Baba noticed that the police officer had occupied more than half of the three-foot-wide passage, narrowing it further. Hence, he pulled the luggage down from his shoulders and held the bags in his hands. He turned to his side and moved past the cop as quietly as he could. One after the other, we followed him—our backs to the wall, our hearts hammering, and our breaths missing. Then, as we left our home, we ran.

A tight-lipped moment informed me that my life was about to change. It wasn't the decision that preceded this instant, nor the preparation that led up to it, or the awareness that it was to arrive. Despite all that sentience, this moment showed up as an unexpected thunderbolt, its roaring lightning conversing with me, but with limited lexis. It announced a change in the course of my life, but not whether it would serve me or shatter me. It varnished my skin with a coarse uncertainty, and it turned my heart attentive, my mind soft.

The thunderbolt arrived as we hid behind a bus parked on the road outside Dharavi. My backpack felt heavier, and soon, I realized it was my body, reacting to the bitter, bitter medicine of a new reality, a snide chemical robbing me of my alleged disease, my yesterday. I looked around, scanning my family's face, searching for the gloom of abandoning our home, but it did not show. They were all busy hiding their bodies, oblivious to the lightning bolt, as if it hadn't just torn up the skies.

As we crouched behind that bus, my mind wandered to our first day in Dharavi, a summer afternoon four years ago. It was a sixteen-hour journey from Rajasthan, the first train ride of my eleven years. I had stayed up during most of the journey, watching the villages, towns and cities, the day and night of their homes, fields and factories, waving at sleepy strangers on railway platforms, inhaling the forests, streams and rivers that I'd only seen on celluloid, and galloping with a bright cheer, the exhilaration of discovery.

As soon as we saw Baba after alighting from the train, Happy jumped at him, and I wrapped my arms around him. Ma held back. It was too 'advanced' for her, the public embracing, too 'forward'. She smiled coyly, stealing glimpses of his face. We were seeing Baba after two years. He hadn't visited us, as he was saving for our move to Mumbai. Apart from the train tickets, we would also need money for our expenses until Ma found work.

'Let's go to the beach,' I told Baba as soon as we broke the hug. To me, the beach was one of the most attractive features of our shift to Mumbai. It's the same for everyone in the desert—the sea is a dream, and the dream is the sea.

'It was a long journey for you, Gudiya,' he replied. 'You must rest for a while. I'll take you tomorrow.'

As we walked towards the station's exit, I noticed that the railway platform had as many people as all of Balhaar, perhaps more. However, unlike our village, they moved about each other without exchanging courtesy smiles or acknowledging nods. They were busy, those people, all of them—the human mules shouldering travellers' luggage, teenaged boys selling tea, men hawking fried snacks, chips and water, and passengers, who were rushing in and out of the station with the urgency of an imminent bomb explosion. To be honest, Madam Journalist, I was a little scared at that platform. Mumbai's busy railway stations, as you're aware, are pet targets for terrorists. That way, Balhaar is safer. No one bombs it.

During our forty-minute bus ride home, I sat by the window with five-year-old Happy on my lap. We clutched the side rails and watched the passing city of iron and ironies—the slums and skyscrapers, the ritzy cars and bullock carts, the men in suits and those in rags—all in one frame, as if a mystical land of lunatics, oblivious to the earthly habits of caste and creed. The television images of my dream city came alive, and I felt a strange connection with the metropolis in those first few minutes. Over time, I've realized that Mumbai tends to have that effect on people. It has that bad-boy charm.

The bus dropped us outside a cake shop in Dharavi. Happy and I raced to open its door, and a whiff of cold air rushed at us. It was the air conditioner, like winter caged in a box. We gawked at the display of chocolate-draped cakes and sugar-laced pastries. Our noses brimmed with the aroma of fresh cookies, and the air tasted better than anything we had ever swallowed.

While our eyes stayed glued to the confectionaries, the baker smiled and Baba's forehead creased. I could tell my father was wondering about the cost—the dilemma of a buyer who prays for clear price tags. It was understandable. Refusing a purchase after knowing its price tells strangers of one's limited means, even their handicapped ends. The depth of one's pockets, I'm told, should be a secret, including the holes at its bottom.

'How much?' Baba asked, almost afraid, pointing at a Black Forest pastry. It had the perfect white-cream frosting, a scarlet cherry, and layers of rich chocolate drizzled with more chocolate.

'Twenty rupees,' said the baker.

'Okay. One, please.'

We devoured the pastry within seconds and started walking home. Our slum looked spirited, wreathed with pockmarked roads and aged buildings under reparation and re-reparation. Rectangular flowerpots painted with the Indian tricolour divided the four-lane road into equal halves. Their plants, however, were missing, replaced by colourful laundry of slum dwellers. As we walked, I noticed that everything in Dharavi was selling something. There were advertisements on walls, auto-rickshaws, downed shutters and loaders' carts, peddling a host of items—fertility pills, private tuitions, job openings and pest-control services. Every ad signified a dream, and every dream seemed to be on offer.

As soon as Baba opened the purple wooden door to our shanty, I wondered where the rest of our home was. It was a 100-square-foot space, Ms Farah—a tin with bright yellow walls. I was disappointed. Although our home in Balhaar cannot boast of concrete, it is spacious, with three rooms divided by mud walls. We also have a small courtyard. In one of its corners, Baba built a toilet with the city money a few years ago. Our grandparents would not let him have it inside the house. 'Can't crap where you eat,' they had said. The other end of the courtyard, meanwhile, houses our animals:

1. Two goats: Salman and Shah Rukh, who always squabble with each other, named after Bollywood superstars.
2. One sheep: Calm and gentle, named Sachin after the Master Blaster of India, Sachin Tendulkar.

3. One sacred cow: Vishnu, labelled after a god because Grandma would have it no other way.
4. One stray dog: Mirchi, named after chilli powder for his red-orange fur.

Having grown up in that airy house, I was upset that our Mumbai one could barely accommodate our luggage. Polythene bags hung from hooks in the walls to create storage opportunities. The kitchen, living room, bedroom, were all one—the gas stove lounged in the bedroom, and an old chest lived in the kitchen. To create the illusion of space, the innovative landlord had divided the shanty's length into two. The overstretched loft hung low, and Baba announced that the mezzanine floor was Happy's room and mine.

This isn't a room, I wanted to say. *This is its mirage.*

I kept mum. Happy, who was on a sugar high, gambolled around the place, too peppy to care about the corrugated shack. Ma, the liar, took centre stage.

'It's beautiful,' she said.

Baba smiled. I did not.

I kept scrutinizing our new home. Since the loft covered most of the ceiling, the house did not have a fan, except for a small one that sat on the floor, next to a rolled mattress. A piece of rag covered the window and the ground was made of grey, rectangular tiles, stiff like the ones on pavements. A five-foot iron closet occupied one corner, with a television set sitting atop it. Ma and Baba would have to strain their necks to watch TV, but Happy and I would have the perfect view from our 'room'. I was pleased.

'Most homes in Dharavi have television sets,' Baba boasted. 'More satellite TVs than all of Balhaar, plus ten neighbouring villages.'

'What about the toilet-bathroom?' I asked.

'There's one nearby, I'll show you,' he said. 'Carry coins when you go. One rupee for number one, two for number two.'

As promised, Baba took us to the beach the following evening, and the sea lived up to its hysteria in my fancies. It had the innate ironies of Balhaar's dunes. It was both alluring and intimidating, its waters both soothing and deceiving. As soon as I saw the sea, I wanted to lose the shore, dance with the waves and rush to the horizon, where the skies kissed the waters. Grinning at the thought, I spread my arms, and as the wind blew through me, I heard her voice. The unfamiliar sea sounded a lot like my desert, and it spoke the same language. It told me of its travels, its adventures, and it asked me who I was. As we exchanged our stories, I realized that the desert and the sea can cull out one's darkest secrets, one's deepest desires, and one's wildest dreams, like mine at the time, of a desert by the sea.

As I hid behind that bus outside Dharavi, thanking Mumbai for turning our saga into a fairy tale, albeit a low-budget one, Baba phoned Om Uncle, the only dependable friend that the city had lent him. Happy and I call him Candy Kaka, for he never met us without a treat, always winning us over with sweetmeats in flavours like orange, mango, tamarind, cardamom and coffee.

A construction labourer, Candy Kaka also belonged to Rajasthan, a tribal village in its southern region, and he moved to Mumbai as an adolescent fourteen years ago. At the time, he had a populated family back home—grandparents, parents, four siblings, including three sisters awaiting capital investment for their weddings and working capital for their marriages. He dropped out of school to assist his landless father when he was twelve, earning ₹100 a day as a raw farmhand.

As the boy planted, cultivated and harvested, operating tools and machinery with gifted ease, his father decided to cash in on his strength. He forged his son's birth certificate to prove he was an adult and packed him off to the urban wild when he was fifteen. Soon, Candy Kaka found work as most day labourers in Mumbai do—sitting for sale in labour markets, milling about motley groups on road pavements, and thronging city squares to lure contractors. With his tall, brawny frame, he was a popular pick at the labourer's corner, called 'mazdoor naka' in local parlance.

Accompanied by unskilled and semi-skilled daily-wage labourers, including construction workers, masons, painters, helpers, loaders and tile polishers, Candy Kaka would reach the pavement in our nearest labour market at seven each morning. Dressed in frayed trousers and a threadbare shirt, he would smoke his bidis and sip on tiny cups of tea. His eyes would scan the faces of pedestrians for prospective bosses, and as soon as he spotted one, he would take off his shirt. He had to beat hundreds of other labourers at the market, and he believed that his broad, hairy naked chest could help him with it. The days the contractors pointed their beckoning finger at him, usually twenty-four times a month, he would make ₹350 to ₹500 per eight hours, melting at construction sites across the city.

Candy Kaka was doing well. He got all his sisters married, and was still sending ₹5000 home each month. He, however, decided to return to Rajasthan after the labourer's corner recently turned into a beggar's junction. Despite the Covid-19 curbs, Kaka would walk to mazdoor nakas across the city, hoping to find work, only to return with testimonies of assault from armed men in khaki uniforms. As he could no longer afford to pay rent, his landlord drove him out, and he moved to a space offered by a local sweatshop owner, surviving off khichri from charities. With the state extending the lockdown further, there was no hope for the labour market's revival soon. Candy Kaka, therefore, had to start walking home. He was a day ahead of us, having left with seven other migrants from his village yesterday.

'We're out of Dharavi,' Baba told Kaka over the phone. 'Eastern or Western?'

'I took the Eastern Express Highway,' he answered. 'It's safer. The police have set up many checks and blockades on the western exit to the city.'

'Where have you reached?'

'Vasai, almost.'

'Only fifty kilometres in twenty-four hours?'

'The cops caught us, yaar.'

'Where? On Eastern?'

'Yes,' said Candy Kaka. 'But I'll tell you the details later. Phone battery is crucial.'

Before Baba could disconnect, Kaka added, 'Call me when you're about to reach the Mulund check post, twenty kilometres from Dharavi. You'll see the orange-red edifice from at least five hundred metres away. It has heavy police deployment and it is where the cops caught us. I'll arrange for you to get past it.'

Baba did not tell us about the cop cavalcade that awaited us at the exit to Mumbai. Ignorant of the threat, we started walking, passing by the padlocked doors and downed shutters of Dharavi's stores, workshops and factories. The railway station and the bus depot, the busiest areas around our slum at every hour, lay despondent. Stray dogs slept on pavements and atop parked cars. Some even lounged in the middle of the roads, having observed the recent peace of the deserted, locked-down streets.

As we moved further towards the highway, I noticed that the canines morphed into men, women and children, asleep on sidewalks and handcarts, under bridges and by open gutters, on hard stone and worn bedding rolls. Their bodies dissolved in the summer heat, and their few belongings lay next to them, tied by fragile threads to their wrists. Soiled cloths and homemade masks covered their faces, more to evade the stench of the ageing garbage around them. As I moved past those people, I noticed that a sour silence had swathed Mumbai, as if the city were sentenced to a still gloom, forced to mourn those humans and their hard lives.

We treaded along the access road to the Eastern Express Highway, and as we crossed the Sion Fort, my heart lost strength. Baba would take us to the old castle on many Sundays. Seated atop a hillock, the fortress offers a panoramic view of our alpha world city—its hulking concrete, its human ocean, and its triumphalist displays of smoke-belching factories. Dingy and dilapidated, the fort's rooms are in ruins, bushes grow stupidly, and the walls stand battered with graffiti—colourful hearts and love notes etched in stone—'I LOVE SNEHA', 'Fuck me, Deepa', 'You want the good time? Call 7825...' It's not all wreckage, though. There's also an old canon, a history and our memories.

During our visits to the fort, we would spend most of our day in the garden at its base, admiring its unusual birds—the parakeets, tailorbirds, sunbirds and the butterflies with gaily coloured petal-wings. The vast garden has an open-air study centre, where students from our noisy shantytown find refuge, spend their days immersed in books. In the evenings, a group of dancers from Dharavi replaces them, hard at work to become India's finest performers. With hip-hop numbers blaring on portable speakers, they perform their complicated tuck jumps, aerial cartwheels and monkey flips. They leap, they fall, they rise, as scores of visitors watch them inch closer to their dream, one tumble at a time.

This audacity to dream, irrespective of the size of one's home, is what I admire most about Dharavi, Ms Farah. Ambition abounds in the myriad lanes of this ghetto, each person toiling to rewrite their story, to paint their canvas with colours of their choosing. You do not give up on your home and family in the village, or move to a strange, unforgiving land if you were not chasing something; and our rickety shacks in the slum, they provide the perfect fuel for these restless flames. They offer a long, hard look at our place in the world, at who we are. They incite us to alter that place, choose who we become.

Over the years, I've realized that Dharavi is a factory of the human spirit, ma'am. It embodies the very essence of evolution, altering and re-altering our heritable natures until we become fit to survive. It has a billion-dollar economy, which accommodates 20,000 big and small businesses, including leather, pottery, embroidery, soap, garments, trolley bags, electrical appliances and aluminium bricks. It also hosts artists, mural-makers, photographers and entrepreneurs. We have adolescent girls creating mobile applications, digitally organizing residents' visits to the communal tap. We have ragpickers creating symphony from the dump, using instruments like plastic barrels and glass bottles. And we have windowless attics doubling up as training academies for India's many film industries: 'A1 Bollywood, Mollywood, Tollywood Acting School—Become a SlumGod Millionaire now.'

Of course, it's undeniable that Dharavi has the squalid poverty and hardscrabble lives immortalized across culture. They shine as bright as the sun. However, there is so much more to our labyrinthine slum. Despite the hundreds of thousands crammed in two square kilometres, the sweat and tears do not dampen our ethos. Men and women work in airless sweatshops, toxic as the innards of a furnace. Boys train to be cricketers in playgrounds where children relieve themselves. Turds are easy to step on, so is muck. The unmistakable smell of sewage hangs heavy over the streets as piles of trash mature, grow older than time. However, none of them, not *one*, takes away from the dreams in our ramshackle homes. As Baba says, tragedy is obligatory in Dharavi, not misery. That remains optional.

'Small homes, big dreams,' the tourist guide tells every foreigner who opts for his poverty safari in our slum. Scores of children chase after the exotic men and women, offering enthusiastic hellos and namastes. The amused visitors respond with smiles, waves and, at times, a few rupees. Their heads bent low to dodge the dangling wires, most cover their mouths to evade diseases, or perhaps, the smell of hardship. All of them arrive with wonder at our lives and leave with gratitude for theirs. 'Small homes, big hearts.'

The guide charges ₹1000 per person for a personal tour of our slum, the thief! He walks the foreigners through our back alleys and black streets, showing them around our unsanitary hovels and undignified workplaces, our unkempt clothes and hungry children. For an extra ₹500, he throws in a home-cooked lunch with an English-friendly local family.

'Asia's largest slum, this,' he keeps boasting.

As we walked past the Sion Fort, I wondered if we would ever spend another Sunday at the 350-year-old edifice. Baba, as if hearing me, prodded me with his elbow.

'Why are you so slow?' he demanded. 'And why do you keep turning around? Walk faster, don't look back.'

The road was golden; a river of asphalt brightened by the creamy yellow glimmer of street lamps, stringing a necklace around the night. The endless, free highway stretched into the horizon before us, as far as we could see, replacing the narrow streets of the city's suburbs. The six-lane motorway, Mumbai's north–south artery, lay empty, as if haunted. It was unlike the pre-lockdown days, when the highway would bustle with tens of thousands of vehicles each day. The tarmac used to be so busy that strays kept off and birds refrained from flying low. Today, however, the fauna attended, resting along the expanse, on a journey of their own.

As we walked onto the freeway, I noticed tiny figures in the distance. Men and women, young and old, slender and sturdy, all marching like mules, lugging their inexpensive worlds in cheaper rucksacks and shoddier cloth bags. Fathers had perched their children on their shoulders, and mothers balanced their luggage on their heads. Dressed in all colours of the rainbow, the burdened beasts moved with a resolute purpose—to flee the city they built and reach the solace of their real homes, where their escaping could cease.

A few metres into our walk on the freeway, about two hours after we left Dharavi, Baba pointed to a public toilet. 'Go if you want to,' he told us, shying from eye contact with the women. 'I don't know when we'll find the next one.'

Four stairs led to the blue-walled lavatory, a partition dividing the space into two—one for gentlemen, the image of a moustached man with broad shoulders painted on its entrance, and the other for gentleladies, identifiable through the picture of a petite woman, her sari covering her head. As in most of Mumbai's public urinals, the toilet greeted us with the inimitable whiff of ammonia and destitution. The odour turned me sceptical. Only two months ago, the septic tank of a public toilet had exploded in Dharavi, injuring five men from our slum.

Happy and I were on our way to school when, around 7 a.m., we heard a loud explosion, and then another. We ran, assuming it was one of those bomb blasts, as debris came flying out of the toilet. Pieces of brick and mortar cascaded down the air, attacking the sleepy, innocent men, who were waiting to empty their bowels during the morning rush hour. Officials, who examined the toilet later, said that some gases had accumulated in the urinal, and their pressure blew off the tank's cover. It landed five men in hospital, handing them bills they could not pay.

Although hesitant, I walked in because Ma pointed out that the toilet had no attendant, the blessed human entitled to unlimited free excretions, and the one amassing ₹1 for number one and ₹2 for number two. The opportunity was tempting, my first gratis piss in four years. I entered but soon realized that the washroom was out of water. The lord of loos had taken the pledge 'Save Water' painted on the toilet's exterior too seriously. 'Water Smarter. Every drop counts.'

The washroom's walls were sprayed with graffiti, again lovers paying their compliments. I wondered why they take to such odd places for their proclamations—walls of ghettos and highway barriers, abandoned forts and public urinals. What is it about such places that reminds them of their love? I'm fifteen, ma'am, and I do not know all about this breed of attachment yet, but Ma says it's the absence of fear. She loves Baba because, unlike many women in our village and our slum, she's not afraid of him. She was expecting fear, perhaps still does, but our father has managed to surprise her.

I do not understand Ma's logic. It's the opposite of what I've seen in every Bollywood film, where men fear rejection from women. Macho heroes romance about trees with randy eyes, eulogize their heroine's bodies, and walk on burning coal—all to impress their female love interests. After the successful stalking, it's the Swiss Alps in chiffon-crusted dances, confident heroines gyrating in the rain, their hair flying in the wind, and their saris blowing off their chests to reveal strategic volumes of bosom. Then, the fear still missing, the couples ride into the sunset.

As we emerged from the washroom, Baba turned to us with fresh zest. 'The aim for the day is to walk until night,' he declared.

Happy, in response, flung his body to the ground. The boy was already tired. He left Balhaar when he was five, and he remembered too little of our village to tolerate this arduous journey. He did speak to our grandparents over the phone, but they did not seem motivation enough. Baba tried to fire the boy's imagination, reminding him of our pet, Mirchi, saying that the dog was a tug-of-war whizz. He also promised dunes, camel rides, campfires and an endless vacation from school.

'Let's go,' my raw little brother was convinced.

We spent the next three hours walking until we spotted the Mulund check post at a distance. Every time a truck passed us by, Baba and Proton Uncle tried to stop it, hoping to thumb a ride. None waited. One almost ran them over, so we decided to stick to the shoulder of the highway, walking along its side in a single, straight line. I noticed that the empty road told many stories—of migrant men, women and families like ours, who travelled by the highway in the past few days. Their slain footwear lay strewn on the sidewalk, with their empty water bottles and newspapers that had doubled as plates. Footprints of all sizes carpeted the muddy walkway, as the sun rose, illuminating the shoe-shaped epitaphs.

'How much more do we have to walk?' asked Happy. 'It's been a thousand hours since we started.'

Baba lifted him in his arms. 'Don't you remember what I told you, sweet boy?' he said as Happy rested his cheek on our father's shoulder. 'Once we're through this, you get to meet Sachin, Shah Rukh, Salman, Vishnu and Mirchi, and everything else I've promised you.'

'You're my strong boy, aren't you?' Ma patted Happy's cheek.

The boy did not respond. He did not care about strength, just wanted to rest. Baba suggested that we wait under the shade of a tree. He also had to call Candy Kaka, now that we were close to the Mulund check post. As father dialled his number, I narrowed my eyes to get a better view of the toll plaza. Three parallel lanes led to the edifice, which guarded the exit to Mumbai. Although cars were absent, a crowd of dozens of people had gathered around it. The chorus of their uproar was faint at that distance, but it turned into silence after the sound of an explosion. A cloud of smoke serenaded the border thereafter, and the people rushed towards us, screaming. Police officers, armed with wooden batons, emerged from the fog behind them, also rushing towards us, screaming.

'Baba, look.' I sprang up.

'Run,' he answered.

With Happy still in his arms, Baba paced towards Mumbai and we followed him. It was stupid. With our luggage weighing us down, the cops would reach us in minutes. Proton Uncle recognized the threat and jumped into a gutter that ran parallel to the highway. The depression was a road drainage system, created to collect rainwater, and since it was summer, we were safe from the wrath of its overflowing muck. All we had to navigate were dry leaves, human and animal faeces, plastic bags, sanitary pads and the occasional rat carcass. We jumped in.

'Duck and keep moving towards Mumbai,' said Proton Uncle as another explosion tore the air, turned it whiter. 'We must reach that enclosed skywalk, climb up and hide behind its billboards. It's only a few hundred metres away.'

'Light steps, light breaths,' Baba agreed.

Yours,
Meher
Still waiting near the exit to Mumbai

3
Kalyug

17 April 2020
Dear Ms Farah,

Even as a fifteen-year-old, I'm no stranger to fear. There was fear of child marriage as a child, considering Baba's farm debt and Balhaar's moneylenders with their cash-for-daughter policy. There was fear of losing my schoolbooks to the blunder we call culture, and the disease we call poverty. There was fear of losing Baba to suicide in our parched village, or accidental death in accident-prone Mumbai, or even murder during the recent baton-charge. At times, there was also fear of the world running out of bananas, of going to bed hungry and never waking up.

As established, I'm well acquainted with fear—my old, tiresome friend. I even understand fear—a feeling that interrogates my soul, enquiring if I have the courage to look beyond the dread, into the abyss, or if I'd rather look away, squeeze my eyes shut. With this mild musing, I assumed I knew everything about fear until the cops hurled those tear-gas bombs towards us. Then, I discovered an unmapped side of it—a kind of fright that swallows the abyss, leaving just tightly shut eyes and tighter, pounding hearts.

Our luggage hanging against our chests, our group of seven crawled through the three-foot-deep gutter. We could hear the mayhem inch closer as dozens of migrant labourers rushed towards us, chased by armed police officers. Their moans and groans made our palms and knees move faster, quieter. As we paced, I felt cold in the summer heat, even as streams of sweat ran all over me. My body, I knew, had gone berserk, and my mind, my mind was singing. A poetic rhythm governed the moments of silence and shrieking inside it: *They're coming for you.* Hush. *They're coming for Happy.* Hush. *They're here. They're here. Are they here?*

It's still a haze to me, our 300-metre crawl in that narrow trench of dirt and despair. In a way, the garbage helped. Navigating that assorted variety of grime kept me busy. It curtailed moments when I peeped outside the trough, glimpsed at the khaki-clad aggressors, and ran into a colossal tizzy. When I did look up, it was much later, only because Proton Uncle was up on his feet. He held his filth-covered hand between his temples, gazed at the police army, and announced we had left the cops behind. The helmet-clad, masked hunters had now besieged their game. It would have been easy, winning that blood sport. The police's prey lacked focus, coughing and sneezing, and temporarily blinded from the shelling.

'Get down,' Electron Aunty shrieked between murmurs, pulling her husband back to the ground. 'Down until we reach the skywalk.'

Within a few metres, we were near the foot overbridge that snaked over the wide sea of asphalt. As we jumped onto its stairway, consumerism lent us a cloak of invisibility, with billboard after billboard concealing our ascent. Once we were atop the elevated expressway, we rushed to its centre, the hoardings still veiling us. We dropped to the tiled floor and heaved a collective sigh of relief.

From atop the skywalk, I had a good view of the police force that garrisoned the exit to Mumbai. They were like a hungry pride of lions, or maybe, a pack of wolves. They had surrounded their prey in a tactical group, capturing their large kill with ease, deboning anything that came in their way. More like wolves than lions, I thought, for their dominant leaders—the alpha wolves—howled over loudspeakers. Although group hunters, every predator in the pack appeared to be a formidable killer, clasping its game by the neck. As we stood on the overbridge, I felt safe. Our herd of herbivores had eluded the carnivores, at least this once. Relieved too, Ma was busy thanking every supernatural avatar she could recollect—the deities and demigods, gods of the five elements, celestial celebrities and ghosts of dead ancestors.

I noticed that our refuge site, the blue metal overpass, was roofless, allowing in a soft, remedying breeze. Had it been any other day, Happy would have tethered a polythene bag to a thread, flown it in the wind like a kite. Today, however, he lay flat on his back, his arms and legs stretched, as if someone had fastened his limbs to four ends of a tiny bed. His eyes stared at the blue sky, looking at nothing. Since the boy appeared comfortable, our bodies, without instruction, started mimicking his. We lay scattered around the three-metre-wide overpass, and our luggage too seemed to be taking a breather. After a few minutes of silent panting, the elders sparred, with little physical energy, but an amplitude of fury.

'It was a stupid plan. It was stupid since the moment you thought of it. Stupid, stupid, and oh, did I mention, STUPID.' Electron Aunty sat up. 'Do you even realize how much danger you've landed us in?'

Proton Uncle, burdened with the demand for a response, pushed himself up. He rested his back on a billboard along the bridge's side-rail, perhaps one advertising mosquito repellent sprays. I imagined the poster. It probably displayed half a dozen dead mosquitoes, lying at the feet of a Mosquito Man. The gnat-superhero could be wielding an over-sized bottle of the repellent, likely enriched with the goodness of dry-fruit oil. 'How will you dream if mosquitoes won't let you sleep?' the ad copy might have created tension before relieving it: 'Worry not. Mosquito Man is here. One spray, the mini-beasts will pay. No delay, buy today.'

'I'm talking to you,' Electron Aunty cleared all doubts if any. 'Are you even listening?'

'It was Gopal's idea too, you know,' said Proton Uncle, pointing at my father, as if Aunty did not know which one he was. Baba sat up, probably resting against a billboard advertising men's-deodorant-cum-sex-pheromones. I need not describe this poster for you, ma'am. It'd be pretty standard: two to four women in tiny skirts and crop tops, their waists in the male model's arms, attesting to the spell-work of his aromatic armpits. Grandma would slip into a coma if she saw that hoarding in the middle of the road, that too, in broad daylight. 'There's no god left in those half-naked girls,' she'd say, certain that the lords fled the women's pin-up bodies as soon as they put on the skirts. That makes me wonder, ma'am, how do deities deal with body odour?

Baba, although attentive, did not speak, not until Ma sat up too. Then, within seconds, he started babbling. Although Mother hadn't uttered one word, I knew her deep almond eyes were talking for her—the most effective means of spousal communication I've seen so far. As a result, Baba started counting and recounting every reason why the long walk was wise.

'So, you see, staying back wasn't an option,' he reiterated. 'Had it just been Jairaj and me, we would have managed in Mumbai. But we could not have risked your lives.'

'But that's exactly what you've done now, risked our lives,' countered Electron Aunty. 'What if the cops got us? What if those bombs hit us?'

'Those weren't bombs, biwiji,' said Proton Uncle, using the honorific ji after biwi, which turned his wife into Respected Wife.

Over the years, I'd noticed that the suffix was Uncle's involuntary defence mechanism, which came into play every time his wife threatened to destroy their intra-atomic stability.

'Those weren't flowers either,' said Aunty, unimpressed by the postfix. Happy, Neutron Sameer and I continued to lay flat, our gazes glued to the clear summer sky, now chasing after its only cloud—a puff of white magic amid acres of bright blue. *Flowers*, I thought. *Those definitely weren't flowers.*

As Electron Aunty continued to screech at the men for their 'dumb, hasty, life-threatening, so-stupid-that-it-makes-dining-with-tigers-look-sensible' decision, Baba jumped to his feet.

'Can't you see we would have died in Mumbai?' he barked, his voice like subdued thunder. 'Do you know the cops assaulted your husband and me twice? This was in addition to the lathi-charge when we went out to get groceries. They were beating everyone back to their shanties, even if they stepped out to use the loo. Did they not threaten you as well? For how long could we have waited in that airless box? Without food, water, washrooms, and without a word on when this horrific lockdown would end.'

'And what after we ran out of money?' he continued. 'We'd be on the street, standing in those humiliating queues, waiting for the bite-sized khichri handed out by community kitchens. Even there, locals get preference over migrants. Hindus don't get food from Muslim donors, and Muslims don't get help from Hindu charities. Then, what would you have us do? Beg strangers for pity food? Turn into urchins?'

'Accepting charity does not make you a beggar,' Electron Aunty grunted, slowly losing power.

'It does,' Baba snarled. 'We're men of dignity. We are not just migrants, we're migrant workers. We work and earn our meals. We don't depend on alms, and we do not stand with open palms and empty bowls on the street, awaiting charity. We're short on money, not integrity. We crave respect, not sympathy.'

Responding to Electron Aunty's silence, he went on: 'And, apart from the police beatings, even the locals in Dharavi threatened us. Did you know that? About six of them, when we were returning home after the lathi-charge. They held Jairaj and me by our necks and said, "if any of you filthy outsiders gets infected with the virus, no one will be spared, we will bury you alive." It's time you realize that Mumbai wasn't ours, but the biggest delusion of our lives, the greatest mirage.'

'It was after the threat that we decided we must leave for home,' Proton Uncle looked at his Respected Wife. 'That was the final blow.'

'Do you know, Jairaj? Two of those six men were Muslims,' Baba added. 'I'm sure they instigated our Hindu brothers against us.'

Proton Uncle did not comment. He does not share Baba's resentment for India's largest minority, probably the only ideology where the two differ. Instead, Uncle said, 'What's the plan now? How do we dodge the cops at the check post?'

In response, Father started strolling on the overbridge and called Candy Kaka, who had covered another thirty-two kilometres in the past five hours, as opposed to our twenty-three.

'No, no one is hurt,' Father assured Kaka after informing him about the tear-gas shelling. 'Now, tell me how to get out of here.'

Once he disconnected the call, Baba shared the plan with us: 'Om is sending us a guide. The man will walk us through a broken wall that leads off the highway, so we can bypass the check post. He'll take a few hours to arrive, and it'll cost some money, but it's better than staying here all day, hoping that the cops would leave at night. Also, Om insisted that we must pace up, use the ample energy of our first day to cover as much distance as we can.'

'Can we eat?' answered Happy, still lying on his back, his eyes still busy with that lonely cloud.

The wall was too high to be climbed, too deep to be tunnelled under, and too wide to be broken into, as if the hard-set, impenetrable shield of ideology around atheists and fanatics. Glass shards spangled its top, attracting and dissuading prospective trespassers, but its concrete body seemed friendly. Marked with chequered holes, it offered a glimpse into the world within—rich families with rich children playing with rich gadgets. The wall guaranteed their privacy and protection, ensuring they remained safe from intruders like us. Yet, here we were, invading their world, escaping the one we called ours.

'Are you sure your name is Banjo?' Neutron Sameer asked our guide as I shut my notebook after writing my first two letters to you. 'As in, the musical instrument, Bulbul Tarang?'

'Money first,' replied Banjo, essentially a human smuggler. 'Hundred rupees each for two husbands and two wives, fifty each for three children.'

'Five hundred and fifty rupees to cross one toll post?' Baba was stunned.

'Okay, round figure, five hundred,' said Banjo, scanning us from top to bottom. I think the smuggler was using a pseudonym. It'd be unfortunate if he wasn't. I mean, imagine naming your boy Drum, or Trumpet, or Xylophone. Hell, imagine Saxophone! His classmates would tease him dead.

Banjo wasn't older than twenty-five, and he looked like he still lived in the decade he was born, the nineties. Dressed in a skin-fitted T-shirt and high-waist jeans, he had a leopard-print bandana around his forehead. He was fair and tall and had dyed the front of his spiky hair golden, likely at home. His mouth and nose, meanwhile, were covered with a skull-face mask.

'Make it two hundred and fifty,' Baba bargained.

'Boss, don't waste my time.' The guide was irked. 'I'm risking my life for you here. If the cops catch you, all they will do is send you back to Mumbai. But with me, there will be hell to pay. Not a rupee less than five hundred. Tell me quick. Go, or no go?'

'Go, go,' said Proton Uncle. 'All going.'

Baba handed him the cash, and the smuggler was at ease. We got off the skywalk and followed Banjo as he walked along the concrete wall, which separated the suburban settlements from the highway. He led us onto a wide footpath strewn with odd, eclectic garbage—water drums, red bricks, scrap metal, batteries and sheets of plastic foam. As we trailed him, walking away from the police check post, I noticed that we were far from our predators, at least three parts of a kilometre. I felt safe at that distance, and within minutes, we reached our covert, coveted hole—a crater amid the chequered part of the white concrete, covered by a sheet of white plastic to camouflage the unauthorized route.

'I built the hole at night,' said Banjo, almost boastful. 'I even polished the edges, so the broken concrete won't scrape your skin. High-class, top-quality, world-best hole.'

We climbed into the cavity and emerged on its other side. There, I spotted a man seated on a red-and-silver armchair, meant for brides and grooms at wedding receptions. I kept looking and realized it was indeed a wedding setup, now gathering varieties of fungi. The mandap, the sanctum sanctorum of wedding rituals, lay battered. Its huge, dome-shaped canopy sat morose on the muddy ground, so did its four pillars. Even the agni kund, the pot of sacred fire, had lost its fervour.

My eyes kept scanning that forlorn, forgotten world, the superstore of scrap, only to discover more wreckage—mangled cars, decaying refrigerators, moth-eaten furniture and outdated industrial equipment. It was a playground of obsolete dreams, that place, older than the rest of the world, and I wasn't surprised to spot a few shanties at its far end—conical homes held together with bamboo and plastic. Men idled inside the huts, women cooked on clay stoves outside, and children played with the rusting, oversized toys.

As my mind searched and weaved stories around the life of that junkyard, the man in the groom's seat walked to us. He exchanged pleasantries with Banjo and informed him that two more 'guides' had commenced operations in the area. With the update, I deduced that the man was the smuggler's deputy.

'Where are their passages?' Banjo asked.

'Further away from the toll post,' said the groom-not-to-be.

'Our business is safe then. Our cavity has a strategic location—far enough from the toll post for migrants to avoid arrest, and close enough for them to spot the cops and shit their pants. Just find out their rates and which officers they've paid.'

'Okay, bhai, done.'

'Is the road clear for us?'

'Yes,' said the deputy. 'The police's patrol van was on its last round five minutes ago. Safe for at least half an hour.'

'Good. Now, keep this cash,' said Banjo as we began to leave. 'In case they bust us, I don't want them to find more than a few hundred rupees.'

The human smuggler led us out of the wreck-yard, and onto the street that ran parallel to the highway. It lay deserted, dead as dry grass, although annexed by advanced civilization—grand grey building after grand grey building, more under construction, an English-medium school, and hordes of school buses parked along the pavements. With children locked up inside their homes, the playground looked lonely. It stretched for about half a kilometre, and Happy walked with his eyes glued to its swings, slides, seesaws, merry-go-rounds and giraffe-shaped ladders. I could tell he was aching to jump onto those rides, run in zigzags around the ground.

'So, where are you headed?' Banjo asked as we trailed him.

'Balhaar,' said Baba, 'Rajasthan.'

'*Baap re!* That is far.'

'I know.'

'Sad, what's happening,' the smuggler said after a few seconds, again injecting words into the comfortable silence. 'I'm helping so many people cross this check post every day. You're lucky to have found me. Else, by now, you'd be walking back to Mumbai.'

'Why?' asked Neutron Sameer, always up for small talk.

'Because it's a national lockdown, boss, biggest in the world. Leaving home is a crime.'

'But we're leaving *for* home. Is that a crime, too?' Electron Aunty made a rare valid point. 'This is Kalyug, I'm telling you. The age of total decadence, the era of nature's wrath, and the epoch of universal downfall.'

No one argued. It probably is.

Grandma often talks about Kalyug, quoting passages from Hindu theology penned thousands of years ago. She says we're already living in the Dark Age of Kalyug, the fourth and final epoch of human civilization. At the end of this, it's all doom, followed by a new world. To be honest, ma'am, I have my doubts about such prophecies. I've been fooled once already. Do you remember when they said the world would end on 21 December 2012? It was some Mayan prediction. I was seven at the time, and I remember the cold winter's night well. Ma had cooked all our favourites for the last meal of our lives; we slept with our cattle inside our house, my favourite goat in my blanket, and we took baths before sleeping, so we could die clean. I even avoided studying for a spelling test in school—all in anticipation of the cataclysmic event. The apocalypse, however, never showed.

'It was never going to happen,' Dadi said the following day. 'These are foreign gimmicks. What do those meat-eaters know? According to our ancient Vedic wisdom, we are at the beginning of Kalyug, which will last for about five lakh years. No need to panic until then.'

Thereafter, Dadi went on to relay several prophecies about Kalyug. Over the years, she's repeated them many a time, every time she caught me doing something 'immoral', like talking to a boy, attributing my alleged depravity to universal decay. I never agree with Grandma, ma'am, but many of those Dark Age predictions ring true for the contemporary world:

- Weather and environment will degrade.
- Famines and droughts will be common.
- Diseases will spread.
- Wealth alone will decide a person's social standing.
- Political leaders will consume citizens.
- Priests will become devotees of their genitals.
- Cities will become warzones.
- Thieves will become kings.
- Kings will become thieves.
- Humans will openly display animosity for each other.
- Filling the belly will become the goal of life.

Spooky, isn't it?

While Grandma is a big advocate of Kalyug and its best friend, moral rust, Dadoo, my grandfather, has a more simplistic view. He says that kal means tomorrow while yug means era, and the essence of this epoch lies in its nomenclature. 'Kalyug is when people live in tomorrows, and for tomorrows,' he told me once. 'It's doom because it's the era where worries of the future rob the present of its joys.'

Dadoo is my greatest ally, much to the surprise and chagrin of many in Balhaar. A tall man, he dons a proud white moustache that tickles his high cheekbones, and matches his white kurta-pyjama-turban. He has soft, kind eyes and softer, old skin. The vices of time live on his face, his furrows deeper than his flesh. They crumble when he smiles, a toothless smile that runs straight to his eyes. I must tell you, ma'am. I like Dadoo much more than Dadi. He's much nicer than my grandma, and Baba says it's because, like most old men in Balhaar, he smokes one magic pipe every day. What else, marijuana.

'It makes him calmer, kinder, even wiser,' explained Baba.

Grandma should smoke ganja too, I wished, and asked Dadoo about the magical powers of his chillum. He sat smoking in our courtyard, the thick fumes personifying his owlish, solemn air. Upon hearing my query, he laughed. 'The magic pipe only helps with questions,' he said, pulling a long drag. 'Answers are my own to find.'

After a few moments of thought, Banjo seemed to agree with Electron Aunty's Kalyug theory. 'This has to be the Dark Age,' he said. 'The things I've seen in these past few days, it couldn't be anything else. Pregnant women, old women, old men, men with fractured legs, and children so tiny, all walking hundreds of kilometres in this hellish heat. Heck, one woman gave birth on the road, and within hours, she was up on her feet again. Some conviction you have, wanting to go home.'

'And you're exploiting that conviction, aren't you?' said Baba, unperturbed by his empathy. 'How many people do you transfer every day?'

'About a hundred.'

'So, at hundred rupees per person, you're earning ten thousand a day. Kalyug seems to be working well for you.'

The smuggler did not respond. A phone call saved him. It was his deputy, alerting him about a police vehicle approaching us. We started running back, hoping to hide behind those parked buses. Too late.

As two police officers jumped off their motorbike and charged at Banjo with kicks and blows, the Grave Sniffer's words echoed in my ears: 'You got money, the cops are yours, and so is their testimony.' If there was any truth in that statement, and I knew there was, we were safe. Baba and Proton Uncle had thousands of rupees, and these were traffic cops. Dressed in white uniforms, they were unauthorized to weaponize bamboo sticks or fling anything that looked like bombs.

The officers pushed Banjo, slapped him and pinned him against a wall, as I thought about the Grave Sniffer's proclamation birthed on a summer morning three years ago. Ira, my best friend, and I had been awaiting this day for weeks, and the messenger of its arrival, as anticipated, was a police official. The cop was at her doorstep, looking for her father, Ehsaan. Someone had dumped a fresh corpse in the Mithi River. The police had failed; the fire brigade had failed. Only Ehsaan Uncle, popular in Dharavi as the Grave Sniffer, could rescue the human cadaver.

'It's severed, the man's body,' the police constable informed Uncle. 'Head dismembered, all four limbs separate, torso wandering around on its own. We must leave now, before the parts get washed to the sea.'

'At once,' said the Grave Sniffer.

Ira rushed to my home to inform me of the summons, and together, we hurried to the banks of the Mithi River that flows through Dharavi. Over the years, Ira had told me countless stories about her father, how he dives right into the murky waters, wades through the muck and sludge, before emerging in triumph, a corpse in his arms. The Gravc Sniffer had recovered thirty-three bodies over the preceding decade, and everyone in Dharavi knew about his flair for sniffing out the dead, salvaging them from their distasteful water burials. It's his idea of social responsibility, he told Ira once, a deed for the deceased.

Since we're in Mumbai, ma'am, you can imagine that the Grave Sniffer is a busy man. News channels often complain about the dead, unclaimed bodies that keep showing up around town—murdered bodies, bodies killed by accident and suicide, and bodies that just stopped living. They're everywhere—footpaths, railway platforms, skywalks, playgrounds and flyovers; and of course, in the sea, rivers, nullahs and gutters. The Grave Sniffer, hence, is an important cog in the Mumbai police's investigation machinery. If the cops do not require the corpses for inquiry, the man also organizes funerals for his finds. Formal farewells for informal departures.

'But how do you know if the deceased was a Hindu, Muslim, Sikh or Christian?' Ira asked her father once. 'How can you tell what kind of rites to perform?'

'I alternate between the four,' the Grave Sniffer had replied. 'Religion is a weapon of the living. Corpses, even gods, are much less communal.'

The eighteen-kilometre-long Mithi River, recently named the most polluted one in all of Maharashtra, is a perfect hideaway for the gone. A Petri dish of infections, it's too toxic for aquatic life to survive, and it deadens the corpses some more. Traversing through slums and industrial complexes, the sewage drain lies choked with household waste, untreated garbage, human excreta, animal excreta, industrial effluents and sludge oil. Yet, hundreds of thousands of slum-dwellers wash, bathe and clean utensils with its water every day. Many others make a living from the cesspit, fossicking through its grime for hours, hunting for sellable metal and plastic.

Upon reaching the riverbank, Ira and I learnt that the fragmented body belonged to a twenty-nine-year-old man, a worker in a wax-printing unit. No one knew his name, as the cops referred to him as 142/17, his case number at Dharavi police station and the year 2017. Everyone, however, was aware of the motive behind his murder—the man was a roadblock to the union between his wife and her paramour. The cops were quick to zero in on the killers. It was easy. Murders over love affairs are the most popular kind in our country, at least on our many crime shows: *Beware, Love is in the Air; A Murder Made in Heaven; Love, Sex and Slaughter.*

As we stood on the bank, I spotted the killers: the woman and her lover, standing with each of their wrists handcuffed to different police officials. Murmurs among slum-dwellers, who had gathered at the bank, told us that the duo had slit the man's throat in his sleep. They split his body inside his home, stuffed the parts in three polythene bags, and flung the bags into the river. The wife, confident of getting away with the murder, filed a missing person's complaint with the police herself. Investigators, however, saw through her deceit and found her paramour. When confronted by a few zealous women officials, she confessed.

'Do you think they look remorseful?' I asked Ira, pointing to the couple that stood a few metres ahead of us.

'Put that finger down,' she hissed, and added after observing the lovers for a few seconds: 'I don't see regret. They're casually pointing at the waters where they dumped her husband.'

About half a dozen police officials waited by the riverside, their mouths covered with handkerchiefs to evade the scents of the fetid Mithi. A few fire brigade officials also stood on standby. Upon indication from one of the cops, the Grave Sniffer removed his trousers and T-shirt, revealing an older pair. He unhooked his boat, tied to a pole on the bank, and jumped on it. He'd built the boat himself, now loaded with the paraphernalia for his search operation—one pedal, a long wooden stick and a bamboo rod. As he tied a handkerchief around his mouth and put on a pair of rubber gloves, the cops pushed his boat into the river.

Once he had pedalled to the spot the murderers had pointed to, the Grave Sniffer used his stick to navigate the sludge until his skilled hands sensed relevance. Confident of a find, he plunged into the sewage, only to emerge with a dog carcass. He placed it on the boat to avoid further false alarms. A few more attempts and animal cadavers later, he surfaced with a human skull.

'The bags have given away, and the body parts are all scattered in the river,' he shouted from his boat, wiping the muck off his eyes. The kerchief around his mouth was drenched in grey goo, and he replaced it with a new one. 'This will take a while.'

Since it was the summer holidays, Ira and I waited. As minutes passed, more slum-dwellers congregated around the river. Spotting a business opportunity, enterprising hawkers started selling peanuts and roasted chickpeas along the bank. People sat discussing the plummeting morality of women, the rocketing murders, the Mumbai heat, and of course, the advent of Kalyug.

About four hours later, the Grave Sniffer had only found a skull and an arm, and everyone—the audience, the hawkers, the police officers, even the killers—seemed exasperated from the wait. Most of the cops now lay on newspapers at the bank, and the accused, too, had managed permission to rest their feet.

'Got it, I've got it,' the Grave Sniffer announced after combing the river for another hour. The spectators clapped and whistled, only to learn it was just another arm. By the end of the day, the final recovery count stood at one skull, one torso and two arms. The legs were on their way to the Arabian Sea.

'You may stop now,' an officer told Ehsaan Uncle. 'That's enough evidence. The DNA from these parts will nail the two.'

I glanced at the killers to check their faces for emotion, but they only looked tired. The cop thanked Ehsaan Uncle and offered him some cash, but he refused.

'Keep me in your prayers,' the Grave Sniffer, also a tea vendor, said.

For days after the search operation, Ira and I would follow television news reports for information about 142/17. We wanted to know his name, and if his killers were brought to justice. News reports never mentioned them and Ehsaan Uncle did not share details, despite all our pleading and pestering. One day, he surrendered.

'The man was too poor for television,' he said. 'An orphan too, so no one missed him when he died. No one to burn candles in public demonstrations, and no one to demand justice. The cops saw scope. In exchange for some money from the killers, they declared that the man's was an unidentified body, murdered by unidentified persons over unidentified reasons. Case closed.'

'But what about all your hard work?' Ira asked.

'The case is still open with uparwallah,' he said, pointing to the sky, meaning the one above, meaning god. 'But with cops, if you have money, you can buy their testimony. Lawmakers and lawbreakers work together in our country. That's why I do not charge those officers for the dives. It's good sense to have them in your debt.'

After that day, I started looking for evidence of the Grave Sniffer's money-testimony theory, and soon, I started seeing it everywhere. It was so obvious, Ms Farah. I was embarrassed I hadn't noticed it yet, especially since I aspire to become a shrewd, observant journalist like you. The cops, many of them, are accepting bribe left, right, centre, top, bottom, east and west—as a payoff to spare erring motorists at traffic signals, as commission from street vendors for permitting their subsistence, as bribe from bar owners who wish to sell hooch beyond the clock, as rent from the homeless who sleep on footpaths, and as protection money from cannabis sellers who dislike lock-ups.

Empowered with the Grave Sniffer's findings, I was confident that we could buy the cops who had busted us near the exit to Mumbai. Of course, this would mean playing the local sport of bribery, but I was beginning to realize that this game was such—if you don't play, you lose. If you don't pay, you're on the news.

There were two officers for sale—one tall, crabby cop, the Conductor, and another short, calm cop, the Insulator. I knew their thermal properties the moment they spoke. The Conductor was hard and sonorous like electricity-conducting metals, while the Insulator was soft and porous like the heat-resisting cotton. They proved my supposition when the Conductor beat Banjo with his fists, and the even-tempered Insulator tried to protect him from the heat.

'Maderchod, Banjo,' the Conductor roared. 'I warned you yesterday that I will shove this road-sign up your ass if you plied more people across the border.'

'No, no, sahib, you're getting it wrong,' said Banjo, his palms joined in prayer and his knees bent to prove his subservience. 'These are my relatives. They were getting bored at home, so I'm taking them for a walk. Casual stuff.'

'You think I have wood for a brain, don't you?' The Conductor slapped Banjo. 'If they're your relatives, why do they have luggage? Achcha, tell me, tell me the names of these three kids.'

When Banjo fumbled, he received another smack, this one on his head.

'Sorry, sahib,' the smuggler pleaded, his previously bent knees now kissing the ground. 'They're poor. Please let them go.'

'And who are you? Some cheap-ass Robinhood? No way I'm letting them pass. They're going back to Mumbai, and you, my friend, you're going to prison. This time, for one full month.'

'Okay, enough now,' the cottony Insulator intervened. 'It's a lockdown, brother. Understand. The whole world is desperate.'

'Exactly, it's a lockdown. What they're doing is a crime.' The Conductor remained committed to his metallic properties, his high melting point.

After a few more minutes of scuffling, Banjo managed to win a personal audience with the Insulator, as we waited with the other cop. Our bodies wept under the harsh Mumbai sun, rivulets of sweat trickling down our torsos. Do not get me wrong, ma'am. Balhaar, too, is hot. Summer temperatures rocket up to fifty degrees, and heat rises off the baked dunes in shimmering waves. The dry air, however, does its job. It descends upon the earth and sucks up the water. In Mumbai, even the air is busy. Clogged with vapour, it has no room to help sweat-purged travellers or dry their damp bodies. The wind, meanwhile, is married to the sea, does not like venturing far from it.

As we waited by the roadside, I could not hear the conversation between Banjo and the Insulator, but I did see our smuggler slip a few notes into the officer's palm. The duo returned soon, and the cop announced that we were free to walk home.

'Last warning,' said the Conductor, shoving Banjo one final time. He then jumped onto his motorbike and sped away with his cotton lump.

After a twenty-minute walk, we emerged on the other side of the toll post. As we began to leave, Banjo returned ₹300 of the ₹500 that Baba had paid him. I do not know what took over the man. He had clearly lost money on the gig. When probed, he said, 'You'll need it. There will be more cops on the way. And I don't want to be the biggest villain of your Kalyug.'

'Banjo Uncle, where did you get that skeleton-teeth mask?' Happy asked him.

The smuggler pulled out a bunch of fresh masks from his pocket and presented one to the boy. 'Side business,' he told Baba. 'Do you want one? I also have other designs—one with a king-sized moustache, another with big, red lips, and a third with bunny teeth.'

'No, we're fine,' said Father. 'Thank you.'

'My real name is Arjun,' Banjo added before walking away.

While the smuggler left to traffic more migrants across the border, we had managed to leave Mumbai. It came with a sense of relief, the kind that broke my heart.

Yours,
Meher
Somewhere near the Maharashtra–Gujarat interstate border

4

Farewell

18 April 2020

In the jungle, the mighty jungle
The lion sleeps tonight
In the jungle, the quiet jungle
The lion sleeps tonight

A-weema-weh, A-weema-weh, A-weema-weh, A-weema-weh
A-weema-weh, A-weema-weh, A-weema-weh, A-weema-weh

Near the village, the peaceful village
The lion sleeps tonight
Near the village, the quiet village
The lion sleeps tonight

This song has been running in a loop inside my head, Ms Farah, with the lifelike animals in its visuals frolicking around my mind, filling it with fear. They're also making this mighty jungle around me seem mightier. I'm sure you know the upbeat song, ma'am, which, I'm realizing now, is a well-mannered euphemism, a euphemism so polite that it also has a merry melody backing its sobering verses.

I first heard the cautionary tune in *The Lion King*, one of my favourite films ever. The animated movie is a journey into the African savannah and has photorealistic creatures galloping through grasslands, scaling cliffs and hills, tumbling and wrestling and romping through rivers and drains. I loved it! It was a storybook come alive, and not the flimsy one that our paper scrap–dealer in Dharavi sells, but a rare deluxe edition with thick, gilded pages and full-colour artwork.

It was a rainy evening in late July last year, and Happy and I were thrilled to watch Simba, Pumbaa, Timon, and their whole lot, on the big screen. Until then, our only cinema-hall experience was in Balhaar, when Celluloid Bro—because he says 'bro' too much—would visit our village. The city-bred twenty-something was a movie pirate, who recorded films on a camcorder in cinema halls. On the second Sunday of every month, he would go around our hamlet with a megaphone in his auto-rickshaw, inviting villagers to the screening of his latest theft. Kids would chase after his tuk-tuk, as he riveted all with cliff-hanging peeks into the film's storyline—'Identical twins separated as children reunite as young men, but the problem is, both want the same girl. One bro is rich, the other kind. One bro fearless, the other wise. Who will land the heroine? And will the bros survive this storm? Come tonight, bros, find out!'

The children, including me, would reach the village square much earlier than the elders. We would watch Celluloid Bro as he set up his screen, projector and DVD player, entertaining us with stories about the film's star-cast, and if he was in the mood, their scandals. Villagers would know that the show was about to start upon hearing his portable speaker, blaring with top musical numbers of the film.

He'd start the movie as soon as the sunlight died, and for ₹12 per viewer, he'd turn the village into a roulette of emotions—scores of villagers laughing and backslapping, mortified through the intimate scenes, misty-eyed in the emotive ones, and breaking into Bollywood dancing, a lot of Bollywood dancing.

I missed Balhaar's open-air theatre after we moved to the city. Baba never took us to a cinema hall in Mumbai. Unlike its on-the-house beaches and forts, the city's theatres were not complimentary. Even *The Lion King*, our first English movie and our foremost visit to a multiplex, Ms Amber afforded them to us. A Bombay girl, who moved to the UK with her parents when she was little, Ms Amber Patel offers free tuitions to kids in Dharavi, teaching us English, math and science. Although the film had released in four languages in India, including Hindi, she had insisted on the English version (with subtitles, of course). It would be good language practice, she said.

Ms Amber is an angel, and not only because she looks like one, with her deep brown eyes that appear more alive than the day, her light skin that turns pink in the sun, her smile that compliments all it sees, and her perfume like a special bouquet, a bit of lemon, a bit of tangerine, some jasmine, some lavender and a few old books. Ms Amber is why I love English, also why I have a grasp of English, especially pronunciations. For instance, while our schoolteacher would pronounce 'psalm' as 'pa-sa-lum', Ms Amber told us it's pronounced 'saam', the letters 'p' and 'l' silent. Similarly, tomb is pronounced toom, plumber is plummer, and sword is sord. Sord.

I can write ballads about Ms Amber, ma'am, but I'll tell you more about her later. I just realized that in all my crosstalk, I've drifted far from the song I was talking about—*In the jungle, the mighty jungle, the lion sleeps tonight...* The reason why I cannot get this song out of my head, Ms Farah, is because we're in a jungle, a mighty jungle, and there might just be a lion, a leopard actually, sleeping close to us tonight. As the lyrics go, we're also near a village, a peaceful village, where a leopard might be sleeping tonight. *A-weema-weh, A-weema-weh*... Ah, stop!

Our group of seven has swelled to twenty, and we are in an abandoned structure in the middle of this wildwood. It looks like the erstwhile home of some rich landowner, but spiders seem to be its oldest residents. Shrouded in a darkness punctuated by the booming calls of owls, it has a thick, tree-covered canopy that has blocked out the ore-gold moon. The only source of light here is a fire torch that we plan to burn through the night.

'We shouldn't deplete our phone batteries if we can make fire,' Baba had said. 'And one torch is enough. More will attract animals. As the villagers had warned, the day belongs to humans, but the nights ... the nights are the leopard's.'

The window frames of this ancient, time-worn house are still intact, but their glass appears burdened with a thick layer of grime, untouched in years. The mouldy walls stand firm, but the wooden door is hanging loose on its hinges. It's as if someone fled this house in a rush, too afraid to look back. Since the door wouldn't shut, we've stacked our bags to block the entranceway. However, through the gaps between our belongings, I can still see the dark forest outside, the darker birds like ghosts, and the wind dancing in the trees. There are also fireflies and starlit skies, as in *The Lion King*, but it's the film's naturalistic beasts that have robbed my peace. This journey has ruined the movie for me, ma'am, turning its peppy anthem into the signature tune of wild brutes, a knell.

Since Happy was petrified, Ma lulled him to sleep, assuring him that big cats, too, might be asleep at this hour. Downright plagiarism. I do not know if she has watched the movie, ma'am, but her words bore an eerie resemblance to those in the final verse of the song:

Hush, my darling, don't fear, my darling
The lion sleeps tonight

Hush, my darling, don't cry, my darling
The lion sleeps tonight

Now that I look around me, everyone seems drowned in a deep sleep, limbs all over, no tossing, no turning, plain snoring. Each of us is fatigued after the travails of the past thirty-six hours, and yet, I am unable to rest my eyes. I keep thinking about the day that passed, and the night that this might become. My mind has developed a mind of its own—Mind, The Second—an unruly bunch of neurons that keep venturing into the wild. Mind II, also creative, weaves varied scenarios in this exact wooded landscape, setting us up against its wild cats, wolves, snakes, sloth bears, or ghosts, or all of them together, and in no climax does it make us win.

I'm writing to you, ma'am, because writing silences Mind Junior. I think I'll keep going until I tell you how we landed in this wilderness. I could also go on about the horrors of this moment instead, but none of it will make sense if you do not know what preceded it. Hence, for the sake of chronology, please allow me to return to the Mulund check post.

Wait! Ma seems to have woken up. She cannot read English and thinks I'm writing a diary, which she does not like. I talk non-stop, she says, and that I take to writing only because I've exhausted my mouth from all the chattering. 'Two ears and one tongue,' she keeps admonishing me. 'So we can talk less and listen more.'

Mumbai's aura has a fifteen-kilometre radius. Although we had left the city behind, we could see its legacy in its satellite town of Thane. Flanked by frost-white skyscrapers, it had multi-speciality hospitals that looked like ten-star hotels, and swanky car showrooms exhibiting high-end, luxury vehicles, probably worth a parliamentarian's ransom. It was as if Thane was trying to recreate the city of dreams, banking on an audience eager to lead the Mumbai life, but at bargain prices. I know because most billboards here sold space—homes and offices, offering low-cost luxury and the 'Real Mumbai life, minus the traffic, plus the savings'. A world of second-bests.

As we walked by those edifices, which appeared like monuments to the desires of India's middle-class, I wondered why, unlike here, Dharavi did not have those jumbo real-estate hoardings. Perhaps because it would take years of editing and enhancing before the shanties looked irresistible on king-sized posters. 'Real Mumbai life, minus the toilets, plus the vector-borne diseases.'

The highway, I noticed, had many flyovers, and Happy insisted that we walk over them instead of taking the roads underneath. The cement-concrete overpasses were like titanic slides to the boy, and Baba did not mind granting him this little joy. They were better for our safety too, as we could now spot police officers and their barricades from afar. A similar flyover, for instance, also preceded the Mulund check post. Had we been atop it, we could have noticed the cop cover from a much safer distance.

I, too, liked the elevated roads better. They offered panoramic views of the world around us—boom-towns-turned-ghost-towns, boarded-up storefronts, empty crossroads, desolate pedestrian walks, and mountains painted on the horizon. There was one problem, though. The top view also offered a close-up peek into the shopping malls along the highway. The boxed bazaars started fiddling with my thoughts, reminding me of our trip to the Mumbai mall where we watched *The Lion King*. The recollection choked my nose with the buttery aroma of the mall's multi-cuisine food court, and as if on cue, my stomach growled.

It's not that I was starving. Only a few hours ago, we'd had chapattis and cooked potatoes. We're also carrying biscuits and some dry snacks, but Ma insisted that we finish the perishable items first. This means two more meals of the horrid potato. I sincerely hope they go bad, ma'am, and so does Happy. It isn't unreasonable, our wish. If you ever cut us open, all you would find is 1. Bananas, 2. Potatoes, 3. Miniature versions of us, begging you to save us from the first two.

'It's so hot,' said Happy, the regular-sized one. 'I think there are two, or maybe three suns in the sky today.'

'No, no,' I answered. 'There's only one sun in our solar system. Planets are many, moons are many.'

'It was a joke, didi. What is wrong with you? Are you thinking about food again?'

I laughed. Happy knows me well.

'No, I'm thinking about Mumbai,' I said after a few seconds. 'The time we went to the mall.'

'It was nice,' he replied, nostalgia missing in his voice. 'I had fun. But Baba told me not to think about Mumbai. He says winners look ahead, losers peep behind.'

'But you cannot see what lies ahead, while everything behind has such a clear view,' I countered and realized that I was still swirling in my whirlpool of gloom over leaving Mumbai, and now, I was dragging my little brother into the vortex. I decided to drift a bit, take him elsewhere, to space: 'Did you know, Happy ... even the sun, when you look at the sun, you're peeking into the past, looking behind?'

'How is that?'

'Sunlight travels through space, right? It takes eight minutes and twenty seconds to reach us. Therefore, when we see the sun, we're seeing it as it was eight minutes and twenty seconds ago. Hence, we're looking back in time. Isn't that cool?'

'Yes, but it'd be cooler if you could look ahead in time. Do they do that?'

'No, that's the problem.' I sighed. 'Also why we're on this journey.'

To shield him from the midday sun, I tied a handkerchief around Happy's head. The fireball shone right above us, bathing us in its fiery heat. As we walked, it got angrier, and over the next few hours, the arduousness of this journey started dawning upon me. All of us drank too much water, looking for public lavatories time after time. As we drifted further from Mumbai, more washrooms appeared locked. The boys and men managed. The entire country and all its walls seem to be their urinals, especially ones with the 'No Peeing' signs. The female of the species has no such benefit. We ran into shrubs and bushes along the highway, squatted amid ants, mosquitoes and caterpillars, and felt exposed.

About fifteen kilometres after the Mulund check post, the road narrowed, turning serpentine. It gave birth to hills and hillocks, clearer air, and privileged trees that had managed to live out their long lives in peace. The skyscrapers and hospitals disappeared. The malls became a memory, but the shrines remained as many—those dedicated to a single creator as well as multi-chambered ones with assortments of divinities, those built with stone as well as ones with golden canopies. Every time we encountered a house of god, Ma and Electron Aunty would remove their slippers, join their palms, and mutter a brisk, abridged prayer. They coaxed us to do it too, but we refused after the first few times. The sweltering earth was too hot for naked feet, and we knew that gods, too, might be busy looking for air conditioning.

As we moved along the winding road, it revealed the biggest temple we had encountered on our journey. Seated atop a hill, it watched over the thoroughfare, its tall, white spire stretching into the sky. When we neared the shrine, I noticed that a flight of stone steps on our side led to its entrance. Ma and Electron Aunty climbed a few stairs, perhaps to feel closer to the upraised deity, and performed their routine. Although I found it comical, their holy communing in the middle of a highway, I suspect the Almighty was listening. Within seconds, a boy as old as Neutron Sameer and I, appeared on the steps, running down towards us.

'You walking to village?' he asked, panting. The teenager was too poorly dressed to be a divine saviour—tatty shorts, fishnet vest and rubber slippers, but I let that pass. Heavens, I assumed, did not believe in sartorial judgement.

'Why do you want to know?' asked Baba, now careful with every stranger, even adolescents. I think he was suspecting the boy to be a police decoy. Although Baba did not show it, I knew he was anxious, especially after our recent confrontation with Conductor-Insulator and the preceding tear-gas shelling.

'Because I help,' the boy answered.

Father called out to the women of our group, and we began to leave.

'Okay, no problem. Don't listen me,' the boy added, still stingy with his conjunctions, prepositions and articles. 'But how far will you go? Big check post in ten kilometres, it is exit to Thane. You go north India, only route is that. Go, go; say hi-hello to policewallahs from me also.'

The teenager started walking away, hoping to add to the tension he had just created. It worked. Baba whistled at him. 'Aye, boy, wait,' he said. 'How can you help?'

'You see river on opposite side of road? My father, he is angler. He take you in my boat, drop you on other side of check post. Twenty-minute ride cost money, great scenery free.'

'How much for the ride?'

'Hundred rupees one person, so one, two, three, four … seven hundred rupees. Little boy free if sitting on lap.'

Baba excused himself to make a call. He spoke to Candy Kaka, who said that although he hadn't encountered cops at the toll post, they could be manning it now. He suggested that the boat would be safer.

'Make it three hundred for all of us,' said Proton Uncle, having learnt nothing from our bargains with Banjo, our previous contrabandist.

'Arre, uncle,' said the boy, 'that no cover my fuel also. We charge full minimum only, Mummy promise. Five hundred last, special rate, just for you.'

The men agreed, and we followed the boy onto the opposite side of the road. Although I was suspicious about him, I forgot it all when I saw the waterfront. It was wondrous, Ms Farah—a river flowing through the backdrop of blue-golden skies, sheltered by wooded mountains on both sides. The water looked like it was made of glass, and I'd believe it was if it didn't breathe, rising and falling with rhythmic ease. The wind, too, lived here, moist and a little savoury, but a welcome relief to our sweat-soaked bodies.

Accompanying the vista was a pristine promenade, with shipshape plants and saplings, and a gigantic pergola. Every tile, every flowerpot, and every lamppost appeared intact, and as I looked around, drowning in the tranquillity of that river, I realized it was much calmer than the sea. It also seemed to evoke its stillness in me, as opposed to the sea's gift of vigour. Baba's decision to leave Mumbai was as unprecedented as the lockdown, and it had robbed me of the opportunity to say goodbye to the sea. This landscape, hence, felt like a conspiracy, one masterminded by Mumbai, my city's endeavour to bid me a perfect farewell.

We walked for about 200 metres along the river before the road revealed a more believable site—a swampy shore flanked by hutments. The walls bore spray-painted instructions like 'No shitting here', and amid the writing, I spotted a placard with the waterfront's name: Gaimukh Chowpatty, or Cow-face Beach. We followed the boy into the miniature slum, and I discovered a warren of about two dozen shanties. Most of its residents were anglers, operating from an unofficial dockyard nearby.

As we passed by the hovels, I was stunned at the number of migrants sitting on the pathways between them. Scores and scores of them, and yet, I hadn't heard one sound of their presence when we walked into that web. They sat with their children on their laps, their luggage on their sides, and the fatigue of their journeys on their faces. Some fanned themselves with old newspapers; some ate, while others slept, their necks unsupportive, and their chins collapsing on their chests.

'Shhh,' said the baby smuggler. 'No-noise zone, this. Cops be like dogs, great ears.'

'We haven't spoken a word,' said Neutron Sameer.

'Free advice, take,' the boy replied. 'And now tell, you want food? Big menu I give—sandwich, rice, dal, chapatti, chutney, even the Chinese. For drink, tea, coffee, all brand of black soda.'

'We don't want anything,' said Sameer.

'Okay, buy water?'

'Just take us to the boat.'

The boy laughed. 'Three hours waiting minimum,' he said. 'You see this people? All wait for boat.'

The teenager allotted us a spot in one of the slum's by-lanes. We laid our bags down and sat under the restful shade of a gigantic tarpaulin sheet that crowned the labyrinth. Even as others complained about the delay, I felt relieved. Half a day had passed since we started walking, and I could use the three-hour wait to rest my feet. I stretched my arms and legs, while the grown-ups continued with their murmurs, fearing that we'd soon run out of money if we paid ₹500 per check post. *A legitimate concern*, I thought, but their voices had already turned distant to my ears. The words vanished once the salty wind started with its song. It soothed my sore body, and my fears began to retreat, graceful and light-footed. Then, along with my consciousness, they flew away.

It's the poor man's artist, the setting sun. It creates great art every evening, across the canvas of the turquoise sky, painting it with rich hues of reds, yellows and oranges, colours at the heart of a fire. As we waited along the shore for our boat, I kept watching the star at the horizon, as it moved between the mountain crests to take a dip in the golden waters. The pot of molten lava seemed sociable at this hour, as it allowed me to gaze at its radiance without retinal woes. It filled the air with a soft warmth, and it coloured me with hope, whispering in my ears through the breeze, saying that if we'd come this far, we'd make it to dawn.

'Do you see those colours, son?' Ma spoke to Happy, resting her arm on his tiny shoulders, pointing at the sky. 'Each of those shades has a meaning. Red is the colour of soil, representing the joy of harvest. Saffron is wisdom and purity, the colour worn by our monks. Yellow symbolizes summer, its light, its warmth. And blue, do you know why these colours adorn the blue sky? Because they're praying to blue-skinned gods—Krishna and Rama and Shiva, before the skies turn black, and the lords drift into sleep on their silver moon beds. But even when night does fall, my child, remember that the world will light up again tomorrow, with as many colours and as many blisses.'

From those words, I could tell that the unwelcome interlude had helped. Everyone seemed energetic after the break, waiting for our boatman to arrive, and sail us into the horizon. The angler appeared soon in the waters, on a traditional craft with a pointed bow, essentially a planked canoe. Made of teak, it wasn't longer than ten feet, with an angry engine that roared and rumbled inside a box. Although the vessel had a broad hull, it could not accommodate more than ten to twelve people. I stood disappointed at its size, as the ferryman anchored the boat on a pole in the waters, and pushed it onto the shore. I noticed the vessel's name painted on its teal body. She was the angler's Kripa or blessing.

I jumped into the canoe first, trying to identify the best seat. That's when I discovered the best thing about boats—every seat is a window seat. I chose the one closest to the bow, assuming it would offer the best view. Once we were settled, another family followed in—a pair of grandparents, a pair of parents, and one girl. Saleha, the girl, looked a little older than me, and when she smiled and introduced herself, I knew she encouraged familiarity, was pretty in an approachable way. Once everyone had boarded, the boatman pushed a button, pulled a string, and brought the cranky engine to life.

'Why isn't that vessel moving?' I asked the angler after spotting a fishing trawler parked in the middle of the river, a few minutes after we left the shore. Ma widened her eyes at me, pointing at her two ears and one tongue, asking me to shut up. Baba, however, placed his hand on hers, sanctioning my curiosity.

'People inside,' the ferryman said, gathering the chewing tobacco in his mouth into a lump, so he could speak with ease. I noticed the angler was a grown-up version of his son, dressed in a similar fishnet vest, shorts and rubber slippers. Although he was slender with a gaunt face, his arms were muscular, probably from the years of pulling and throwing nets, and lifting and transferring heavy loads. His hours in the sun, meanwhile, had dyed his skin black. 'People living inside, like you, migrants.'

'Since when?' I was surprised.

'Start of lockdown.'

'But why?'

'Arre,' whined the angler, spitting the globule into the waters, realizing I'd have more questions. To be audible above the engine, he had to scream and the tobacco was not helping. 'Those men, they return to land after fifteen-day fishing trip. Late March. By then, lockdown already happen. No export chance, so they dump fish back in sea. No work, so they want to go back to village. But trawler owner, old man, big belly, big heart, let them stay on boat.'

'But why didn't they go home?' asked Saleha.

'Home so far,' he said, and I realized that like his son, the ferryman, too, was averse to grammar rubrics. 'Also, land no safe. Water safe. No cop, no corona.'

'How are they managing food?' I asked.

'They got kerosene stove inside. We give supplies when they call. They no call too much. Phones charge when engine on. Engine on eats fuel.'

'Didn't they ask NGOs for help?' questioned Saleha, intelligent in expression.

'How many people will NGO help?' he said, spitting again into the waters; this time, in anger. 'Many thousand migrant anglers like this, live in trawlers or more small boats after lockdown, all anchor in coast of Maharashtra. This, only Maharashtra. Many more states in India, many more anglers like this. No food on boat, no water for drink, no talk to families, no income now, maybe not so much also later. Still, no one care. Why care? Billion people in this country. Some learn fishing after they die.'

While others were unperturbed, Saleha seemed to share my concern for the fishers. Her forehead creased, her jaw clenched a bit, and her dark eyes looked angry. I liked that look on her. I was incensed because I'm an aspiring journalist, and I have a heart that can feel no other way. But I wondered why she was enraged. Did Saleha, too, want to be a reporter? I decided I'll ask her once we were off the vessel, away from that conversation-hogging engine.

As our boat glided into the setting sun, it splashed water on our faces—liquid drops of diamonds, ablaze with golden fires within. I looked around and noticed that an orange haze had come to live on the waters, while the wind brimmed with the fragrance of nearby woods. Silhouettes of birds flew across the sky, and I imagined leaping off the boat, falcon-winged. Flitting and fluttering, I joined the birds, soaring over the mountains. When I looked down from my flight, I noticed that everyone in our boat was aglow with the sun's golden rays, their faces bearing the semblance of a smile. I kept hovering in silence, letting them enjoy that moment of farewell a little longer.

We crossed the river around twilight and reached a paradise of swamp. As soon as I stepped foot on the shore, my shoes sunk into the marshy soil, soft like ash. At first, I assumed the mud appeared waterlogged because it sat at the edge of the island. However, as we walked further, I discovered a soggy wasteland, a barren, ravaged world. Undisturbed mountains of trash dotted the landscape. Shrubs and reeds littered the ground, while the trees stood naked. They looked dead, those trees, standing tall only to avoid collapsing on those boggy tracks. *Careful*, I told myself. One misstep and the mire would swallow me whole.

'Wait, don't move,' said Baba, and walked a few steps to strip one of the trees of its branches. It bowed and yielded without a fight, and father returned with walking sticks for all of us.

'So, where's your village?' Saleha's grandfather asked Baba after thanking him for the cane. The man and his wife looked like old angels, at least one and a half centuries between the two. They had wizened faces, the kind that have riveting stories to tell. Toothless with silver hair, both their backs hunched a little, their bones appeared exposed under their thin skins, and their eyes seemed burdened with the wrinkles on their lids.

'Rajasthan,' replied Baba.

'Oh, good,' said the grandfather. 'We can keep you company. Our village is only a few kilometres away from the Rajasthan border, near the temple-town of Shamlaji in Gujarat.'

'Are you prepared to walk that far, kaka?' Proton Uncle asked.

'No, we're not walking,' said the old man. 'We'll take a truck soon.'

'Yes,' said Saleha's father. 'Why don't you join us? We're forty people, all travelling to Gujarat or Rajasthan. We belong to the same slum in east Mumbai, but we're moving in separate groups because it's safer that way. About ten kilometres from here, we'll gather at a spot where a trucker will be waiting for us. He'll drive us up to Jaipur.'

'How much is he asking?'

'One lakh rupees for the truck and we can have up to fifty passengers. It'll be around twenty-one hundred per person for the forty-seven of us, but we can bring him down to at least two thousand. We'll also tell him to let the child travel free. So, twelve grand for the six of you.'

As soon as Saleha's father mentioned the amount, all of us, perhaps even Happy, got busy with mental math:

₹7400 (Cash with Baba) + ₹6900 (Cash with Proton Uncle)
= ₹14,300
₹14,300 – ₹200 (Smuggler I/Banjo) = ₹14,100
₹14,100 – ₹500 (Smuggler II/Boatman) = ₹13,600
₹13,600 – ₹12,000 (Smuggler III/Trucker) = ₹1600

The numbers had spoken; we could take the truck. The driver's last stop was Jaipur, and if we got off at Parasli on the Rajasthan highway, which is on his route, our home would be less than 200 kilometres away. The remaining ₹1600 would be enough to get to our village from the highway. I was pleased. Saleha and her family had saved us from most of the walk.

'Isn't Saleha a Muslim name?' Baba asked after agreeing to the truck ride.

'No, it's Sanskrit,' the girl answered as I melted in embarrassment. 'It means noble.'

'Good,' said Father, visibly relieved. 'I wouldn't want to travel with *them* on this already dangerous journey.'

Baba's resentment towards the Muslim community is older than I am, and I could never get hold of its twisted roots. I suspect he was born with the antipathy, a wildly mutating hatred gene found in abundance in our country. For instance, only nine months ago, Baba—a man too busy with the nuts and bolts of his daily grind to care about politics—was overjoyed when the Indian government revoked the special, semi-autonomous status of the northern state of Jammu and Kashmir.

The Muslim-majority state, as every Indian kid knows from super-hit films, has been the subject of two wars between India and Pakistan. Now, with the new announcement, Kashmir had essentially become a part of India. Many, including my father, celebrated—the traditional, smoky fireworks and the customary, raucous drums. Many others danced on the streets, waved the tricolour and distributed sweets. Puzzled by the celebration, especially my father's, I asked my history teacher about Kashmir. He did not comment on the out-of-syllabus enquiry, just said that the festivities were because 'Pakistan has lost, India has lost, and Hindustan has won.'

I do not know all about Kashmir, ma'am, although I studied it last year. My Class Nine history textbook mentioned the disputed region under the broad topic of Indo–Pak relations, stating that, 'Pakistan considers Kashmir as the biggest hurdle in establishing relations with India.' It, however, summarized the two wars in two sentences, adding that the nature of the Indo–Pak conflict has now changed to terrorism.

Of course, I'm too little to comprehend every geopolitical and historical complexity ingrained in the strife. But I have learnt plenty about democracy, ma'am—and the images I saw on TV after they scrapped Kashmir's special status, they did not look like democracy to me. Kashmiri homes had turned into prisons for its politicians, cities became ghost towns with army-enforced lockdowns, and jails welcomed thousands of new entrants. A sinister silence reigned over those lives, relieved only by the rumbling engines of paramilitary vehicles.

'Is this fair?' I had asked my father at the time, pointing at the televised images of Kashmir's deserted streets, abandoned playgrounds, and the lengths and lengths of barbed wire that divided its neighbourhoods.

'What's right might not always be fair.'

'Do you know, Baba? They have the national pledge printed on the front page of each of our textbooks. It says, "All Indians are my brothers and sisters. In their well-being and prosperity alone lies my happiness." Is this well-being? Or prosperity?'

'This is suffering that precedes prosperity,' he said, firm as if stating a fact. 'The two always work in that order, no exception.'

I wonder if Baba would say the same today, after having lived through the loss of livelihood, the violence, and the unprecedented curfews that we saw in Kashmir—at a time when there was no pandemic for an excuse. I know he still would, and that breaks my heart.

I often wonder about the genesis of my father's passionate hate. No, he was not born with it, of course not. He has *learnt* to hate. But from where? Is it a colonial residue of the British Raj's 'Divide and Rule' policy? It could not be, he wasn't even born at the time. Is it something he picked up in Balhaar? No, because Proton Uncle, also born and raised in the same village, does not share his bitterness. Then maybe, someone is brainwashing Baba, injecting communal poison into his veins, and that of many, many other Indians. I wonder why they would do that, ma'am. Wouldn't it prove to be lethal? As our history teacher once said while discussing the World Wars, 'Hate is heavy—a secured debt, where the country is held as the collateral, the borrower is every citizen and the interest is blood.'

The marshy wasteland stretched for about half a kilometre before merging with the state highway. The six-lane motorway lay deserted, with only a rare vehicle whooshing by every few minutes. The road was also unlit, its darkness dissolving into that of the night, but the walk felt safe. The missing light had lent us a cloak of invisibility, and although I could not see much, I could tell we were walking amid greenery. There was a conspicuous drop in temperature, a woodsy fragrance lingered in the air, and I could hear the trees rustle in the wind. I could also hear crickets, the long-horned grasshoppers playing amid bushes, humming their characteristic jingle, 'tsitsi'. At times, Happy would join their song, and they'd go quiet, only to start again with much more gusto. *Tsitsi. Tsitsi. Tsitsi.*

After a few kilometres into the walk, Proton Uncle, who was leading our cluster, tumbled to the ground. He asked us to be careful, saying he had tripped over a rock. As he rose, Baba pointed his flashlight at the obstacle, so we could sidestep it, and we realized it was a man. Curled like a foetus on a worn-out black throw, he did not wake up when Proton Uncle's foot hit him, nor when we uttered a collective yelp upon spotting him. His eyes and mouth were half-parted, his clothes and hair were drenched in mud, and his face appeared twisted with agony. We could tell he was alive only because of his heavy breaths in the silence of that night.

'Are you awake?' Baba poked the man's arm with the tip of his walking stick. When he did not respond, Father tried to nudge him awake with his hands.

'Don't touch him!' Ma jumped. 'If he has the virus, it'll hop onto you.'

I noticed that the young man, who appeared to be in his early twenties, was trembling at intervals. He had a tattered mask around his mouth, and his feet were naked. A bag lay next to him, with a sealed packet of biscuits. Baba sprinkled some water on his face, and he woke up in a trice.

'I'm just going home,' he said, incoherent and dazed. 'I have an ID.'

'Are you drunk?' Father asked him.

'No, I'm just going home. You can see my ID.' The man sat up to prove he was sober. 'Do you have some water?'

Since we had limited bottles of water, Baba did not hand him one, but asked him to open his mouth. As Father poured the water down his throat, he gulped some of it, but soon broke into a bout of coughing. He pulled out a piece of cloth from his pocket and tried to stuff it in his mouth, perhaps to stop the coughing, or snub the jarring sound of his struggle for breath. It helped with neither.

I felt sorry for the man, the way his body shuddered with the fit. I, too, have a sore, painful history of cough. While the bhopa or medicine man of our village believes it's an inheritance from some past life, doctors in Mumbai say that it's some sort of dust, dog or pollen allergy. I, however, know it's something else, something more. The coughing spells have been with me since I was little, they kick in every few weeks, and they get worse during the physical training sessions in school, during winters and monsoons, during the flu seasons, and at times, simply because the sun has set and night has fallen.

When the fit occurs, I break into a long, irrepressible bout of coughing, where my throat tightens, my breath shortens, my chest threatens to implode, and my face turns pale. It takes many minutes before the spell subsides, and many more before the wheezing stops and my breaths regain normalcy. Ma gives me a crystallized lump of sugar to stop the coughing or a piece of clove, but when it persists for days, we have to see the doctor for a round of antibiotics. The way this man was coughing, I knew he was in need of antibiotics.

'Do you want some food?' Baba asked the man after he had composed himself, handing him the bottle of water.

'No, I cannot swallow,' he said, still groggy. 'My throat hurts.'

'For how long have you been here?'

'I don't know. Few hours, I think.'

'Do you have a fever?'

'Yes,' he exclaimed, suddenly energetic. 'That's why the motherfuckers threw me out of the truck.'

'What truck?'

'The truck I paid for, that truck. I boarded it last morning in Bengaluru, where I work, to get to my home in Gujarat. I got a fever after a few hours into the drive, and the passengers bought me some medicines from a town on the way. But my body did not stop burning, and they threw me out of the truck. They threw me on the road. Out of the truck. The motherfuckers!'

'Looks like he has corona,' said Father, and we all jerked back, as if we had spotted a streak of tigers. I felt guilty soon after, and I think Baba did too because he asked the man if we should dial a hospital for him.

'No,' he screamed between his coughs, clutching his chest, as if trying to squeeze the pain out of his heart. 'You won't be calling doctors, you'll be calling cops.'

'Listen, you need a doctor,' Baba tried to convince him. 'You're weak, you have a fever, and that cough is getting worse every second.'

'Get out of here,' the man howled, still breathless. 'Be on your way, now.'

'But you'll die on this road,' my father persisted.

'I won't,' he answered. 'I will only die at home.'

Many of us tried to persuade the man, asking him to let us call an ambulance, but he got angrier. Since he could not assemble the energy to stand up, he started flinging mud and stones at us. We decided to leave him alone.

Even as we walked away from that migrant, my disobedient mind refused to leave him behind. Mind II kept running back to him, thinking how, despite being so ill, he was determined to keep himself alive, only so he could die at home. I wondered what built that conviction in him. I wondered what built that conviction in the millions of migrant workers across India, who were walking hundreds of kilometres to get home. I could understand the need for it, the necessity that you must return home because the city isn't affordable any more. That, I understood. It was also why I was on the road. But I could not understand the want for it, this fatal romance with one's permanent address.

The man was foolish, I told myself; his longing, irrational. Convinced, I tried to silence Mind Junior, but my eyes got in the way, the image of his sunken face vivid before them. His face stayed with me even as I boarded our truck, even as the truck came to a halt, and even as cops aimed those flashlights in my face.

Yours,
Meher
In the wildwood

5

Stars

18 April 2020
Dear Ms Farah,

After we encountered that migrant worker on the highway, resolute to skirt death until he reached his home, I got thinking about Balhaar, my home, and what it meant to me. I tried to force affection onto my memories, some colour, but despite all that effort, home only meant doom to me—a laggard dust bowl that had once pushed my father towards suicide. It meant a thief, who was determined to rob me of my future, had I not escaped it in time. It meant a netherworld, where bias ruled the days, and anguish, the nights. The more I thought about my home, the more fortunate I felt for having fled it, for having built a new one in a land where hope was still legal.

It all started on a Tuesday, when an uncle in my village, also a farmer like my father, hung himself from a tree in his pearl millet field. I remember it was a Tuesday because Grandma was busy writing Lord Ram's name, the only word she can write, hundreds of times in red ink. Her notebooks always reminded me of my school punishments, where teachers, every time I jabbered too much, asked me to fill pages with 'I will not talk in class'. Dadi's notes, however, were far more commercial. Once deposited at the temple, the writing would oblige Lord Ram—the primordial lord of all lords, the slayer of demons, and the conqueror of three worlds.

Do you know, Ms Farah? There are banks dedicated to pleasing Lord Ram with bad handwriting. Perhaps, you could do a news report about them. Foreigners from every continent, except Antarctica of course, hold offshore accounts with them. The banks distribute free paper and keep the inscribed ones as deposits, trusting that Lord Ram will respond to the dust-laden reams. Hell, there are entrepreneurs selling varieties of paper for the holy scribble: hand-made paper, first-rate high GSM paper, revolutionary eco-friendly paper, and acid-free paper for bonus purity. Their other speciality: tiny chequered boxes and grids that perfectly accommodate the lord's three-lettered name. Ram, Ram, Ram…

The banks, if you ask me, are offering a decent bargain. All they want in exchange is this: hopefuls must write the lord's name 125,000 times while abstaining from onion, garlic and non-vegetarian food. I do not care about meat; I'm a vegetarian by inheritance. However, I did ask Grandma about the ostracism of onion and garlic once. Her response: aspiring yogis and soothsayers avoid the two because they stimulate the nervous system, can rupture vows of celibacy. They get the men too excited, she said, especially garlic, a natural aphrodisiac.

'Girls your age must also keep from too much excitement,' she added, staring me down through those thick glasses. Then, she ordered a tireless yearning in me for the sacrilegious excitants: 'No more onion and garlic for you, not until you're married.'

That Tuesday afternoon, I was walking home from school when I saw Kalu Uncle hanging by a noose from a tree—his loose, open palms idling by his thighs, his naked chest melting in the desert heat, his dry tongue sticking out, and his half-parted eyes accentuating his deathly demeanour. Aeons of donkey work in the field had shrunk his body of thirty-four years to a papery frame, and he was underdressed for death—just a soiled loincloth around his waist.

Kalu, the Hindi word for black, is one of the most popular names in our village, and Kalu Uncle earned it because of his ebony skin. The man's colour or his melanin levels never bothered me. But that afternoon, as he hung from the tree, his skin first caught my eye. It glistened in the afternoon sun, as if a million stars danced on his flesh, as if the universe had cast a spotlight on him, cheering him as he put on a show. His cadaver looked healthier than his living body ever did, and as I neared his corpse, I smiled. Kalu Uncle had become a star.

You might think I'm nuts. In my defence, I was eight at the time, ma'am, and I knew little about death and its ill-mannered finality. I believed Dadoo when he said that once people die, they become stars, stars that watch over us when night falls. He reasoned that there are billions of stars in the universe because there are billions of dead people on earth. Kalu Uncle had wanted to become a star, I told myself. It made sense. Have you ever witnessed the night sky in a desert, ma'am—the tens of thousands of stars scattered across the black canvas like moon-dust, breathing life into it with their platinum shimmer? They gaze back at you, those stars, twinkling and chattering, and luring you to their distant galaxy. Who wouldn't want to be among them?

Soon, however, Kalu Uncle's glimmer faded. I realized he had been selfish. While he merrily left to join a constellation, his family fell to pieces. Over the years, the farmer had drawn a loan of ₹38,000 from a private moneylender, hoping that the pesticides he was buying and re-buying, and the bajra he was sowing and re-sowing, would save his fields. But Balhaar is a desert, ma'am, one where the rain plays and wins at the game of hide-and-seek. We haven't seen a generous shower in years, and water is the coin of this land. Women and girls make daily trips to the beri, a traditional percolation tank, and hide their full pots to avoid theft. There are fights over water, and there are allegories about water—stories of abundant lakes that once dotted the thirsty landscape and legends of those that never dried up, continued to cradle civilizations. Kalu Uncle should have used that money to dig a tube well. The uneducated man he was, he didn't, and with no way to feed his family, he fled to the Milky Way.

A day after his death, the moneylender—an angry bison–like, moustached man, who knew he would not get his money back, took Kalu Uncle's daughter away. Kalu Aunty was happy to let the twelve-year-old go. One less growling stomach in the house and she would have to marry the girl off in a year or two anyway, as soon as she got her first period. The humped moneylender had saved her from the dowry payment and pardoned the loan—an irrefutable deal for Kalu Aunty, two birds with one bison.

I know Kalu Uncle's story might not surprise you. Dozens of farmers die by suicide every day in our country, and as a seasoned journalist, you've seen it all—the financial distress, the nooses, and the loan sharks that feed on farmers as well as their carcasses. I, however, was pained when they took the daughter away. I saw her, Ms Farah, and I had kept looking. She did not want to go. She wailed, begging her mother to keep her, pleading with her star-father for help. Her baba did not show up, and the village council watched in silence. She bit the bison's hand to escape his grip, and Kalu Aunty slapped her. Then, she boarded his SUV—the echoes of her cries frozen, the tears in her eyes silent, and every grain of fight in her, forfeited.

After Kalu Uncle's suicide, I would follow Baba to the fields. I would skip school and watch him from behind a few bushes as he ploughed and sowed. Every time he neared a tree, my heart would jump. My eyes would search for the criminal rope and the pile of bricks he would use to climb up to the noose. I was afraid that my father, too, would become a celestial object, aware that he, too, was scheming for a spot in the skies.

Cannabis. It's god's own medicine, the gateway to enlightenment, a hallucinogenic blessing. That's how Balhaaris describe it. They swear by its holiness, associating it with Lord Shiva, the greatest among gods, the unvanquished master of elements, and the supreme lord of the three worlds. No, no, do not confuse him with Lord Ram. Although they have similar identifiers, Lord Shiva appears the coolest in his portrayals. He sits on a tiger skin, garlanded with a serpent, body smeared with ash, and a trident in his hand. A few depictions also paint him with a smoking pipe, one brimming with marijuana, Balhaar's darling narcotic that celebrates every sprout of life, and mourns every speck in the dust of death.

'You're not distributing cannabis. You're handing out Shiva's prasad, his sanctified blessing,' said the sadhu, who was officiating Kalu Uncle's funeral. The man had wrapped his long, matted dreadlocks in a leopard-print scarf. Dozens of rosary beads groped his neck, and his body was white from ashes borrowed from cremation pyres. After spending decades in the Himalayas, the ascetic, dressed in an ochre loincloth, had now become the resident guru of Balhaar. He smeared some of Kalu Uncle's ash on his forehead, and announced, '*Bum bum bhole.*' (Praise be to Lord Shiva.)

Sitting next to a small, smoky fire, the sadhu packed a conical clay pipe, called chillum, with the weed that Kalu Uncle's family had gifted him. He pulled a long drag, and the smoke rushed out of his mouth and nose, clouding his furrowed face, and mingling with the little bonfire. His red-rimmed eyes turned fiery.

'Oh, the creator and destroyer. Oh, the unborn and the deathless. Oh, the auspicious one. Accept Kalu into your heavenly abode. Bless his soul,' the sadhu orated, puffing and coughing. 'Bless it.'

Men and children from most of Balhaar's seventy lower-caste families had gathered for Kalu Uncle's dazed send-off. The upper castes, obviously, were absent, as the deceased's family, like ours, is proletarian. The rich live in a cluster away from ours, their elite neighbourhood housing the revered and the brainy—the artisans, scholars, priests, landowners and moneylenders. Our lower-caste vicinity, meanwhile, resides on the other side of Balhaar's invisible line of control, accommodating the poor and the impoverished—the labourers, manual scavengers, barbers, blacksmiths and domestic servants.

If you ever visit Balhaar, ma'am, you could identify our plebeian homes with ease—exposed mud walls, roofs thatched with straw, earthen floors coated with dung, do-it-yourself furniture and zero whitewashes. The upper crust's homes, meanwhile, are tip-top and top-notch—roofed with concrete, in-house bathrooms, and elaborate courtyards filled with white SUVs. The aristocrats also have separate corrals for their pet camels, cows, bullocks, goats and sheep, and at times, even horses. Rich animals, snug sheds, and delicious fodder.

As the mystic performed the funerary rituals, the bereaved family distributed cannabis leaves among mourners. Men sat smoking in circles, their thick fumes snaking into the sky and dissolving into the dusk. It was a grand funeral, one could tell. The drug aside, the family, like the upper castes, had also hired professional mourners—women weepers, selling tears for cash. Dressed in black, the funeral celebrities sat surrounding Kalu Aunty. They wailed, howled, and beat their chests, and soon, their fat tears stained their cheeks with kohl. Kalu Uncle had a lower-caste life, a lower-caste death, but an upper-caste funeral.

'How did they afford all this?' Baba asked Proton Uncle after we returned home from the service. The two sat on a charpoy outside our house, smoking a chillum, as I lay with my head on Baba's lap.

'The old, furry moneylender gave them twenty thousand rupees for the girl,' said Uncle. 'He's marrying Kalu's twelve-year-old.'

'And they spent all that money on the funeral?' Baba was stunned. The marriage, given the science of marriages in Balhaar, was sound.

'Looks like it, but it's okay. They'll get five times the amount once the government pays them for the suicide.'

'Rubbish.' Baba spat after lighting the chillum. 'They're getting nothing.'

'It's the law of the land, brother. You kill yourself, you get one lakh rupees. You live, you get balls.'

'Even if you commit suicide, you get nothing.' Baba exhaled. 'How will the widow prove that Kalu killed himself over agricultural distress? There's no suicide note. And like most of us, he borrowed the cash from a private lender. Moneybags isn't stupid to keep an official record of the debt, and risk arrest under financial laws. With no documents, how will she prove that he was a genuine farmer, who genuinely committed suicide over genuine farm distress?'

'Agreed,' said Proton Uncle, pulling the chillum from Baba's hand. 'But don't fret. With this huge cannabis offering, Lord Shiva will take care of the compensation.'

'What's with this custom of ganja funerals anyway?'

'What's the problem with it?' said Proton Uncle, a little irked. 'What's the problem with you?'

'Our scriptures don't mention or recommend it. And the man has passed. What's to celebrate?'

'His life, his memory, the end of his suffering, what else?'

'Nonsense. This is no celebration-velebration,' said Baba, pulling the pipe back, his eyes now turning red from the green leaves in his chillum. 'Villagers will turn your life into hell if you do not throw the ganja party. Don't you remember? That Navin did not host one for his father because he could not afford the narcotic. They haunted and taunted him, saying he did not love his old man, not enough to send his soul on a spiritual trip with Shiva.'

'True. But when people turn up in large numbers for these funerals, as they did today, it indicates that the deceased was a good man and that many have shown up to mourn him.'

'To mourn or to get free weed?'

'What did you go for?'

'To grieve,' answered Baba. 'Well, mostly.' After a few puffs, he added, 'I also went to see what transpires after a suicide.'

'And what did you see?'

'More debt for the family, party for the rest.'

'Including us.'

'Yes,' said Baba, handing the magic pipe to Uncle. 'But that's not the point. The point is, I do not want to kill myself any more. I had been thinking about it for months, and I was going to do it yesterday, but they found Kalu's body before I could make my noose.'

Proton Uncle did not respond, exhaling, and compelling Father to elucidate, bridge the silence with words. 'The same reasons as any other farmer,' Baba continued. 'Debt has mounted and droughts of the past few years have dried up all the money. There's no hope this year either, and in a few weeks, I won't have enough to feed my children. All I have is this useless piece of land, which isn't good to sow or sell. Suicide seemed rational.'

'Nonsense.' Proton Uncle slapped Baba's cheek. 'Firstly, suicide takes courage. And you, my friend, jump when you spot a spiny-tailed lizard, even if it's in a picture. Second, it isn't the solution. You can fight for your family, your corpse cannot. Third, you know I've been down that road, and I regret treading it.'

'I'm not doing it,' said Baba, speaking more to himself. 'I saw Kalu's widow and her children. I could never do that to my family.'

'Good,' replied Proton Uncle. 'I'm in the same drowning boat as you are. We'll look for a shore together.'

I was little, Ms Farah, and at the inkling of Baba's death, I started crying, louder than the professional mourners did. Baba could not become a star or unleash lustful bison on us. No, no. I sobbed and wailed, and Ma rushed out of the kitchen.

'Baba wants to suicide,' I told her, tears rushing down my cheeks. 'He wants to suicide.'

Ma stood staring at Baba, her eyes disappointed but unsurprised, as my grief ballooned into a cough—my first coughing spell, as far as I can remember. It grew uncontainable in seconds and I began to struggle for each breath. I could feel my ribs contract, my lungs emanate a harsh, high-pitched sound, as inhaling turned laborious, and then, impossible. I knew I had to stop crying, so I wiped the tears off my face, while Ma brought me a glass of water. Although the cough wouldn't allow a moment of respite, I forced the water down my throat, and my narrowed airways pushed it back out. As I vomited, I realized that I had to wait for the fit to pass. It was a few minutes before it died, and when it did, every ounce of energy in my body had perished with it.

Father hugged me after I regained composure. 'I thought you were asleep, my child.' Noticing how weak I'd become, he added, 'I'm not suiciding, Gudiya. I'm not going anywhere. I would never, never leave you.'

Although Baba pledged to live and kept repeating his pledge, the family wasn't convinced. Dadi started writing more pages for Lord Ram, and Ma exhausted all her savings of ₹200 on our trip to the Sati Devi temple. We had to change three buses to get to the shrine, but Ma insisted that it had to be done, that 'praying to this goddess has a hundred per cent guaranteed results.'

Once we reached the small, nondescript hamlet, I noticed that a former cremation ground doubled as the devi's temple. The idol was a golden trident draped with a long scarf or dupatta, standing firm on a brick platform. The spear signified feminine virtue, the priest told us—the golden radiance emanated by an eighteen-year-old girl, who burnt herself alive at her husband's cremation pyre and turned into an instant goddess.

'This was four decades ago,' the priest recollected. 'The couple had been married for less than a year when the man died of a sudden illness. She saw his body, wept for a few minutes, and then left to put on her red wedding sari and her bridal make-up. After they lit the husband's pyre, she climbed onto it. The flames engulfed her, as she sat unmoved, chanting prayers. Hundreds of onlookers cheered her on—the epitome of a dutiful wife, one who followed her husband to the afterlife.'

Three months after the temple visit, Baba moved to Mumbai with Proton Uncle, giving up on the farm and his suicide bid. I cannot tell if it was Dadi's extra pages for Lord Ram, the leafy blessing of Lord Shiva, or the prayers to the specialist goddess for husbands, but something had worked. Baba was in Mumbai, far from the desert of destitute stars, snorkelling in the sea of survivors until this novel, zoonotic tide threatened to swallow him.

It was a little after midnight when the cops took us captive. We had been travelling in the truck that Saleha's family had arranged for us—seventy-eight men, women and children, crammed in that eighty-square-foot space, like cotton balls stuffed in a polythene bag. The trucker with the red lorry had picked us up from a secluded spot off the highway. About five metres long, the vehicle had a sheet of paper pasted on its windshield, proclaiming, 'Essential Goods Duty.' As we climbed into its cargo space, we discovered thirty-one passengers lying on gunnysacks, their luggage hanging on a rope line suspended across the truck.

'You're cheating us,' our group confronted the truck driver. After we met more residents of Saleha's slum on the highway, our number had increased to forty-seven, and we were not expecting further company on the drive. 'You'd said you'll have fifty people in the truck, and now, there are thirty-one more.'

'No, I said you can get up to fifty people,' the trucker stated. 'I never mentioned the total number of passengers.'

'Do not twist words,' someone barked. 'You're a crook.'

'Are you coming or should I leave without you?' The driver was unperturbed. I could not see much of the trucker's face under that dark night, but his moonlit silhouette informed he was a heavyset man—tall, square-shouldered, buffalo-necked, pot-bellied. He could knock any of us out with his pinkie.

'Come on, come on, let's take the truck,' one of the migrants waved a white flag, probably thinking of the driver's pinkie. 'It'll be uncomfortable, but we can manage. Think of it as our slum on wheels.'

'No,' said another. 'Why should we pay full money for half the space? Reduce the price, or we're not going.'

'I cannot,' the trucker softened. 'My boss, the vehicle owner, has decided the rates. I'm only a driver. You will have to pay twenty-one hundred and twenty-eight rupees each, so I can have one lakh from the forty-seven of you.'

'Make it fifteen hundred per person.'

'Impossible,' the driver stood his ground. 'I'll have to pay the difference from my pocket. My boss is an angry man.'

Our group persisted too, leading to a round of diverse outbursts among our people—blabbering, stomping, screeching, cursing and name-calling. Their emotions followed no particular order, dancing a motley, asynchronous dance of tone and pitch. None of it worked, so a more mannerly set of humans from our cluster took the stage.

'You're like a brother to us, bhaiya,' the group appealed to the trucker in a perfect chorus, as if they had rehearsed their opening line in advance. 'Have mercy on your distressed brothers and sisters.'

'You're unlike your master. You're not a leech,' went the second arrow from their emotive armoury. 'You're human like us, and you must help your kind.'

'God is watching, bhaiya,' the group pulled out nuclear arms for their third strike. 'You do not want to earn his wrath.'

After tenacious guerrilla warfare, the driver agreed on ₹2000 per person. He also let Happy travel free after Electron Aunty turned our men's pockets inside out, proving they were empty. Our remaining ₹1600 were safe with Neutron Sameer.

Huddled in the truck's goods compartment, our human cargo struggled for space. It smelled like spices, the carrier, and I could tell it was on its way back to Rajasthan, the Seed Spices Bowl of India, after delivering its famed seasonings in Mumbai. Spices make everything smell like spices, and they'd wrapped the truck with a heady, savoury smell. Coriander, cumin, garlic, ginger and turmeric, I could identify, but there could have been more.

The men occupied one wall of the truck, while women stood by the other. Kids filled the intervening space, their faces packed between our stomachs. As the heavy vehicle galloped on the dark highway, I felt like I was standing in an overcrowded, peak-hour local train in Mumbai. Do not get me wrong, ma'am. I'm no stranger to crowds; I've lived in Dharavi. In fact, I'd say that life in the slum often resembles that on a Mumbai local—airless, congested, buzzing with Bollywood and spiritual songs, animated with gossip and card games, and a bustling galaxy of cursing, pushing, shoving, slapping and hair-pulling. However, I'd also say that favelas are much easier to survive than Mumbai's trains.

As we stood packed like sardines in that truck, I remembered my first experience with the Mumbai local, the city's lifeline and the world's busiest and deadliest railway system. It was the morning rush hour, and the crowd wouldn't allow Ma and me to board the women's compartment. We entered after everyone in the world had plunged into that hole, and the only space our feet could find was the footboard at the edge of the bogie. We hung by a pole at its gate, and as a railway station approached, the train slowed down, but we did not disembark, waiting for the driver to pull the brakes. To my stupefaction, that irked a few commuters.

'What are you waiting for? The train to stop?' an aunty shrieked, before pushing us aside and leaping off the train.

That day, I learnt that Mumbai, a city that is always on a deadline, is home to countless geniuses, experts at beating the laws of inertia. Jumping off running trains is a popular sport here. It leads to broken bones at times, but more often, like the aunty in our bogie, the whizzes get away without hitting the ground—running on railway platforms for a few minutes after they leap, and matching the train's velocity until their bodies are fit to stop without tumbling.

In addition to the overpopulation, there was another similarity between our truck and train rides—both the journeys had brought a diverse range of travellers together, sharing a common goal: reach their destination on time, and with some luck, alive. However, unlike the train, the truck's ceiling was made of plastic rags, devoid of grab rails for support. Every time the trucker drove over a pothole, our bodies would jump up together, hitting the luggage above us. Every time the road turned, we'd all turn with it, swinging and swaying, as if a single piece of mass, a cube of clay.

Less than two hours into the drive, the truck came to a screeching halt. We were expecting the break. Before we boarded the vehicle, the driver had informed us that we'd reach the interstate border between Maharashtra and Gujarat soon. Should he spot police deployment there, he would ask us to get off the truck at least 300 metres before the check post. We'd have to cross the border on foot thereafter, through the fields by the highway, and meet him on the other side.

As we waited for the driver to open the door, I heard an array of noises, including those of batons pounding against the vehicle's body. Men screamed in anger, and a man screamed in pain. The breaths inside our truck grew quieter, the prayers more earnest, and each of our bodies melted with tense sweat. Within seconds, the door was open, flashlights illuminated our guilty faces, and we knew all was over.

'Another human consignment,' declared the police in-charge, dressed in a khaki uniform and a mask pulled down to his neck. Five cops accompanied him, but I could tell he was the bull among the sheep. Tall and moustached, he was brawnier than his flock, furnished with a muscular jaw and aggressive arms. His masculine shoulders had three silver stars sparkling on them, more radiant than those in the sky.

'Bring the motherfuckers down,' the Bull ordered, banging his baton against the truck, as if penalizing the vehicle.

Once we had alighted with our luggage, the sheep counted us, revealing twenty-four women, forty-three men, including the driver, and twelve kids, including a six-month-old.

'No one's going to beat you,' the Bull responded to our pleas for moderation, 'assuming you cooperate. You disobey, you pay.'

'Yeah, you disobey, you pay,' reiterated a sheep, probably pleased with his boss's rhyme. In a belated imitation of the Bull, he also banged his wooden stick against the truck. I could tell this one was the ram, the leader of the four lambs. He stood close to the Bull, with a similar soldierly moustache, the colour of burnt wood. His eyes were fierce enough for his dominion over the flock of baby sheep, but it also had a tinge of docility, a sign of his submission to the cattle leader.

'Aye, where's the driver?' the Bull bellowed as we stood under the serene, star-lit skies playing music for our eyes. It was naked, the highway. Dressed only in the green robes of nature, it had no building, street lamp, signpost, or any other retrofit, except for the motorway, which looked like a bald stream running through a lush scalp. Other than the tarmac, the highway stood raw, silent, until the lambs started bleating.

'Get him, get him,' the lambs cried as our driver loped into the bushes along the highway. We watched the trucker's futile flight as the baby sheep caught up to him, as they grabbed him by the nape of his neck, and then kicked him back to the highway. The natural orchestra of the night tapered off, now replaced with the trumpet of synthetic expletives.

'We're doomed, aren't we?' I asked Baba, who stood in the men's line parallel to ours. 'Now, it's either jail or a migrant camp or Mumbai.'

'Don't worry,' Father replied without looking into my eyes. 'The officers will arrange for us to get to Rajasthan.'

Baba's fraudulent response irked me. I understand that he was trying to shield me with that lie, but he must know I'm not little any more. It was obvious that we were standing in the line of fire, and should the missiles come flying, I'd rather be prepared. The truth would help me in that case, not his airy hope or his white lies. I was pissed, but I stayed mum. This was no time to turn against each other.

That night, as Baba stood in that queue of the ill-starred, I watched him. He's a tiny man, my father—no taller than five-and-a-half feet, skin the colour of milk chocolate, and velvet-black, determined eyes. His veins compete for attention on his hard, farmer's hands, and his tired shoulders hardly droop. Back in Balhaar, he used to have a long, gravity-defying moustache that curled towards his nose, just like Dadoo's, but he got rid of it once he moved to Mumbai. 'Too country,' he said. Now, he has a small, bushy one, like Mr Albert Einstein's, wild but lovable.

Ma, too, made a few post-migration changes. In Balhaar, she would wear the traditional Rajasthani attire—a full-length, pleated skirt called a ghagra, a choli or blouse embellished with beads and sequins, and a three-metre-long embroidered dupatta that covered her face and torso. It's imperative that she hid herself behind that stole, especially her face. Villagers believe that the ghoonghat or veil represents her honour, her modesty, and protects her from the lecherous eyes of strange men. Of course, it's hot inside the veil, especially in the desert heat. Of course, she could see better without the fabric clouding her view, but these are cultural hangovers, ma'am—they're greasy and they stick. We keep hearing about ghoonghat revolutions in neighbouring villages, where women dare to walk unveiled before unfamiliar men. However, Balhaar, as our panchayat or village council says, 'is still safe from that profane, demonic influence.'

Ma has two halves—one modern and defiant, another traditional and a burden to her. Once in Mumbai, she shunned the ghagra-choli, started wearing saris, and then sewed herself a pair of salwar-kamiz—loose trousers with a knee-length tunic, and a short dupatta that did not smother her face. Two years later, she got bolder, wearing jeans, thigh-length tops, and no dupatta. You should have seen her when she wore those tops, ma'am. There was a mini rebellion in those cotton blouses, and each time she put them on, she was a revolutionary—her against the disorder of social order, warring and wearing on behalf of her mother, sisters, every woman in Balhaar and all of India. Of course, she would not dare to wear those clothes in our village. Her mutiny had limited geography, the Mumbai Metropolitan Region.

While Ma gave up on the veil after moving to Mumbai, she continues to don other markers of married Hindu women—a long line of vermilion-red powder in the centre parting of her hair and the mangal-sutra around her neck. While the red pigment is to ensure spousal longevity, the thread of black beads doubles up as a protective sheath, guarding her marriage against evil forces. My mother believes in amulets more than she does in evolution, and she has tied black threads around all of Happy's limbs, even his neck. I don't need protective talismans; she says, 'The evil needs protection from you.'

'Why do you keep saying that?' I asked her once.

'Just,' she answered, 'look how you talk; look how you talk back. You do not need amulets. You can chase demons away with your words.'

'It's still better than being a pseudo modernista,' I told her. 'You know those blouses are fake empowerment, right?'

She laughed. 'See, I told you.'

It's no secret that Ma loves Happy more. With those dimpled cheeks, long eyelashes, and two of his front teeth now missing, the three-foot boy has a cherubic charm. Happy's official name is Vinod, meaning happiness, and for him, joy is simple—a ₹10 chocolate bar, a few minutes of batting while playing cricket, or fantasizing about his principal dream, a remote-controlled toy car. Happy turns unhappy only when he's hungry, but he's always a bit of a drama queen. 'I get nightmares when I drink milk before going to bed,' he says to get away from the beverage. 'I think I should keep away from it.' When the parents don't listen, he adds, 'Don't you say that children are god's avatars? You must listen to god.'

As for me, I, too, am tiny for a fifteen-year-old, and my most prominent feature is my nose ring. It's just a golden hoop, but it talks too much. In Mumbai, the moment teachers saw it, they knew I've come from a village, likely illiterate. In Balhaar, the moment anyone saw it, they knew I was ready to bear children. Girls usually have their nostrils pierced after they get their first period. It's believed that nerves from the left nostril rush straight to the reproductive organs, and piercing it eases childbirth.

'You'll be thankful later,' said Grandma when I got mine.

While Ma loves Happy more, Baba favours me. Unlike Ma, who thinks that life cannot be led in metaphors, that life is too deep for metaphors, my father and I enjoy the hidden parallels of life. While I'm still learning the art of postulation, inspired by my geometry textbooks, Baba has his routine of mirage analogies. Every time he likens the optical illusion to life, he glances at me in expectation, waiting for a slow nod with pursed lips, expressing approval, even wonder. I nod, I purse.

I think Baba adores me also because I study hard, and I'm always among the top rankers in my class. He knows I aspire to be a reporter, and I think he feels proud. Until a year ago, when I had wanted to become a broadcast journalist, he would pretend to be the cameraperson as I held a rolling-pin microphone in my hands and delivered my mock news reports. He would say, 'lights, camera, action,' and he'd say, 'cut,' despite repeated reminders that those were filmmaking commands. I think my ambition excites Baba, perhaps because he could never dare to dream. When you live in a ten-by-ten-foot home, you hope niggardly and dream calculatedly.

As I watched my father, standing on that highway, the lambs assaulted the trucker, tore his pockets, and snatched every rupee he had, including the money we had paid him for the ride. They handed the cash to their leader, and upon spotting the fat stack, the Bull attacked the driver with his horn-like baton. He kept battering the man until his cries grew into wails, and his breaths turned into gasps. He pocketed the cash, and showed the tearful trucker to the front of the men's line, like a mischievous kid forced to the classroom's foremost bench. The Bull then led our group off the highway, and as we walked with flashlights guiding our feet, I spotted the barricaded interstate border in the distance. We were moving away from it though, towards Mumbai.

Yours,
Meher
In the wildwood

6

Sugar Ants

19 April 2020

I was wondering, Ms Farah…

Have you ever felt little? Perhaps, like a sugar ant. No, exactly like a sugar ant. I mean, it does not matter that you're harmless, that you'd never sting, or that even if you bite to defend yourself, it wouldn't hurt. It's insignificant that you'd never leave your home in the heaths and the forests, had you not been desperate for food. It's nugatory that the worker ants of your family toil, sweat and slave, foraging for food, protecting it from predators, and building nests. It's of zero consequence, whether you're a queen ant or a larva, a good ant or bad. What matters is that you're little, and you can be crushed. In some cultures, you must be crushed.

When police officials doused our bodies with those chemicals, ma'am, I felt like a sugar ant. It was irrelevant that I was a good student, a decent daughter, and that I hoped to be a diligent journalist someday. It was worthless, the honesty that my parents thrive by. Trifling, their obedience for every man-made institution of terror—government, god, karma, hell and superstition. Trivial, their non-violence, the fact that they would never hurt anyone, not even an ant. What mattered was the depth of Baba's pockets, and the lack of it, somehow, coloured us fit for oppression. We could be crushed, no problem.

After the cops apprehended us near the Maharashtra–Gujarat interstate border, the Bull and his cattle escorted us to a ground, a twenty-minute, unlit walk from the highway. I cannot recall the exact route as it was too dark, but I know we had entered a village. I'd seen the nude, yellow bulbs illuminating the little porches of little huts, and I'd heard the tetchy fans inside concrete ones. Soon, the lights and sounds had disappeared, and under the veil of that black, silent night, we walked, as if blind, as if deaf.

Dawn found our seventy-nine bodies asleep, supervised by four police officials. Our bags were at work as our pillows, our spare clothes made for our mattresses, and the blanket, the blanket was a knitting of fear. The Bull and the Ram had left as soon we reached the ground. The lambs stayed, noting our names, addresses, phone numbers and identity-card details wherever available. As we dictated our particulars, our fears erupted into questions, fogged the air, but the sheep refused to clear the haze. The cloud of doubt stayed through the night, got denser by daybreak: 'Let us go, sahib.' 'Our parents are waiting for us, sahib.' 'I haven't seen my children in two years, sahib.' 'We would have died in the city, sahib.' 'No, please don't beat us, sahib.'

The cops, however, stuck to their sticks, and every query found an answer in the colonial weapon for crowd control. Soon, a labourer fell to the ground while escaping the lathi, hit his forehead on a rock, and bled. He stood up within moments, rubbed some mud in his wound, and returned to his questions. Innocent blood, says history, creates either patriots or tyrants, poets or prophets, warriors or scoundrels.

In our case, it did nothing. It was not real, the migrant's blood. It was cheap, red sweat.

Once the Bull and Ram returned, the chaos paused. Dressed in fresh uniforms, their hair was still moist from their showers, and both had a pair of black aviator sunglasses shielding their eyes, as if cops pulled out of a Bollywood reel. They jumped off their motorbike, and the Bull took to a megaphone, instructing us to queue up. He had food for us, he proclaimed. We'd be home soon, he promised. We obeyed, and a lamb went about us, noting our body temperatures with a contactless, pistol-shaped thermometer. Happy, who was asleep in Baba's arms, was startled when the cop pointed the device at him. The boy mistook it for a firearm, and Father had to calm him, apologize for his warranted fright.

After we collected our packets of puffed rice, the Bull informed us that it would be a few hours before buses arrived to drive us home. 'We need clearances from the Gujarat and Rajasthan state governments, so you can cross the border without trouble,' he explained over the megaphone. 'It's nine in the morning now, and everything should be in order by two in the afternoon. Until then, do not bore us with questions. The food packets have been sponsored by a huge-hearted, very noble politician, and he'll be here soon to click pictures with you.'

It was not generous, the food, but it was hot. We mixed the rice with our last batch of cooked potatoes and guzzled our meal. I wanted to use the washroom, but I knew that as earlier, I'd have to walk to the woods that fringed the ground. I decided against it and lay on the mud for some rest. Surrounded by trees, the circular space had enough shade for all of us. A few huts stood nearby, and curious villagers often lurked around, observing our affairs. Most left in minutes, disappointed with the lack of entertainment.

The humoured bellies lulled a few migrants to sleep. Eyes rested also because the Bull had seemed genuine in his last address, even his promise of delivering us home. He could not stand the weight of his conscience, we assumed, perhaps because of the barrage of news reports in the past few weeks. They told stories of millions like us, who had set out on foot for their villages—mowed down by tempos, killed by fatigue, massacred by heat, and murdered by hunger. 'Indian migrants are dying to get home,' informed a news headline. 'India is walking home,' stated another.

As I waited for the afternoon to arrive with our buses, Saleha lay down next to me, and we got talking. Dressed in a peacock-blue salwar-kamiz with pink embroidery and a matching dupatta, the girl was beautiful in the conventional way—ruddy complexion, features like artwork, and midnight-black hair that touched her waist. She wore an air of aplomb around her long, firm bones, and I could tell that her poise did not originate from the sculpture of her skin, but somewhere deeper.

Since I'm usually the most talkative one in any room, I told Saleha all about me, and discovered that she was no fan of brevity either, as she, too, offered an uninhibited peek into her life. She was twenty-four years old, she told me, much older than her delicate face suggested. An arts graduate, she lived with her parents in a slum in the eastern Mumbai suburb of Govandi, home to tens of thousands of daily-wage migrant labourers.

'The coronavirus lockdown added a deeper colour to our slum's despair,' said Saleha, her brown, aware eyes looking as if they had seen things. 'It struck us like a hammer, burying us deeper into the ground.'

'Of course, like Dharavi,' I said.

'No, nothing like Dharavi,' she corrected me. 'Dharavi is the superstar of slums and Govandi is its much poorer shadow. My ghetto sits near the Deonar dumping yard, where Mumbai sends thousands of tonnes of waste every day. They say that the junk has piled up to a height of nearly twenty floors. Dharavi, I'm sure, has no such monument to boast about.'

'Oh yes, I know Deonar.' I was reminded of a news report. 'There was something on TV about how those mounds of waste stink, and how the city was planning to buy lots of herbal deodorant to kill the smell.'

'Yes, that's the one. That's my home,' she said. 'And the mounds do more than that. They catch fire and cause diseases—tuberculosis, skin issues, so many other ailments. Only living near that dump makes sure your life ends before you turn forty, as opposed to the life expectancy of nearly sixty years in Dharavi, and over seventy in the rest of Maharashtra.'

'Then why do people live there?' I was surprised at the statistics, and the revelation that poverty, too, suffers from hierarchy.

'Cheapest housing in the city, what else. A hundred-square-foot home in Govandi rents for about two thousand rupees a month, as opposed to five thousand in Dharavi. Also, the landfill is a source of income for ragpickers. Many slum-dwellers venture into the dump and bring back saleable material, which sells at twenty rupees per kilo.'

It was believable, making a living out of garbage while using a dump yard for an office. As Ma once observed, the god of bread and dough runs Mumbai. The moment you set foot in this city, its lights blind you to the standard deities. You realize that gods do not exist, none of the 3,30,00,000 Hindu ones, or those overseeing other religions, except for one who hasn't made the list—the liberator of the downtrodden, the vanquisher of all misery, the skeleton key to all doors—money. There's only one religion in the city of dreams, survival and the one demon: surrender. There is no wrong way to please the god of coins, and only the rock-ribbed find home in his kingdom. Survival of the lionhearted. Glory or death.

'How do you know all these numbers?' I probed, a little intimidated by Saleha's knowledge. Even I'm pals with current affairs, but I don't have figures memorized.

'I work with an NGO, which runs a community kitchen in Govandi. It's called CBGB, an acronym for Chapatti Brigade, Gravy Battalion.'

'Wow.' I was impressed. 'Were you involved in the Covid-19 relief work as well?'

'Yes, of course,' she said, her eyes lighting up.

'What kind of work?'

'Our response was mainly focused on ensuring that every slum dweller had food. A few were able to manage at first, as they had groceries for a day or two. Then the stock ran out, but they had money to buy essentials. Then, in a few days, the money, too, was over, and almost everyone in the slum depended on charities for food. It was chaos, agony, chaotic agony.'

'In what way?'

'In the most unimaginable ways,' she said. 'I remember walking into a home where a mother had nothing but water, and she was boiling it with salt to feed her children. We had kids looking for food in garbage heaps, and when a milk van overturned, many scooped up the spilt milk from the road, joined by a pack of dogs. We ensured that all these people had enough to eat. These were migrants too, ones who had risked staying back.'

'I think my family and I, we would be in the same situation, had we waited.'

'Yes, mine too. But we're the fortunate ones, aren't we?' Her eyes questioned mine. 'We had money to survive three weeks. Some people could not wait three hours. Within twenty-four hours of the lockdown in India, tens of thousands of migrants had already started walking home, the first wave of coronavirus refugees in the world.'

'Did you also help migrants who were walking home?' I asked the data enthusiast. Although captivated, I was a little embarrassed. While she was out serving society, I was sitting at home, brooding over bananas and my missed examination.

'Yes, we did, once we started getting distress calls from migrant workers stranded on highways. Fifty calls a day initially, and by the end of the first week, about three hundred calls daily. The numbers kept rising.'

'What were they calling about?'

'They needed help with food, wage denial, forced retrenchment, information about how to get home, so many other things. There was such confusion and ignorance at the time that one migrant man, when we gave him a bottle of sanitizer, he asked if it was a medicine for the virus and if he could drink it. Thereafter, our NGO told all its volunteers to specify that the bottles contained disinfectants, which cannot and must not be consumed. It was both harrowing and challenging.'

'I can imagine,' I said. 'NGOs usually respond to emergencies with limited epicentres, whether it's a flood, an earthquake, or even an outbreak. In this case, the epicentre was all of Mumbai, all of India, all of the world.'

'Yes, exactly,' she agreed.

'Weren't you afraid of the virus?' I asked her, my questions telling me that I'd entered my snoopy, journalistic mode.

'I was, at first. Then, the kind of starvation I saw... The kind of hardship and deprivation...' she said and stopped to stare at the sky, as if it were playing a flashback reel for her. 'I remember a migrant, who was pretending to be a madman, talking to himself and flinging stones, so cops wouldn't stop him as he walked home. Another time, we rescued workers who were locked up inside a warehouse without food and water, as their employer did not want to lose labour. Many other stories like these, and together, they drove out every fleck of fear from our minds. The threat did not go away, the fear did.'

'Then why did you leave Mumbai?' I asked. 'You were doing such good work.'

'I had to,' she sighed. 'Financial woes at home and my family just wasn't willing to stay back. They love the city, but they don't trust it.'

Saleha and I were still talking when, around 11 a.m., a van arrived at the ground. I assumed it had brought more police officers, but three men in astronaut-like uniforms walked out of the vehicle—white, hooded jumpsuits, white gloves, white steel-toe boots and white helmets. The space cadets got busy as soon as they arrived, connecting two huge pipes to a steel container, which looked similar to the oxygen tank attached to spacesuits. Once they had set up their apparatus, they appeared ready to jump onto a rocket and shoot off the planet, but they were not here to fly. I knew that when one of the spacemen took over the megaphone.

'Everyone sit up,' the man commanded. 'Sit with a foot's gap between each other. No, not in a line. Sit in rows, ten per row. And shut your children's eyes. Shut your eyes too.'

'Do what he's saying.' The Bull pulled the megaphone from the astronaut. 'You do not want to piss me off.'

In a moment, each of the six alarms of our six senses, especially the sixth one, started buzzing wild. The woman with the infant pressed her baby's face against her bosom, covering all of him with her sari. Happy grabbed my hand, asking if we were going to face real pistols this time. I did not want to be a purveyor of false hope like Baba, so I stayed silent. I pulled my brother to my lap, wrapped my fingers around his eyes, and squeezed mine shut. A few children wept in fear; Happy did not. His nails dug into my thighs, but his eyes remained dry.

'Look down, eyes shut, mouths shut,' the Bull was still hogging the megaphone. 'Do not open them. Aye, dog-fucker. Do you want to die? Shut those fucking eyes.'

Soon, we heard the sound of a machine launching to life. The hoses hissed and started attacking our bodies with mist. The astronauts sprayed us with the curious liquid for about three minutes, and I wondered if it was acid, if this was one of the many acid attacks in our country. It could not be; we would have been ashes by now. I wanted to open my eyes to douse my curiosity, but I did not. The

Bull's curses remained as consistent as the dutiful hoses, deterring anyone who tried to steal a peek. When they did allow us to open our eyes, about five minutes after they stopped the spraying, I saw that the droplets were colourless, but had a strange odour. They also bit the skin.

The chemical had instant consequences. I broke into one of my coughing fits, while many others, including children, had started vomiting, their stomachs in pain, their eyes burning, and their skin inflamed. Some migrants scratched their bodies like monkeys, but I knew we were not that close to humans in the evolutionary process. We were still ants, sugar ants.

'Are you trying to kill us?' a migrant worker howled. His son had developed cherry-red rashes all over his chest.

'I cannot open my eyes,' bellowed another. 'They're burning, they're burning too much.'

'It's your fault,' the Bull screamed over the megaphone. 'I told you to keep your eyes and mouths shut. Now, cry, vomit, repent.'

'Call a doctor, please call a doctor now,' pleaded a worker, coughing, sneezing and struggling to breathe.

'Calm down,' roared the Bull. 'It's only bleach. It'll kill the virus on your body. You should be grateful we disinfected you.'

'If it isn't harmful, why are your men wearing those white suits? Why are you standing so far?' The worker wasn't convinced.

'Are you killing the virus or us?' asked another.

'Are you disinfecting rich people?'

The cops, once again, answered with batons until the crowd settled. The astronauts left soon after and the politician arrived. We tried to tell the leader about the chemical bath, but he was interested in our pictures, not us. He asked the lambs to bring the leftover food packets and clicked images of him handing them to us. 'No, no, do not smile for the camera,' he coached us. 'Look distressed, hungry, especially the children.' About two dozen choreographed pictures later, he was gone.

Ma rubbed her palm on my back and handed me some rock sugar to dissolve my coughing spell, while Baba poured coconut oil on Happy's arms to soothe the eruptions. Some workers washed their eyes and bodies with the little water they had, some fanned themselves with leaves and rags to extinguish the fire on their skin, while a few others lay on their stomachs to ease the abdominal pain. The cops refused to call for medical help, but we did not protest. Most bodies were too weak to fight, discovered victory in surrender.

Minutes melted into hours, but the buses that the Bull had promised us did not show up. Saleha and I sat simmering over the chemical bath, when around 4 p.m., a different source of relief walked in—the press. The dull afternoon became abuzz with the clamour of outdoor news-broadcasting vans, and reporters walked about our group, interviewing anyone who appeared willing or unwilling. As their camerapersons set up the equipment, the journalists fixed their hair and clothes, cleared their throats, and put on grim looks. Then, they spoke loudly, angrily, importantly.

A journalist, with freshly glossed lips, led with an introduction to her report:

'I'd like to inform our viewers that this, behind me, is the exact group of migrant workers that was intercepted at the Maharashtra–Gujarat border last night. The police discovered nearly eighty of them packed in a goods carrier. This morning, officers doused the men, women and children with chemicals, a video of which has now gone viral on social media, with one lakh views already. It shows the migrants sitting on the ground right here, as medical officials in hazmat suits sprayed them with chemicals at this exact, very spot. While we're still awaiting a reaction from the government, the opposition has termed the act "inhumane" and "chemical warfare against India's poor".

'Sources inform that the migrants were sprayed with a diluted mixture of sodium hypochlorite, a bleaching agent known for its hazardous properties. The World Health Organization has warned against spraying individuals with such disinfectants, as it can prove to be poisonous if ingested, can irritate the respiratory tract, and lead to complications like bronchospasm. Health agencies recommend limited use of the chemical compound even when disinfecting surfaces, and here, we have humans sprayed with it.

'Now joining us live is Mr Manohar Pali, a migrant labourer who was a victim of the chemical shower this morning.'

The journalist then turned to the migrant, 'Mr Pali, tell us how you feel.'

The labourer, a lean, middle-aged man, was still groggy after the reporter woke him up from his sleep and shoved the microphone in his face. 'I was vomiting soon after the spraying,' he said, scratching his head. 'I even had a bout of loose motions, but I'm feeling better now.'

And thus went the interview:

Journalist: I understand the cops found you in a truck last night. Where were you going?

Mr Pali: Home.

Journalist: And where would that be?

Mr Pali: A village in the Rajsamand district of Rajasthan.

Journalist: Where were you working?

Mr Pali: In a brick kiln near Mumbai.

Journalist: What kind of work did you do?

Mr Pali: Brick kilns are busy workplaces, madam. We dig pits, moisten them, hack out clay from the wet pits, make the mud mixture, put the mixture in brick moulds, let the bricks dry and then unload them from the moulds. Then, we carry the bricks on our heads and put them in a burning furnace, as big as a cricket pitch, and as red-hot as hell. We also sweep and clean the baking area, hammer coal, keep the furnace fired day and night by feeding it with coal, among other things.

Journalist: No, I mean, what is your exact job at the kiln?

Mr Pali: This is my exact job at the kiln. Everyone does everything in kilns. Our country is booming, madam, and modern India needs bricks to build its buildings, offices and cityscapes.

Journalist: Did your employer help you with accommodation after the lockdown?

Mr Pali: Yes, when I joined work, he had allotted me a space near the kiln, where three other workers and I built a hut. All labourers have huts there.

Journalist: If you had a hut or a place to stay, why did you leave?

Mr Pali: Because I could not eat my hut.

Journalist: Did your employer not help you with food?

Mr Pali: Before the lockdown, our labour contractor would give us two hundred rupees every Saturday to buy food grains, medicines and vegetables. After the lockdown, he went missing. We waited for him for three weeks before leaving.

Journalist: How did you manage food in these three weeks?

Mr Pali: We got help from a local charity, but the NGO soon ran out of resources, and could only provide one meal a day. We said, okay, no problem. We lived on one meal some days, and went without food on others, hoping that work would resume soon. It did not, so we decided to leave. We lost wages of five months, but we still left.

Journalist: How five months? It's been only three weeks since the lockdown.

Mr Pali: This is not your corporate job, madam. We're paid at the end of every season, which lasts from November to May. If you can, please find our contractor and get us our dues. He's a fair, rich-looking man, wears a tie, rides a motorbike, and curses in four languages.

Journalist: How much does the work pay?

Mr Pali: Around five hundred rupees for a set of eleven hundred bricks, so almost half a rupee per brick.

Journalist: Would you know the selling price of these bricks?

Mr Pali: Around six rupees per brick.

Journalist: How much do you earn in a month?

Mr Pali: It depends on how many bricks I make. Usually, five to six hundred a day, so around eight thousand rupees per month.

Journalist: Do you have enough money to get to your village?

Mr Pali: What would be your guess?

Journalist: I can guess, but our viewers cannot.

Mr Pali: They can too, but I'll spell it out for you. My wife transferred two thousand rupees after borrowing it from a moneylender in our village, and I managed another four hundred by pleading with households near the kiln. Since I paid two thousand to the truck driver, I only have four hundred left with me now. I do have my legs, though, and they've promised to walk me home.

Journalist: Didn't you get that two thousand back?

Mr Pali: No. The cops took all our money from the driver when they found us, and I'm sure I'll never see that cash again. If you can, please try to get it back from the officer in-charge. He's a tall, muscular man, bitter as truth.

Journalist: When did you start walking?

Mr Pali: This attempt or the previous one?

Journalist: Were there two attempts?

Mr Pali: The first one was five days ago. I left with six other labourers from the kiln. We reached the Maharashtra–Gujarat border in a day, but the cops caught us, locked us up for thirty hours, and then sent us back to the kiln. We left again yesterday, busted again.

Journalist: Did the cops spray you with chemicals today?

Mr Pali: Yes.

Journalist: How do you feel about that?

Mr Pali: Not as surprised as you are.

Journalist: Why is that?

Mr Pali: Because animals do not fuss over being treated like animals. We might bite back at times, but we don't fuss.

Journalist: Who treats you like an animal? Your employer?

Mr Pali: The cops just did, the world routinely does, but let's talk about work if that interests you.

Journalist: Do tell us.

Mr Pali: Brick kilns, madamji, have children toiling without childhood in their eyes. Employers often rape the women labourers, kick pregnant ones in their stomachs, and beat men for the most human of mistakes. I've seen workers fall into the furnace and turn to dust. And who hasn't heard of the labour contractor who severed the hands of two of his workers? Only because they quit their jobs at the kiln. The goons asked the boys if they wanted to lose their lives, a leg each, or their right hands. Both chose the hand.

Journalist: I understand. But the more immediate problem here is that you still have a long way home. Aren't you scared of the virus?

Mr Pali: I'm only afraid of hunger, madamji. Everything else, I can manage. And I've been working in the kiln for years now. If I can survive the respiratory ruckus there, I can live through this covid-fovid nonsense.

Journalist: Thank you, Mr Pali. Thank you for speaking with us. I wish you all the best for your journey.

As the worker retired to his muddy bed, the reporter turned to the camera. 'As you can see, these migrants are desperate to reach home,' she orated. 'With great risks to their lives, they've set out on these perilous journeys, and yet, their expeditions are met with chemical baths and police brutality. This is Meghna Paul, bringing you the report live from the Maharashtra–Gujarat interstate border, only for News AD, News All Day.'

Although the journalist had continued speaking to the camera, answering questions of her newscaster, I could not hear her above Mr Pali's nonchalance that kept lingering around me. The man's face hadn't revealed one speck of emotion, his voice stayed committed to its monotone, even as he narrated troubling details about his life as a brick-kiln worker. I was enraged this morning because I believed I did not deserve to be drenched with chemicals. He, however, appeared at ease with them. He was even expecting them. I wondered if he was a defeatist or a man wizened by time. I wondered if he was among the vanquished, or someone who had already won the war by refusing to fight it. I wondered if he was too afraid to fight the world, or above all fear. But most of all, I wondered if I was in the wrong, overreacting, expecting too much of fellow humans.

After concluding her interaction with the studio anchor, the reporter moved on to the Bull. As she approached the cop, most of us followed her, looking for our answers in her questions. The officer appeared uncomfortable with her interrogation, but he could not silence her with batons. He was compelled to speak, a beast shrunk to a mouse.

'Sir, what prompted you to spray these migrants with chemicals?' the journalist probed.

'We had orders,' said the Bull.

'I just checked with the district magistrate. The order was to disinfect the buses in which the migrants were supposed to travel. Do you think you were a little over-enthusiastic with the hoses?'

'I'll have to check,' he said, his foghorn of a voice softening. 'It could have been a misunderstanding.'

'It was an expensive misunderstanding, officer. People here have had serious health repercussions, even the children.'

'I will have to check.'

'Have you helped them with food?'

'Breakfast in the morning. We'll serve lunch in a bit.'

'It's almost five in the evening.'

'The food is on its way, madam,' he retorted. 'We also have buses arranged to send them home.'

'What about their money? The cash they'd paid to the truck driver? I understand it's with you.'

'Yes, of course. It was recovered from the driver, who is an offender in this case. He'll remain in custody, and we'll hand over the people's money back to them when they leave for their homes later today.'

The migrants cheered, and as I saw the reporter tame the Bull, my desire to become a journalist strengthened. I want to become an impactful reporter, Ms Farah, someone who affects real change, like this journalist, like you. I, however, hope to become a print journalist, ma'am, not a television one, simply because most people on our 24/7 news channels have flipped their lids. Ma has banned the 9 p.m. news debates in our home, exhausted with the anchors and their bawling, name-calling and mud-slinging. Although she cannot understand English, she says that their sheer demeanour shoots up her blood pressure, makes her brain want to tear out of its case.

'Such animals,' she said before announcing the prohibition. 'They make the drunks in our slum look like gentlemen.'

'All these reporters have gone mental,' agreed Baba. 'Look how he's screaming at his guests. He must spend all the money he earns on lozenges.'

I lowered the television's volume, but that did not help. The anchor was still boisterous, if not in his pitch, his pantomimes. I wondered how one could make a language as elegant as English sound so crass, but the man had managed. I switched to a Hindi news channel, hoping to please my parents with the language of their choice, but things got out of control. A debating panellist mouthed one of the big swear words on national television, prompting Ma to announce an immediately effective veto on news debates. She did not prohibit Hindi news, though, simply because she enjoys the juicy crudity of those stories, ones frosted with spicy headlines like these:

- *Kya* alien *gai ka doodh peete hain*? (Do aliens drink cow milk?)
- *Chudail maangey pyaaz* (The witch wants onion)
- Amitabh Bachchan *ko lagi thand* (Amitabh Bachchan felt cold)
- *Dharti pe aadhe sher aadhe insaan ka saboot* (Evidence of half-tiger-half-man found on earth)
- UFO *ne aasman mein kheench li gae* (A UFO sucked a cow up into the sky)

More than journalism, it's a mix of mythology, science fiction and Animal Planet, garnished with an imagination that defeats the genius of nature. Not that English channels are clean, ma'am, but at least, they do not debate whether aliens have abducted a police commissioner's dog. I'm not kidding. It was a twenty-minute report on a prime-time slot. Google it. That's why, Ms Farah, my chosen language of journalism is English, and my chosen medium, print.

My specialization, meanwhile, would be science, as our country needs a scientific temper more than all else right now, more than even temples and cows.

As I stood smiling, lost in my sunny future as a journalist, the reporters were busy interviewing migrants, most of whom complained without fear. A few journalists also approached my family with queries, but I did not let them speak. I'm saving it all for you, ma'am, because I know how crucial exclusive stories are to reporters.

The media left after the interviews, and although the lunch never showed up, a government bus did arrive a few hours later. The Bull handed our cash to its driver, asking him to settle our dues at the end of the journey. Seventy-eight of us boarded that fifty-four-seater vehicle. Some piled on each other, some squatted on the floor, and some sat on the carrier atop the roof, but no one complained. The Bull had us believe that we were going home.

Meher
Still in the wildwood

7

Black Hole

19 April 2020
Dear Ms Farah,

It was a full moon night six years ago. Balhaar's dunes were aglow with a platinum shimmer, as velvety rays of the fairy-tale moon encased every grain of sand on their bodies. The desert lay drenched in its soft diamond-flames, each of us radiant like stars. I sat in the courtyard of our home, beguiled by the beauty's splendour, oblivious to her insinuations. I learnt later that she shone so bright because she was trying to betray the night, uncloak its dark secret. She failed, and her friend, the sun, rushed in for a rescue. He flooded the world with light, exposing a seven-year-old boy's mutilated body.

The corpse's name was Kirtan, meaning prayer, and his murder weapon, too, was prayer. Hisses of vultures led the police to his body, abandoned deep in the desert, to the appetite of scavengers and demanding deities. When the officers found him, they looked away.

His killers had slit his throat, punctured his cheeks with dozens of needle holes, and bored another at the back of his skull, as if with a drill. A few feet away, lay the paraphernalia for a ritual—metal pots filled with blood, old skulls and bones, a garlanded picture of goddess Kali, and an earthen plate with sweets, sandalwood paste, incense sticks, lamps and ghee. When they saw their son, the parents wailed and the village mourned. Balhaar became dimmer with an airborne melancholy, but it was not a moment of some rude awakening. Everyone knew that human sacrifice, although still prevalent, is a ritual as old as the dunes.

Investigations revealed that Kirtan's paternal aunt had perpetrated the crime. She picked him up from near our school, and the unsuspecting child did not resist. Once they were far from the village, she stuffed a cloth ball into his mouth, bundled him up in a jute sack and a few hours later, tore open his throat. She murdered the child to please goddess Kali because a religious ascetic promised her that the sacrifice would rid her family of their financial woes.

'Just wait till we're done with the ritual. The skies will part, showering gold—biscuits, not droplets,' the godman told her. 'Human blood is considered as maha prasad (greatest oblation) in our scriptures, and sacrificing one child keeps the goddess pleased for a thousand years. Not just you, generations of your family will want for nothing. I've seen the miracle with my own eyes, the generosity of Kali, the Mother and the Warrior.'

The sadhu explained that the sacrificial child must be a young boy, aged three to twelve years, or a girl who has just started menstruating, or a child who was a breech baby. 'The ritual has to be performed on a full moon night,' the godman insisted. 'We'll slice the child's nose and ears, collect the streams of blood in pots, and offer them to the goddess. Alternatively, we could drill a hole in the boy's cerebellum and empty his blood. I prefer the hole. It's less messy.'

Despite the murder, the gold never poured—neither biscuits nor droplets. The tantric absconded soon after, and the aunt landed in jail. No one, however, prosecuted the goddess. I was nine at the time, ma'am, and I turned to Grandpa with my naïve discontent.

'Why is the deity free of criminal charges?' I asked him. 'Why aren't they putting her on trial? Her demand for blood makes her culpable too, you know.'

'The goddess did not ask for it. She barely speaks,' said Dadoo, and went on to introduce me to one of the oldest citadels of prejudice in India: superstition. 'Human sacrifice does find mention in old religious texts. For instance, in the sacred book of Rigveda, a cosmic man is sacrificed to create the universe. However, nowhere do our scriptures mention that deities demand blood. Some of these sadhus, they manipulate religion and its texts, weave falsehoods around them, all for cash. The godman must have charged thousands of rupees for the ritual.'

'But who made him a god's man?'

'He's self-proclaimed, like every other swami,' Grandpa explained. 'Any man can become a holy man in India. All you need are saffron garbs, vermillion paste on your forehead, and a string of one hundred and eight rosary beads. If you have a beehive for a beard and haven't bathed in aeons, even better. Such unqualified sadhus have set up shop in every city, every village and every street of our country. They're hawking superstitions, peddling myths for money, and using god as their tool to build prisons of ignorance.'

'Don't feed her nonsense,' Grandma intervened while milking her sacred cow in our courtyard. Upon hearing Dadoo, she covered the animal's ears. 'By uttering such blasphemous words against our priests, you'll draw the ire of every god there is, even the peace-loving Cow Mother.'

'So you're saying every sadhu is honest-to-goodness,' argued Dadoo, his hands busy with a piece of ancestral engineering—forging clay into a chillum. He shaped the wet mud into a long, thin cylinder, and punched holes at its two ends, one wide, the other narrow. He then let his magic pipe dry in the sun.

'No,' said Dadi. 'But not every religious idea is a fallacy. For instance, the belief that one should not sweep or scrub their home after sunset is a hundred per cent true. Defiance irks the goddess of wealth, shrinks the fortune of one's household. That's why everyone in the world cleans their home in the morning.'

'Half the world does not know your goddess.' Dadoo laughed. 'And do you know where this superstition comes from?'

'It is not a superstition.'

'Of course it is. It's a notion that overstayed its time, grew up to become a superstition,' said Grandpa. 'When this belief originated, there was no electricity. It was only a matter of practicality to finish your cleaning in daylight when everything is visible. They added the wealth angle to create fear. Nothing gets work done faster than fear, especially one of losing money.'

'You're an infidel,' countered Dadi, lacking a better comeback.

'Yes,' said Dadoo. 'And I wish I'd been one sooner, before I lost a grandchild to my fidelity.'

Dadi did not argue, and Dadoo dodged my subsequent questions. I decrypted his statement only three years later. It was Krishna Janmashtami in 2017, one of the major Hindu festivals, celebrating the birth of Lord Krishna—the eternal spiritual charioteer, popularly known as the butter thief, married to 16,108 women. Balhaaris, like all of India, commemorate the day with an enormous jamboree. Priests and religiose volunteers embellish our temples with flowers, leaves and lamps, and the entire village gathers at the shrines—lower castes at the lower-caste temple with stone idols, and upper castes at the upper-caste temples with gods made of gold.

At the stroke of midnight, the priests bathe Krishna's idols with milk, dress them in silk garbs and peacock-feathered crowns, and present the statues with calorie-heavy birthday meals. Grapevine has it that the aristocrats offer the chappan bhog or fifty-six delicacies, prepared with the lord's favourites, butter and ghee. The feast includes paneer, cooked greens, dals, deep-fried bread, pickles, poppadums, chutneys, yoghurt, savouries, nuts, fresh fruits, dry fruits and desserts—a multi-course meal, yummier than the most ravenous of my imaginations.

On the day before the festival, almost everyone in Balhaar keeps a vigil, fasting until midnight, the traditional hour of Krishna's birth. Ma, a renowned abstinent, fasts two days every week, fifty-two weeks a year, to win favour with two different deities. However, she does not keep from food for Krishna. I did not know this, not until we moved to Mumbai. During our first Janmashtami here, in August 2016, I noticed that Ma ate without restraint. She did not accompany us to Krishna's temple at midnight, nor did she bathe, dress, or offer sweets to the idol at home. Her rebellion piqued my interest, but she refused to reveal her cause. When it showed up again the following year, I persisted.

'It's because Krishna did not save my child,' she said. 'Had he protected him, my boy would have been eight today. You'd have two brothers, not one.'

It was July 2009. I was four, and Ma was in the final month of her pregnancy. Her baby, my first sibling, was due around the day of Janmashtami, which fell on 13 August that year. However, three weeks before the date, on 22 July, Ma complained of severe stomach pain. She had suffered an accidental haemorrhage, was bleeding internally, but she refused to visit a doctor. 22 July was the day of the solar eclipse that year, the longest of the twenty-first century, and eclipse-related superstitions had bound her with many restrictions—do not look at the sun, or your child will be born with a cleft lip; do not hold a knife, or it'll scar your baby with spots and blemishes; do not leave home, or the infant will have to battle deformities. Ma visited a doctor only the following day. She gave birth to my brother, and he succumbed within hours. Her life, too, fell in jeopardy, and Baba rushed her to a hospital in the city of Jodhpur. She returned after a fortnight, frail and ruined.

Ma sobbed as she spoke, and her tears burdened my heart. I hugged her and wept with her, but a shade of repulsion polluted my grief. I felt angry because, unlike Dadoo, Ma still blamed Krishna for her loss, not the savage superstition that killed her son. I never took it up with her as she still aches for her lost child, but I did tell Ms Amber about it during one of our evening classes. The altruistic educator had also volunteered to be a friend.

Ms Amber is only a decade and a half older than I am, and her name is the colour of her heart, a warm honey-yellow. She first came to India on a vacation, and after one of those poverty safaris in Dharavi, she took up work with an NGO in our slum. It was only a six-month project, but she ended up staying for five years. At the end of each programme, she would return to London, proclaiming that she was going home forever, only to reappear in a few months. Every time she left, I would bet with her on her return, and I won five of those gambles. The sixth time was late last year when she flew home for New Year's Eve and did not return. I'm sure it was the coronavirus that held her back and I'm also sure that she'll return to Dharavi soon, as soon as this carnival of death and disease is over. She'll knock at our shanty, the prize for my sixth win in her eager hands. This time, however, I won't be there to open the door or match the glint in her eyes.

Ms Amber had bought me five gifts from her five trips home—a mug with the picture of a red bus, saying I LOVE LONDON, a piggy bank shaped like a red telephone booth, a tall blue hat with a Union Jack print, a London-themed stationery set, and the fifth one, a blouse from a label called Primark. All her gifts were first-hand, their price tags intact, only the cost struck out with a black permanent marker.

'I hate that Ma cannot see what killed her child,' I told Ms Amber after narrating the story of her loss. 'She still believes in superstitions, and she still cannot perceive their deceit. For instance, Ma is the eldest of six sisters, and her parents, who produced six kids hoping for a boy each time, named their fourth daughter Unchahi, or unwanted. They believed the superstition that naming their daughter so would tell the gods that they did not want girls any more. The fifth one, too, was a girl, named Kaafi or enough, while the sixth one was called Bharpai or penalty. Grandma never gave birth to a boy, and Ma never took offence at her sisters' names. She doesn't even realize they're offensive.'

'It's the lack of education, Meher,' said Ms Amber, trying to calm my ruffled nerves. 'It can blind one to oppression.'

'It can also make one oppressive, miss,' I said, still angry. 'Every time I get my period, Ma treats me like a pariah. She forbids me from sitting close to others in the house, rebukes me if I touch their food, clothes, or any of their things. I have to sleep alone on the loft because she keeps Happy away from me. And not just me, she imposes the same restrictions on herself, oppresses herself too.'

'You should talk to her, an honest conversation,' said Ms Amber, unsurprised at the ovarian prejudice in my home. Being a woman of Indian origin, she had heard plenty about it from her mother. 'Tell her what you think, about the baby, about your monthlies, about everything. I can join you if you like.'

'No, miss,' I said. 'It's not just Ma. It's all of Balhaar. In fact, it's worse in Balhaar. There, we spend the three days of our courses in the animal sheds of our homes. We sleep on the floor, stay hungry until someone brings us food, and use a hole in the ground, separated by a sari, for a toilet. It's because villagers believe that menstrual excretion occurs to punish women for their sins. They say that we must leave home because gods and ancestral spirits dwell in homes, and they do not like sinful women. If we stay in, our kin and livestock would die, and our crops would be destroyed.'

'No way!' she exclaimed, surprised at the rural extent of the insanity. She then quoted one Mr Voltaire, 'Superstition is to religion what astrology is to astronomy: the mad daughter of a wise mother.'

'Yes, exactly. And you must tell your Mr Voltaire that in some parts of India, the daughter is beyond crazy—a raging lunatic armed with hacksaws and daggers,' I said and went on to tell her about poorer girls in Balhaar, who spend their menses in a communal hut outside the village, as they do not have animal sheds inside their homes. A few years ago, a drunkard raped one of them, left her for dead. Another girl lost her life due to excessive blood loss, as there was no medical aid in the period hut, and she could not leave it to seek help. After that instance, a few women in our village protested against the banishment, but the village council threatened a social boycott against their families.

'As Dadoo says, such traditions are a bitter aftertaste of the past, and I want to do something about them, miss. I want to nudge my family, my villagers, and all of India awake, point them to the line between religion and superstition, and tell them that the latter is smoke and gunmetal, toxic and deadly. Grandpa understands how dangerous these ideas can be, but no one else does, despite crimes like human sacrifices rooted in such beliefs. Even Ma remains blind, despite having lost a child to them.'

'Superstitions age well, Meher. They're in the past, present, and they're already awaiting us in the future,' said Ms Amber. 'And it's not just India; they're prevalent all over the world. For instance, people in several countries believe that a broken mirror is a bad omen, as the glass pieces are a preview of your soon-to-shatter soul. What an idiotic belief. The shards are bad news simply because you'd have to clean up the mess. The penny you found on the road is lucky because you got it free. A black cat crossed your path because she's probably out looking for meat. And if either of your palms is itchy, it's perhaps because your skin is craving moisturizer. This is common sense, but the antidote to common sense—superstition—is more strong-willed. It lingers, it transcends time, and it wins.'

'So how do I fix this? How do I crown sense as the victor, at least in my country?'

'You're too young to fix it, child.' Ms Amber smiled. 'But you can study well and become a journalist someday. It's the journalist's job to dispel darkness and herald change, and I know you'll make a conscientious one.'

'Why aren't you a journalist, miss? You studied to become one, didn't you?'

'Yes, but I'm doing this. Journalism does not mean reporting. It means serving, and I'm fortunate enough to be serving my country, my roots, and wonderful kids like you.'

'But aren't you British?'

'According to my passport, yes,' she said. 'But my heart belongs to India. Where does your heart reside, Meher? What makes it sing?'

After that conversation, I plunged deeper into my desires, and I knew I had discovered my dream—I was going to be a journalist, yes! I would say it to every uncle, every aunty, every teacher, and every person who responded to my adolescence with a 'So, what do you want to be when you grow up?' My answer would have the gleaming halo of a humane purpose, a worldly duty, and a wee bit of pride. I've known my dream for three years now, Ms Farah, but the wish snowballed into a resolve only recently—as I sat in that steel-bodied bus after the chemical bath, as the Bull barged in with his cattle, as they flung us into a black hole.

When the cops pinned me to the floor, dragged me by my hair, and tried to silence my insurgent body, I travelled in time. I fled that moment, that fleeting moment of the present that was quickly turning into the past, yet remained unforgiving. I fled the world, which had dropped to its knees in that instant, gushing with barbarity. I fled the pain, the cries of the girl in my head, who screamed as if she were being murdered over and over again. I jumped onto a swing, my time machine, and I oscillated between the past and the future—a distant evening, where I lay with my head on Dadoo's lap, asleep, at peace, as he ran his leathery fingers through my hair, and another one in the future, where I lay buried under the ground, asleep, at peace, as moths and beetles feasted on my corpse. Of course, it was abnormal, my reaction to my first encounter with violence, but *it* was abnormal too, the violence.

It all happened an hour after we passed the interstate border between Maharashtra and Gujarat. As soon as we crossed the check post into Gujarat, children clapped and hoorayed like they'd spotted cake, adults whistled and yahooed like they'd spotted gold, and everyone's teeth showed. The momentary victory brought sleep, assisted by the creamy wind that blew in through the bus's open windows. I woke up only when the driver slammed on the brakes, and my face hit the seat before me.

I assumed the driver braked in a hurry to save a stray dog, pig, donkey, or buffalo strolling around the highway, but in seconds, different species of animals—the Bull and his sheep—entered the bus. I rubbed my eyes to check if I was awake. All doubts vanished when the cattle started charging at the men in our bus, beating them with fists and batons, attacking their faces, necks, arms, legs, chests, hands and every other speck of skin. The terrified children crouched between the chairs, their heads covered with their tiny hands, their stomachs sunken, and their breaths cold.

'Bastards,' roared the Bull, standing in the middle of the bus. 'We gave you food. We gave you a place to sleep. And how did you repay us? You farted to the press. You said words against us. You thankless goat-fuckers.'

The Bull's spit-rich monologue continued until the Ram interrupted it with his own. He pulled Mr Pali up by his neck, the brick-kiln labourer who had spoken to a journalist at length. 'Son of a whore!' the Ram tried to choke the migrant. 'The disinfectant made you vomit, is it? You're shitting water, is it? Let's see what this does to you.'

Mr Pali struggled for breath. His body trembled as he kicked the air with his feet, and used his hands to loosen the Ram's grip. The animal, however, was determined. 'Don't forget you're a pest,' the Ram spoke to Mr Pali's shutting eyes. 'You were born like pests, you'll die like pests, and you'll eat chemicals like pests. Where is that journalist madam of yours now, haan? Don't you want to hide in her bosom any more?'

Mr Pali began to lose the world, and the Ram let go of his neck. The Bull gleamed with pride, as his crony turned his attention to other migrants who had spoken the truth. He pulled their hair, punched their mouths, and spat on their faces. He pounded their chests with batons, pinched their testicles, and banged their heads against the bus's walls. The evening turned darker, and the wind turned sad, but no one spoke. I wanted to dissent against the silence. I wanted to extend words to our innocence, scream that we did not deserve that crimeless punishment. I wanted to be heard, so I kept mum. I knew no one was listening, neither god nor government. Warring with words with armed men was foolish, so I hugged Happy instead, turned his eyes away from the violence. My subdued screams, however, continued to bedevil my head. They'd turned into a frozen echo when Happy jolted me back to silence.

'They're asking us to get off the bus, didi,' the boy said. 'They're too-too angry.'

The sheep drove us out of the vehicle, while the Bull cornered its driver, took over the cash we had paid to our trucker, and asked the driver to leave with the bus. As we stood in the middle of that horizonless highway, surrounded by trees and forests, I found it difficult to breathe. The air was beginning to turn to mud, kneaded with sobs and sighs. I stood thoughtless, as the cops divided us into two groups—one for men, another for women and children. The lambs kept landing their wooden weapons on the men as they jumped in pain with a comicality that had no humour.

'You want to go home, you pig-fuckers? I'll see how you get anywhere,' the Bull, once again, bellowed in rage. 'Your verbal defecation on camera has cost me my job.'

Thereafter, the Bull turned into a Mad Bull. He charged at the men with a ferocity that would embarrass thundering skies. He beat each one of them, including Baba, Proton Uncle and Neutron Sameer. My father pleaded, saying that no one in our family had spoken to the press, but the Bull's nostrils flared, and the veins on his forehead threatened to tear open his skin. He slapped my father, and Baba collapsed to the ground.

'What you're doing is illegal.' I rushed to help my father up from the floor. I could feel tears contaminate my angry eyes. 'You cannot do this. I will report you. I will report each one of you.'

'To whom?' laughed the Mad Bull. 'You've already eaten up our jobs. Now, little girl, we're answerable to no one. Do you know what that means?'

'That means you're an animal, a small-brained, anarchic carnivore.'

The Mad Bull grabbed me by my hair and flung me to the ground. I jumped up and spat on his face, disallowing him the pleasure of my defeat. That made him angrier, and he clutched my shoulder, pushed me backwards, swept his leg behind my ankle, and hurled me to the floor. I stood up again, only to taste mud again. As I lay on my back, cursing him, he started dragging me around by my hair, his fingers bearing the force of a thousand gravities, until I turned around and bit his shin. Then, his gorilla arm pinned my neck to the road, while two of his sheep locked my limbs. I mustered every crumb of the fight in me, but I could not push the animals away.

As I struggled, my rage grew into a vicious, bitter taste in my mouth, my limbs started turning lazy, and my eyes began to sleep. I could feel my breath sprint away from my body, the coughing spell approach, and in that moment, I discovered my swing-shaped time machine. When it dropped me back in the present, the Bull stood at a distance, and my father lay at his feet, his palms joined, cheeks tear-soaked, and eyes vanquished. Furious, I barked at the cop, but Ma slapped me.

'Shut up,' she wept. 'Please.'

Baba stared me down with a prayerful gaze. I kept away from the Mad Bull thereafter, and he, too, maintained distance. The caning ceased, but that was more because two trucks had just stopped next to us. The vehicles looked like maternal twins with dull faces—centre partitions in their windshields separated their square eyes, their front grilles made for their flat noses, the headlights looked like their shallow dimples, the rear-view mirrors contributed as their alien ears, and the bumper bars, their toothless smiles. The six-wheeled lorries appeared fatigued, each with a heavy elliptical tube mounted on its back—a gigantic, horizontal cylinder, made of spotless, stainless steel. 'Milk Carrier,' proclaimed the blue writing on their silver bodies. 'Milk not for sale.'

'These trucks will take you home,' announced the Mad Bull. 'Men get in one lorry, women and kids in another.'

That meant an airless death. I could not spot one source of ventilation, not even an air hole, on the cylinder. Our group complained, but the determined cattle started dragging us towards the trucks. Many begged the officers not to split our families, but they pretended to be deaf. When a woman broke into unbridled cries, they hit her with a baton. The Bull then pulled out a smaller, bloodier weapon. 'Get in or die here,' he threatened, kissing the muzzle of his pistol. 'You have ten minutes. Then, I start shooting.'

The drivers of the two trucks hurried at the ultimatum. The duo, enveloped in a sad aura, looked like they were betraying their will, as they leapt off their cabins, climbed the steel ladders at the rear ends of their trucks, and opened the manholes atop the cylinders. The forty-two men of our group stood near one lorry, and the twenty-four women and twelve children around another. As the migrants climbed up the ladders of their respective trucks, the Mad

Bull beat their backs with an avid rage, commanding them to walk faster, 'not like dainty brides and worn-out widows.'

'You won't get away with this,' a migrant worker growled as he climbed. 'There is justice in god's court, if not here.'

The Mad Bull pulled him by his belt and threw him to the ground. Then, he shoved his pistol into the man's mouth. 'Be grateful that I'm letting you live, you donkey-fucker. Shut up or I'll send you to god's tribunal now, with a bullet-shaped hole in your forehead.'

That was the last one of our protests. I looked at Baba as he began to disappear into the manhole, and he smiled, trying to revive hope that now lay buried in the dark backwaters of my heart. I pulled Happy close, and we started climbing the steel ladder up to our truck. We crawled atop the cylinder, holding onto the handrails that covered its length. We reached the manhole, and then, through a rope ladder, we descended into the dungeon.

It smelt like dead flowers, the pit, and I pressed my mask against my nose. Once the driver threw in our luggage and shut the lid, the children bawled, the women prayed, and everyone screamed for help. But I knew that no one on the planet could hear us. We were light years away from earth, like matter pressed in a tiny space, like cosmic junk dumped into a black hole. Nothing could escape that oubliette, no sound, no light, no life.

'This is how we die,' Electron Aunty grabbed my wrist. 'A matter of minutes.'

I did not respond. I saw rare merit in her pessimism. I was already feeling breathless in that airtight ditch, as if a million needles were poking into my throat, narrowing my windpipe down to a thread. Happy, too, felt smothered. I lifted him in my arms, so he could breathe.

'I'm scared, didi,' he said, locking me in an embrace.

I could barely hear him above the wailing children, but I kissed his forehead, unsure of alternative devices.

'Let me hold him,' said Ma, pulling the boy from my arms.

'Don't worry, my child,' she told Happy. 'This truck is taking us home. But as you know, we're in the middle of a national lockdown, and we must travel secretly. That's why the cops have hidden us in these containers.'

It was a decent alibi, but I knew Happy wouldn't fall for it.

'Then, why were the policemen beating everyone, Ma?' he questioned. 'They slapped Baba and didi too. What did Baba and didi do? Did they lie? Did they steal? Did they say a bad word?'

'No, no, my love. They did not do any of that,' said Ma, kissing his face. She recognized that the boy would see through her smokescreen again, and went for a more acceptable answer this time. 'Sometimes, bad things happen to good people and good things happen to bad people,' she said. 'But only sometimes, when God isn't looking. Nature comes into play when God is away, and nature loves balance. It creates the dusk to balance God's dawn, winter for His summer, a mind for heart, hatred for love, destruction for creation, fire for water, sea for land, valleys for mountains, deaths for births, and demons for deities. Similarly, sometimes, good people have bad experiences because nature is trying to balance the fairness in the world.'

She was right, I thought. Both chaos and peace are part of our lives, probably to align us with the universe, its elemental love for equilibrium. One of the many things that science has taught me, ma'am, is that balance is the master key to everything in our cosmos. Our bodies, our planet, and our universe, they're all built and thrive on balance—time and space, yin and yang, protons and electrons, matter and mind, matter and antimatter, left and right hemispheres of our brains, height and depth, past and future, and inhalation and exhalation. Then, there is the eternal law of balance, Newton's third law of motion, which states that every action has an equal and opposite reaction. And to top it all, physicists believe that the sum total of all the energy in our infinite, unlimited universe is zero, as its positive and negative energies—matter and gravity—cancel each other out. A macrocosm of balance, our universe.

'So, if good people get bad things, and bad ones get good things, isn't it better to be bad?' enquired Happy, pulling me back into the black hole.

'No,' said Ma, now in a quandary. 'And if you keep talking, you'll soon run out of energy. Stay mum and breathe. Slowly, gently.'

It seemed like a morning-less night, our first few minutes in that milk carrier, but as time went by, we got used to its travails, to our miserly breaths and hammering hearts. At first, when the vehicle had just started moving, there were broken sobs and defeated cries for rescue. Then came the tears, the roars, and the communal disorder. Then walked in silence, and the final entrant was the superhero, control. The saviour did not spring from the sorcery of hope, of course not. Its roots lay in the first animal instinct: survival.

We realized that if we wished to survive that cylinder, we'd have to tackle three major challenges:

Obstacle 1: The absence of light.

Remedy: We lit flashlights on as many phones as we could find.

Obstacle 2: How do you stand inside a three-dimensional hollow tube with curved sides and no flat base?

Remedy: Electron Aunty, to my surprise, came up with this one. On her suggestion, we covered the ground with our luggage, creating a flat surface on the floor. The kids, all eleven of us, sat on the bags. The twelfth one, the six-month-old baby, remained in his mother's arms.

Twenty-two of the twenty-four women lined the curved lengths of the cylinder, eleven on each side. Since there was no space to park their feet on the ground, they lifted their backs on the walls behind them and rested their feet on the ones in front. We, children, readjusted to sit between their legs. It then looked like a piano, the inside of that tube, with alternating torsos and lower limbs.

This obstacle had two sub-obstacles: 1. Saleha's grandmother, the oldest woman in our group, could not prop up her body against the curved wall. 2. The woman with the infant could not balance herself either, as she was carrying a baby. We squeezed in a bit and made them sit against the two flat, circular faces at the two ends of the cylinder. The mother had enough space to breastfeed her vexed infant.

Obstacle 3: How do you avoid suffocating to death?

Remedy: The women divided themselves into two groups according to their sides of the walls. They decided to breathe alternately and asked the children to pick the side they liked. The instructions for each group were simple: 1. Remove your mask. 2. Close your mouth. 3. Breathe in through your nose for three counts. 4. Purse your lips like you're about to whistle. 5. Breathe out slowly through your pursed lips to the count of five. A woman on our left did the counting when the right side breathed, and a woman on the right returned the favour for the left ones.

Although our breaths followed a perfect rhythm, like some mechanical regularity, I worried about the infant, wondering how he was handling the finite air. The baby was doing much better than we were, I soon realized. He lay nestled in his mother's arms, inebriated on milk, lost in his drunken stupor, while the elders struggled with the nagging demons inside their fully developed brains.

With the three solutions, we had managed to conquer every major impediment of the black hole. I, however, knew that the tube would soon run out of oxygen, and its air would turn into plastic with the carbon dioxide we were exhaling. The cures were temporary, while the threat of dying in a coffin seemed eternal.

Breathing life into my fears, the truck stopped dead. *This cannot be good*, my nerves rumbled, considering our two recent experiences with sudden brakes. Within seconds, however, the vehicle started moving again. I could tell it was turning around, as our bodies swayed to the left, disrupting the order we'd so artfully acquired. The deceleration, as I'd anticipated, was a force of evil—the trucker had stopped near a divider on the highway before making a U-turn, and landing us back on the road to Mumbai. We resumed our respective positions and banged our fists on the walls. The driver could not hear us; the symphony of breaths was lost, and the walls started closing in. The women reinstated the breath counts, forcing an uneasy calm through the cylinder.

In the other truck, meanwhile, chaos was at work to bring order. The men piled on top of each other, punching and kicking the manhole lid to push it open. The metal cap resisted for an hour, or maybe more, but I know it was until much after we'd crossed the interstate border back into Maharashtra. The men received text messages from their cell phone service providers, welcoming them to Mumbai's home state, adding the strength of elephants and oxen to their blows. The lid gave in.

One of the younger migrants climbed out of the manhole. The men held his legs until he caught hold of the handrails above the cylinder and started crawling atop the tube. It was tricky. There was the wind that jostled him back, and there was the night that stole his sight. There were pockmarked roads, and their bumps that kept slamming his face against the steel. There were also overbridges as tall as mountains, and their descents that threatened to fling him off the carrier, like a human arrow emanating from a slingshot.

It took years-long minutes before the migrant figured a way—he gripped the pair of handrails next to him with his palms, and as he moved towards the tractor, he stuck his feet in those behind him. After four metres of commando crawl, the man was atop the driver's cabin. He kept pounding his fists on the windshield until the trucker pulled the brakes.

Once the men's carrier stopped, the hostages rushed out of the cylinder and breathed. Upon spotting their assembly outside the truck, our driver stopped too. While a few migrants held onto the truckers, others rushed up the ladder of our container, opened the manhole lid, and pulled us out of the great void. As I walked out of that cage, I saw husbands embracing their wives, children squished between their parents, as most eyes looked up, heavenward, nodding, thanking, bowing. Some labourers had a faint smile colouring their pale faces, some broke into shaky laughter, some held their palms to their hearts, some wept, while all seemed relieved. We had just walked out of a black hole, alive.

Even as a few migrants cried for revenge, we decided to let the drivers go, aware that their actions were at the Bull's behest. Once our breaths had resumed their automated functions, Baba suggested that we keep walking towards home. He mentioned that our great odyssey had led to a change of fortunes. We were poorer now, as the cops had usurped all our cash, except for the ₹1600 that was still safe with Sameer. That paltry sum was all we had to cover the remaining 750 kilometres, and the only means of transport the amount could afford was our feet.

As we walked under that inky night, I wondered if we'd have to battle the Mad Bull again, who'd be waiting for us at the interstate border. I wondered if we should return to Mumbai instead, and let fate deal the cards. I thought of talking to Baba, but I saw that he did not share my angst. Not just he, most grown-ups were busy with some mundane banter, discussing the most rudimentary of issues—the sweltering evening, our grubby faces and clothes, missed calls from Grandpa, and the snacks we would eat for dinner. I questioned the insanity, and Baba threw a hackneyed Hindi proverb at me. '*Jaan hai toh jahaan hai,*' he said. If you have life, you have the world.

Yours,
Meher
Still in the wildwood

8

Wildwood

19 April 2020
Dear Ms Farah,

Once upon a time, in a desert as dry as rust, lived a boy named Happy and a girl named Meher. The siblings escaped the baked dunes of their native land and built a merry home near a blue paradise called the Arabian Sea. Soon, however, a great pandemic befell their country, and the children had but little to eat. They rushed out of their coastal wonderland and hurried back to the sandy wilderness. On their way, a witch, angry like a bull, ambushed them, threatened to eat them alive. They escaped her dark, ashen home, which smelt like sour milk, and ran into the forest. Happy left a trail as he walked, so he could find his way back if the jungle turned into a leafy labyrinth. The legend of Hansel and Gretel had wizened the boy. Hence, unlike those siblings, he did not mark his path with breadcrumbs, which would soon turn into birdfeed. He used paper, aware that he wasn't in a fairy tale, and that he did not have bread to waste.

One rainy forenoon, as I walked by the scrap dealer's shack in Dharavi, Cinderella called out to me. She was, of course, in Mumbai, as Balhaar has no fairy tales or fairy-tale retailers. Dressed in an arctic-blue gown with golden hair and glass slippers, the princess hung on a rope on the store's doorframe, suspended by a clothes peg. A pumpkin-shaped chariot stood behind her, and well-dressed mice danced at her feet against the backdrop of an enchanted palace.

Cinderella promised me a tale of magic, fairy godmothers, and upward mobility, and I brought her home. Once I was hooked to her story, she rushed me back to the merchant's shop, introducing me to her contemporaries—Rapunzel, Sleeping Beauty, Snow White, Goldilocks, the frog-kissing princess, Wonderland Alice, the Little Mermaid and, of course, Hansel and Gretel. The girls left me bewitched, as if by a magic spell in one of their tales, and soon, their chronicles turned into bedtime stories for my brother. Happy resisted at first, contesting that all my heroines were babes in the woods until princes or wizardry rescued them, but he soon gave in to the wand-work of my magic tales. When he learnt that we had to walk through the forest, he was even grateful for them.

'Good you told me about Hansel and Gretel, didi,' he said. 'Your nocturnal chitter-chatter is of some use now.'

It was a few hours after midnight, and we had woken up from a brief sleep by the highway. After our great escape from the black hole, we spotted an open area off the thoroughfare, where a lamppost illuminated a restaurant with padlocked shutters—Paapi Pet or Sinful Stomach: Jain Food, Veg Food, Non-Veg Food and Sweet Food; Brakefast, Lunch, High-T and Dinner.

A few buses stood parked outside the joint, and we decided to eat and rest behind their cover, before starting again in the wee hours. Most migrants from our milk carriers had left us, as they did not want to stop walking. Twenty of us waited, including our group of seven, Saleha's family of five, and eight others from her slum—three women and five men.

We decided to walk through the forest upon Candy Kaka's suggestion. The lockdown, he said, had turned the lonely hinterland into a road much travelled, as the dense, unmanned thicket was helping scores of migrants hide their illegal desire to get home. I had my apprehensions about the wild, aware that only a few days ago, a forest fire had engulfed a group of migrants like ours, as they walked through a dry canal in one of the jungles. It had looked like a lake of drifting embers on television, the fire, which soon grew into a red-golden tornado. It swallowed four of the ten migrants, including a woman and a baby girl. I raised the concern with Baba, but he brushed it aside, stating that the wildfire wasn't reported in Maharashtra, but far, far away, in the southern wilderness of our country.

Baba had last spoken to Candy Kaka before we took the ferryboat, and now thirty-six hours later, Kaka was 400 kilometres away from Dharavi, as opposed to our 150. Of course, he had left Mumbai a day before us, but while the Bull and his sheep had landed us back in Maharashtra, Candy Kaka had already crossed the Maharashtra–Gujarat border and was a few hundred kilometres away from the Gujarat–Rajasthan one. Once he crossed into Rajasthan, he'd be home within hours.

'How has Kaka covered so much distance already?' I asked my father once he was off the call. Om Uncle's kismet was colouring me green with envy, a dozen shades deeper than that of the wildwood.

'He got lucky,' said Baba. 'Their group of eight snuck into Gujarat via the fields by the border. They'd walked for forty-eight hours without—'

'One second,' I interrupted my father. 'Why can't we take the fields too? Why do we have to venture into the forest?'

'It isn't an option for us,' said Baba. 'After we escaped the milk carriers, the cops might be looking for us, and I'm sure they've already tightened security at the border. Also, your kaka said that the forest is safe, as many migrants are taking the route. It'll only be a few kilometres.'

As my family nodded in agreement, Baba returned to Candy Kaka's story. He stated that the eight migrants had walked for forty-eight hours with little rest. After a few kilometres into Gujarat, Nihal, one of the men in Kaka's group, started trembling. The shivers matured into a fever and vomiting, and soon, the man collapsed. Kaka tried to revive him by pouring handfuls of water on his recessed eyes and blue lips, but the man had already turned to rock. They took him to a hospital, where he died within minutes. Thereafter, the seven migrants struck a deal with an ambulance driver at the facility, who is now driving them to Rajasthan. Two of the men are lying on stretchers in the emergency transport, posing as patients with saline solutions injected into their veins, while the remaining five are pretending to be their relatives. They started a few hours ago from Vapi in Gujarat and the medical wagon, with the monotone of its wailing siren, is now zooming past the empty highway without trouble.

'How could they afford a private ambulance?' questioned Proton Uncle.

'They paid whatever they had, and promised to give more upon reaching home,' said Baba.

'What about the man who died?' I asked. 'What killed him?'

'The road, what else,' replied Baba, ditching his white lies for the truth this time. 'The doctors informed them that Nihal's blood-sugar levels had dropped and his body temperature had rocketed. He had also suffered a heat stroke and was so dehydrated that he had cried without tears before passing out. They moved him to the intensive care unit, and then onto the ventilator, but he did not live. His exact cause of death, they said, was severe dehydration.'

'What about his body? Will they send it home?' enquired Ma.

'Unlikely. Since the man had a fever, the doctors suspected that he had caught the virus, and collected his nasal swab as soon as they reached the hospital. His reports should arrive in a day, and his body will remain in the hospital morgue until then.'

'What if he tests negative for the virus?'

'Even then, the hospital won't send his corpse home because of the lockdown and the cost. They've built mass graves in an impromptu cemetery near the hospital, where they're tossing bodies of all coronavirus patients. Om said that his friend will end up there.'

'Is Om okay?' Proton Uncle asked.

'He's disturbed. They belonged to the same village, and Nihal, no older than thirty, was like a brother to him. Om informed Nihal's parents about his death. They're inconsolable, and although they've managed to borrow money to travel to the hospital and see their son one last time, local authorities aren't granting them a travel permit, not even to collect his body.'

'So why hasn't Om left with the corpse in the ambulance?' Ma seemed distressed.

'Doctors did not allow him, as they're awaiting the Covid-19 test results. He would have waited, but the ambulance driver refused to accommodate the delay. He would have fought, but their village council, upon learning about Nihal's death, threatened to throw Om's family out of the village if he arrived with the body of a suspected coronavirus carrier.'

Baba added that Candy Kaka had insisted that we must keep drinking water to stay hydrated, and I, once again, proposed that we must return to Mumbai. 'Maybe, there's some karmic debt that's keeping us from reaching Balhaar,' I tried to speak to my parents in their language. 'Maybe, this just isn't what god wants for us.' My words inspired a moment of thought and then fell flat. Thereafter, Baba proposed the wildwood to other migrants in our group. Aware of the Bull's presence at the interstate border, they concurred without hesitance and soon, one of the men found a gateway to the forest. He had walked to the far end of our rest stop to relieve himself, where he spotted an iron gate next to locked shops—a liquor store, a barbershop and one selling deep-fried potato fritters. He unlatched the door and discovered the wilderness.

'It's too dark out there, though,' the man informed. 'Let's wait two hours for the sunrise.'

As the morning twilight heralded the beginning of a new day, our group walked through the gate. Although the bronze sky was about to give birth to the sun, and the night and day were beginning to freeze into a single moment, the forest appeared as eerie as a thick fog on a stormy night. I could not tell what it was hiding, and I hoped I would not find out either—a secret that had best remain a secret.

Minutes into our walk, sunbeams started peeking through treetops, and a misty veil began to clothe the air. Clouds caressed the tops of distant mountains, and the warmth of the rising sun woke up the hornbills and grey jungle fowls, the pigeons and quails, and the cuckoos and parakeets. The world came alive with their songs, as we walked through grass that was taller than men, navigating stones, broken stems and loose rocks.

Since the jungle was just off the highway, it was not free of human refuse—plastic bottles, glass shards, sanitary waste and a variety of wrappers. The biggest challenge, however, was the abundance of minute ticks that had already started crawling up our pants; their bites like burns. To avoid their stings, we stopped to tie plastic bags around our arms and feet. Those who had socks wore socks. We declared it mandatory to be silent in the forest, but Happy felt the need to speak.

'Didi, you're carrying a notebook, aren't you?' he asked.

'Yes, why?'

'I want to tear a few sheets, so I can leave a paper trail.'

'We won't get lost,' I replied. 'There are no turns or bends on this route. We'll keep walking straight until we reach the other end of the check post.'

'Give me the book,' he said, pulling my backpack. 'Lest you become another babe in the woods.'

At the first glance, the wildwood appears sinister, as if the lair of an omnipresent demon—yes, a demon, not a ghost that was once human. At the second glance, it gets worse. Although we were walking parallel to the highway, we had ventured deep into the umber-brown woods until we'd lost all concrete and became invisible to the vigilant eyes of patrolling police officers. We'd also lost cell phone network in our game of hide-and-please-don't-seek, and could easily be walking towards our exotic graves.

The only respite was that the rugged landscape had burst into ancient trees and splendid shades, with flowers sprinkling a rainbow of colours onto the canopies. Squirrels scurried around trees, birds hunted for insects, small rodents scampered through the foliage, and troupes of monkeys made their whooping calls. Our noisy feet flushed a few apes out of their hideout once, and a thrilled Happy chased after them. The puzzled creatures jumped onto the trees, grunting and watching us from a distance.

'Careful,' I warned my brother. The ground lay choked with creepers, climbers and vines, as dark as the forest itself, and one wrong step would plunge his little body into the populated mud.

'Don't be a buzzkill,' he said, pushing my palm off his shoulder, quoting a word he had grasped from older boys on his cricket field.

As we walked on, we heard a stream's murmurs amid the songs of the forest. The earthy scent of wet mud guided us to the brook, its shore slippery with algae fringing its red soil. The rivulet pleased me. Travelling twigs twirled on its surface along with leaf-litter, and butterflies fluttered around its pebbles, their wings aglitter in the sun. I could not see where the brook came from or where it was going, as the trees got closer in the distance, creating a green, leafy horizon on both sides. The rivulet, however, did not seem worried about its course. It hopped over the stairway of mossy boulders, and broke into a little pool before us, like a large, white rose petal.

Four hours had passed since we'd entered the forest. We stopped by the stream to cool ourselves, scooping up water, and sprinkling it on our faces and necks. Then, without provocation, Proton Uncle pushed Baba into the rivulet and broke into raucous laughter. Father, I expected, would be furious, but instead, he pulled Uncle in too and started splashing water over his body. The men, like kids who had just discovered popsicles, appeared giddy with excitement, and soon, they also pulled Happy and Sameer into the stream.

'Do you remember the time we fled home to find a stream in the desert?' Baba asked Uncle, wiping the water off his eyes. Electron Aunty ordered the men to 'stop this childish nonsense right now and get out at once,' but Sameer pulled her in too. Soon, all twenty of us found ourselves surrounded by the torrent of mirth. The water soothed our tired limbs, drank away its fatigue. It also washed away the dirt and sweat of our two unbathed days.

'Yes, of course, I remember,' said Uncle, now drenched in nostalgia. 'We were chasing mirages.'

It was a winter morning in Balhaar. With chapattis and pickles in their tiffin boxes and sipper water bottles hanging around their necks, Baba and Proton Uncle, both twelve at the time, left for their mirage-hunt. In the past, the desert had tricked them with the illusion many a time, and each time, their parents had dissuaded them from pursuing the oasis. 'It's a lake made of the sweetest water on the planet, sweet as a rosy evening,' the grown-ups would quote the local folklore, 'but it's guarded by a sand-skinned monster, a vicious rakshasa. The demon will transform into a gigantic whirlwind if you go close, and it will swallow you whole.'

The forbiddance added honey to the sugary water in the boys' imagination and, determined to taste it, they set out for their hunt on foot. It wasn't just their dream, the oasis. It was also the dream of the parched sand, the thirsty birds, and the handsome sky, searching for a mirror.

Hours passed before the boys spotted a lake, and when they did, it disappeared as soon as they neared it. They sat atop a dune and ate from their lunch boxes before resuming their quest. Soon, they spotted another lake, this one with trees and sentinel dunes standing at guard around it. The boys rushed, and their feet slowed only when they neared the quartz-blue waters, when the sand started whirling in eddies of wind, roaring and blustering. 'Rakshasa, rakshasa,' the children cried, covering their eyes to keep the behemoth's powdery claws from blinding them. After a few minutes, when they peeked from between their fingers, the monster had vanished with the oasis, leaving no trace of their existence, as if they had been a dream.

'It was your idiotic idea,' a little Baba told a little Proton Uncle as night fell upon the desert, and the boys lay in the sand after squandering every ounce of their energy. Hours of search, and not one drop of the saccharine waters. Dawn to dusk, but only the many sand monsters. 'You always drag me into these mindless misadventures, and I always end up in trouble, always, always, always.'

'That is hardly true,' said Proton Uncle, busy admiring the stars that appeared as bright as hailstones.

'Really?' Baba was irked. 'It was your moronic idea, lacing the goat-feed with laxatives, so they kept shitting for days. Your foolish idea, exchanging cattle of the villagers—holy cows for unhallowed buffaloes and unhallowed buffaloes for holy cows—so everyone kept wondering about the trick gods had played on them. Your half-witted idea, slipping those lizards into the schoolmaster's jacket—not one, but two, and then the punishment ran into three days. My thighs died, standing in that rooster position for half a week, arms behind knees, and head between legs. The blood never returned to my brain, and I think that's why I still keep listening to you. Like your recent stupid idea, building a dune of our own, and now, this stupider mirage-hunt.'

'The dune was a good idea,' said Proton Uncle. 'Imagine, once we'd built it, we'd mark its crest with a flag, with both our names written on it—our personal sandbank.'

'It was a stupid idea, Jairaj.'

'No, we just got the logistics wrong. We had to give up because we got tired of plying the raw material to the worksite. Instead of building the dune near our home, where the sand is scanty, we should have built it deeper in the desert. Like here, this would be a good spot for a dune.'

'Yes, that's exactly why there are so many dunes here and now, we're lost in them. The wind has blown away our footprints, and I have no idea how we'll get back home. We're lost because of you, and now you better figure a way out of here.'

Grappling with the fear of skinks and scorpions, Baba covered his body with a blanket of sand and drifted into sleep under the moonlight. The following morning, a few gypsies discovered the boys and helped them back to Balhaar. Proton Uncle's father, per usual, was too drunk to notice that his son had been missing, but his mother punished his absence with a pitiless whipping. Baba got away with a warning from my grandparents, which, per usual, irritated him.

'Is that all you have to say?' Baba questioned the poor, polite parenting. 'I could have got lost, hurt, or never returned. I could have even died.'

'Yes, I know,' said Grandpa. 'So next time, come to me. I'll help you find the oasis.'

'Why can't you behave like normal parents?' Baba seethed.

'Because you're special, my son,' said Grandma, kissing his forehead. 'And special children cannot have ordinary parents.'

Baba hated being special. He knew his remarkability was rooted in the fact that he had been a stable zygote, who held on tightly to his mother's uterus, grew into a sturdy embryo, then a reliable foetus, and eventually, a healthy baby. He was the fourth child of his parents, and the only one to survive. The first three were lost to negligence, as Dadi did not care for herself during her pregnancies, continued working in the fields until her final weeks. Sitting at home would mean less food on the table; worse, her in-laws and the villagers would brand her lethargic. Moreover, like everyone in the village, she believed in the popular childbirth dictum: 'It's a tiger's cub, it'll find its roaring way out.' Grandma's, however, were human babies, and once she realized that, she turned cautious.

'After my third child died in my stomach, villagers started calling me banjh,' she told Baba once, stating the derogatory term for infertile. 'It's the worst thing a woman can be—a curse, where even the gods think you're not good enough to be a mother. Villagers would leave me out of community celebrations, especially naming ceremonies of children, as they believed I'd cast evil, envious eyes on the newborns. And then, after all that heartache, you arrived, and you lit up our world with your perfect little fingers and your perfect little toes.'

As Baba grew up, Dadi-Dadoo grew more protective of their only child. When he left home to chase mirages with Proton Uncle, my father had already dropped out of school. Balhaar did not offer education beyond class four at the time, and his parents would not let him leave the village to study further. A boy who liked his books, Baba protested but ended up working in the fields. Banal was his parents' winning argument: 'You're only a child. We know what's best for you.'

As a teenager, Baba wanted to move to the city of Jodhpur, and train to be a camel racer. He wanted to participate in the cattle fairs organized across Rajasthan, and win each of their prizes—best camel racer, best-dressed camel, best camel haircut, best camel beard, best camel dancer, and winner of the camel pageant. He wanted to jump onto the carousel rides in those fairs and get lost in the spectacle of colours, juggling with the jugglers, singing with the folk musicians, dancing with the skirt-swirling dancers, and listening to the tales spun by storytellers. His parents, however, did not let him have this dream either. They resisted even when he moved to Mumbai.

'You're abandoning your land, your fields, your parents, your wife and your children.' Grandma wailed. 'What if there's an emergency? What if we died? Would you return to show us to the pyre?'

'I'm doing this for my children,' said Baba. 'And as you did, I know what's best for them.'

My grandparents were not convinced, but Baba did not bother with further brawling. He left with sour words hanging in the air, and I know their bitterness still bite his heart. Perhaps, he hates the ivory sheath that his parents built around him, this bondage of deep love. Perhaps, he blames them for protecting him so much that he never had the chance to succeed or fail, to fly or fall. Perhaps, he had wanted to fly, he had wanted to fall, to get up and then soar.

I can see that Baba tries to be a different parent to us because he encourages me to study, wants me to go to college, and become a tech-friendly, English-speaking journalist someday. Perhaps, it's his dream, more than it'll ever be mine.

'Jairaj,' said Baba, pulling me back from the river of hereditary memories to the forest's stream. 'Did you realize? Like all your stupid ideas, even Mumbai was conceived by your fiend of a mind.'

As we watched in amusement, Baba made his fifth attempt at a handstand. He pulled in a deep breath and jumped into the stream's shallow water. This time, he managed to plant his palms on the bed of the stream, and extended his legs towards the sky. Proton Uncle pushed his feet back into the water, and Baba emerged, coughing and cursing.

'Yes.' Proton Uncle laughed. 'Mumbai was the greatest mirage-hunt of our lives, and this time, we completed the adventure, found our oasis, albeit fleetingly.'

It must weigh at least half a ton, I mused when the wildwood revealed the carcass of a buffalo. The slain animal lay facing us, its eyes open, and its stomach half-eaten. Flies feasted on his remains, and scavengers were probably approaching him for lunch, as the musty smell of his death mingled with the crisp perfume of forest foliage.

Ma started vomiting at the sight, prompting Electron Aunty too, and together, they startled the man who was sprinkling some crystals over the cadaver. The stranger jumped like a nervous cat, picked up his cloth bag and packet of crystals, and began to leave when one of the migrants called out to him.

'Aye, you,' said our man. 'Is there a village around here? Can we find food?'

'Vegetarian food.' Ma elbowed Baba, her palm cupping her mouth and nose.

The stranger, in response, ran, and our men chased after him. Sameer caught hold of him soon and opened his bag. It was hiding metal wire snares. I stole a long look at the man, who claimed to be a cattle grazier. Although he said he was a local tribal, I noticed he did not have the hardened face of deprivation or a skirt of leaves around his waist, as shown in the movies. He was not semi-naked, his clothes—a T-shirt and shorts—exhaled the scent of detergent, and he had leather sandals on his feet, while his young hair and beard appeared friends with hygiene, even grooming.

'Why were you sprinkling salt on the dead buffalo?' Baba asked the man.

He did not respond, and Father examined the packet of crystals that the grazier was now hiding behind his back. From its label, he learnt that it contained a pesticide called carbofuran. It was several minutes of probing before the man heeded our enquiries, confessing that he was in the forest to kill a leopard. *Why?* Because the crazy big cat had wreaked havoc on his village. *How?* It would enter the village, and take away children and dogs. It had also mauled a buffalo only a few days ago at the same spot, one of the many animals that fell prey to the leopard's stealthy stalking and patient ambushes. *So, now what?* The tribal grazier had decided to put an end to the predator's menace. *Ambitious; how would he do it?* By sacrificing one of his older, unyielding buffaloes. He brought the bait to this spot, which the leopard frequents, and let the buffalo graze around until the master of camouflage attacked him. The predator ate enough meat from the rump, but since the buffalo was too heavy to drag into the denser parts of the forest, the leopard left once it was full. *So, a failed plan?* No, the big cat will return for its kill, only this time, its food will be laced with the poisonous carbofuran. *What about the metal snares?* They're a backup, in case the predator smells the poison and does not consume the meat. The wires, once laid on the ground, will entangle the leopard, its neck in the best case. *Poor leopard.* No, no poor leopard. The mad cat had to be eliminated, or more children, more dogs, more livestock would be killed.

'Baba, we should leave.' Happy pulled at our father's shirt, fear of the loony leopard now creeping up his bones. I, too, was thinking about the crazy cat and the fate that awaited it. I could not tell if she deserved her approaching end, if she invaded the village first, or if villagers had initiated the war by annexing her home. The typical chicken-first-or-egg-first conundrum. Either way, both parties had turned prey.

'Yes, immediately,' said Baba, and turned to the grazier. 'Do you live nearby? Can you take us to your settlement for some food?'

'Of course,' he replied. 'I was just leaving. It'll be a few hours before I return for the dead leopard.'

'What's your name?' Baba asked him.

'Vayu,' he said, his eyes beaming with bizarre pride. He explained that his name means wind, and his four siblings represent the other four elements, which, according to some great thinkers, including his parents, form the basis of all cosmic creation—Akash (Space), Agni (Fire), Jal (Water) and Prithvi (Earth).

'What if your parents had a sixth child?' Sameer sounded redundant as Sameer is.

'No, they were mindful of that,' said the tribal man. 'My father got the snip after the fifth one.'

Vayu laid down his metal snares around the dead buffalo and started walking away from the cadaver. As we followed him, he asked, 'What are you doing in this forest anyway? It's dangerous here. Can't you see the leopard scats?'

'We don't know what leopard shit looks like,' said Sameer.

The grazier pointed to some fresh and old dung littered around the grassland. 'See,' he explained, 'that is fresh leopard scat, dark brown, about twelve centimetres long, musky smell, fuzzy bits of fur hanging off it. If the poop were old, it would be white because of all the calcium. And that, over there, is sloth-bear scat. It's the easiest to identify. It's black, much darker when it's fresh, and there's simply a lot of it, as bears are healthy poopers. I also want to show you wolf droppings, but I can't seem to spot them. Just remember that wolf scat is often cord-like, about an inch in diameter. If it's runny, you know that the animal has just finished a bloody meal.'

'So, there are leopards, sloth bears and wolves here?'

'Yes, but we're safe,' said the turd analyst. 'Most animals, if they're hunting alone, will avoid large groups of humans like ours.'

'But we must still hurry,' said Happy. 'Please.'

We followed Vayu through the maze of trees, their drooping branches fighting for sunlight, scraping our limbs and faces, and tearing our clothes. Our feet crunched on the dirt, as they snapped brittle twigs, and tripped over gnarled roots and aged rocks. A healthy forest astir with life, it was home to a gentle breeze that carried the sweet scent of forest flowers—bells and sprigs of white, pink, red and lavender, which added a startling touch of glamour to the green utopia. Birds twittered around us, flying from tree to tree, and disappearing into the sky.

Along the walk, Vayu boasted that he had once killed a leopard with a single arrow of his handmade slingshot. The man was on a hillock with his cattle when the beast lunged on one of his buffaloes from a tree, its jaws open and claws outstretched. 'I aimed the shot right between its eyes and sent the animal rolling down the hill.' The grazier's chest expanded with pride, his arms akimbo. 'The leopard was bigger than the biggest wild cat, chubbier too.'

Vayu also had a sloth bear story. He said he was gathering firewood in the forest once, when he came face to face with a sloth bear. It was too late to lie down and play dead, so he tried to retreat, but the bear charged at him faster than he'd expected. Its teeth dug into his upper thigh and bit deep. The grazier pulled out his knife and slashed the bear's snout. He then scrambled up a tree, as the animal disappeared into the forest, bellowing in pain. 'It took me two months to recover from that wound, but I'm sure the bear took longer,' said Vayu, prouder now, his head tilted back and a slight smile spreading across his face.

Happy was sweating with fear by now, his mouth had turned dry, and he claimed to have three million butterflies in his stomach. Baba asked Vayu to stop with his stories, but the man explained that it was futile to fear the wild or its animals. He also offered an oral manual on animal encounters: If you spot a leopard, wolf, or sloth bear, be quiet. Do not run away. The animal will move away on its own. If it doesn't, retreat while still facing it until you're out of each other's sight. If you see date trees, know that a sloth bear could be around as that is their favourite food. If you spot a leopard before it spots you, stand up wind of it, so the cat won't smell you. In fact, you can identify a leopard trail by smelling their spray. It smells like human piss, and they mark their ranges by spraying on bushes and trees. Most importantly, never forget that you're in the animals' home, and like humans, they do not appreciate uninvited guests either.

'Watch out,' Vayu exclaimed in the middle of his speech, pointing to a glossy, blue-black snake that was sliding out of a rodent burrow. About a metre long, it had black eyes, milk-white bands on its body and a red, wide-forked tongue. Upon spotting us, it coiled its body into a ball and hid its head. Once we were past the reptile, the grazier informed us that the snake was a common krait, one of the four most venomous species in India.

'As you can see, the wild is more afraid of us than we are of it,' said Vayu. 'Like that krait, most animals here can be deadly, but they're also shy and secretive. They hate daylight and prefer eating animals to humans, but the night makes them aggressive. I hope you don't encounter any of them in the shadows.'

As if on cue, Happy started throwing larger pieces of paper along our trail. His pensive eyes peeped into the Hansel-Gretel tale for more adaptable lessons, while his feet moved faster, looking for an expedited happily-ever-after.

It was an emerald-green enchantress, Vayu's village, an artefact of tempting solitude. A natural museum of gigantic trees, it could serve as a laboratory for environmentalists and a treasure chest for botanists. About forty huts stood in a circle around a pond, surrounded by their gatekeepers—sundry trees, plants, shrubs and herbs. A well-manicured flower garden broke the monotony of the green foliage with its large flamingo-coloured flowers. Women cooked on firewood near the pond, men plied logs of wood, and some lay on hammocks, while children played around the banyan, tamarind and blackberry trees, eating fruits off the forest floor.

'Welcome to Sargum,' an old man with a walking stick greeted us.

'Such an apt name,' I said. 'Your village is indeed a melody for the eyes.'

The man laughed. 'Melody is sargam, child. Our village is Sargum, named after a man who lost his mind or 'sar' after he got lost or 'gum' in this part of the forest. Tell me, what brings you to our wilderness?'

'We were looking for some food,' said Baba. 'Vayu, a cattle grazier from your village, brought us here.'

We turned around to find the man and realized he was missing. He had walked us to the settlement, announced it was his before vanishing without notice.

'What did he look like?' the old man asked. Dressed in a lungi and shirt, he had a turban around his head, and his mature face appeared tanned by the salt of the open air. An untamed white beard tickled his chest, and with his soft gaze and full smile for strangers, he appeared to be a man of ceremonious manners.

'He was tall, medium built, young,' said Baba. 'We met him when he was trying to kill the crazy leopard, one who has been attacking children and cattle in your village.'

'Nonsense,' the old man with the sparrow hands roared. 'There is no such leopard, and the murderer does not belong to this village. He was a wildlife poacher, who seems to have escaped because he knew we would report him to forest officials.'

'And he weaved the crazy-cat story to dodge our suspicion...' Sameer connected the blood-covered dots.

'Yes,' said the old man. 'Animal poaching has more than doubled during the lockdown.'

'Has it?' I was surprised. 'With all those images of animals walking urban landscapes around the world, I assumed the lockdown was a boon for them.'

'Nonsense,' the man thundered again. 'Vigilance in the woods has declined, as forest officials are splitting their time between regular duties and those related to the new disease. This has created a sea of opportunity for poachers.'

'What kind of animals do they poach?' asked Sameer and his frivolousness.

'They're killing leopards and smaller cats for their skins, ungulates for their meat, and monkeys for the medicinal properties of their flesh. Even indigenous people have turned to poaching of late.'

'Why?' Saleha got interested.

'Loss of employment,' said the old man. 'One leopard carcass sells for five lakh rupees. Before the lockdown, the locals would sell honey, flowers, fruits, bamboo, gum and other forest products via traders in nearby cities. With the lockdown, markets are shut and traders haven't visited the forest to collect the produce.'

Responding to our silence, he added, 'Come, let's get you some food.'

The man, who we learnt was the head of the village, led us to the centre of the settlement and asked the residents to ready a meal for us. We told him about the purpose of our journey, and he offered to take us to the village temple to pray for our safe passage. The shrine sat atop a hillock, and having walked through the woods for seven hours, we did not have the will or spirit for the climb. However, we could not refuse the old man's kind eyes. Saleha's grandparents waited, while the rest of us followed him.

The sun-soaked hill was a mosaic of golden yellow, green and deep brown. As monkeys watched us from treetops, we followed an unpaved path through the scanty vegetation, strewn with coconut husks and shells. Baba advised me against the climb, as I tend to get breathless too soon, but I insisted on it, and when we reached the windy summit, I knew the panorama was worth the trouble. The highway stood at a distance, reduced to the width of a pencil, and as I looked around, I felt safe. Surrounded by the great expanse of the green sea, under the parasol of a blue one, we stood in a forgotten land, unscathed by the atrocities of time and the habits of humans.

This is the closest I've felt to a divine image, I found myself thinking.

An ancient tree crowned the crest, and under its shade was a miniature temple. The deity was a rock, representing a god who had chosen to stay in the wildwood, instead of walking the wilderness of human civilization. The tree, meanwhile, was at least thirty metres high, had knotted arms and, according to the village head, was five centuries old. Protected by a platform, it had a bright red fruit, which, the old man claimed, could cure a host of diseases, including dysentery, cholera, arthritis, skin allergies, asthma and pneumonia.

'Where are we?' Baba asked. 'Maharashtra or Gujarat?'

'Maharashtra,' the man answered. 'The interstate border is about twelve kilometres away.'

Baba did the math and announced that we had walked twenty kilometres in the forest already, and that we should be able to take the highway in another fifteen.

'Is that a mosque?' Proton Uncle asked the old man, pointing to a small minaret on the adjacent hillock.

'Yes.'

'I assumed yours was a Hindu settlement,' said Baba.

'It is, and that is a Muslim one. In the middle of these two hillocks is a disputed cave. Hindus believe their god lived in that cave once, and Muslims believe theirs did.'

'Of course,' said Baba. 'First they annexed our land, and now they're after our temples. This is Ayodhya all over again. Muslim invaders demolished our temple in Ayodhya many centuries ago. Then, they built the Babri Masjid on the ruins, on the birthplace of Lord Ram. The blasphemy!'

'Yes, I'm aware,' said the old man. 'Then, almost three decades ago, the mosque was torn down because Hindus wanted to build a temple there.'

'And why not?' exclaimed my father. 'It was our land. Now, we also have official sanction from our country's apex court for the construction. The Supreme Court allotted the site to Hindus only a few months ago. You must go to court. We're fortunate we have politicians protecting our faith.'

'Thank you for the advice, young man. But did you know that the communal violence over that property dispute in Ayodhya killed nearly two thousand people? Hindus as well as Muslims. Colour of both their blood, red,' the old man retorted, surprising me with his knowledge of the world despite the location of his home. 'Thankfully, we're living too far from civilization for politics to corrupt religion here. Of course, our ancestors sparred over the cave, as both sides wanted to build their shrines there. But after decorous dialogue, they decided to build them atop these two hillocks.'

'So the cave is abandoned now?' Saleha questioned.

'No, it has prayer rooms for both faiths and the gods don't seem to mind.'

'Can we see the cave and the mosque?' she asked.

'Yes, of course.' The old man smiled. 'I'll take you.'

'No,' said Baba, his raised eyebrows threatening to fly off his temples. 'It won't be appropriate, and we must leave soon.'

Saleha's father, Hari Uncle, agreed with Baba, and the conversation met an abrupt end. Over the course of the journey, the two men had grown friendly, already conversing with eyes and headshakes. Hari Uncle, we learnt, worked as an auto-rickshaw driver in Mumbai after moving to the city eighteen years ago. His wife and daughter joined him five years later, while his son still lives in the village, managing the family's grocery store.

'My parents also live in the village, and were only visiting us in Mumbai when the state announced the lockdown,' Uncle told Baba. 'They were due to return to Gujarat in March-end, but with the sudden lockdown, their train tickets turned void without a warning. That's how they got stranded in our slum.'

Despite the lockdown, Hari Uncle tried to ferry passengers who were out for emergencies, but after five cash penalties and as many beatings from the police, he gave up. When his earnings plummeted to zero, and the expenses remained as many, he decided to leave for his village in Gujarat. There was also the threat of the new disease looming over the old bodies of his parents.

'Why didn't you drive the auto-rickshaw home?' Baba asked him. 'So many drivers, especially ones with families, have left for their villages in their tuk-tuks.'

'Yes, but many of them have also been killed in accidents. The vehicle is a light three-wheeler, not designed for highway commute,' he said. 'Also, the police checks. I know one driver who was on his way home with his family—wife and two children—when the police apprehended him. He was carrying a plastic container filled with petrol, as he expected petrol stations to be shut. The cops asked him what the barrel contained, and the flustered man said water because carrying loose petrol is illegal. They asked him to take a sip, and when he didn't, they beat him up and dumped the family in a quarantine centre.'

Hari Uncle added that he had been driving a rented rickshaw for most of his eighteen years in Mumbai. He bought his own vehicle only two years ago and was paying ₹6000 as a monthly instalment on the five-year loan. Following the lockdown, the EMI continued, compelling him to sell the vehicle to repay the outstanding loan.

'It was going to be an uncomplicated journey in the truck we'd arranged, but somehow, it turned out to be this lewd boxing match, us against every mother's son,' Uncle lamented.

'Every mother's son,' my father repeated. 'Human and animal.'

We descended the hill and enjoyed a hot meal of potato curry, wheat roti, onions and pickles. As we began to leave, villagers gifted us handmade anti-leech socks, and a bag full of snuff to keep the bloodsuckers at bay. They also gave us a spear, few walking sticks, some kerosene to build a fire, eucalyptus oil to repel ticks and mosquitoes, and a nasal spray to treat snakebites.

'Don't you think you'll be more comfortable, even safer, if you lived closer to amenities like schools, hospitals, roads and markets?' Saleha asked the old man, thanking him for the unusual gifts. 'The government might have offered you resettlement packages, haven't they?'

'Didn't you and your family leave home to resettle too, child? How did that work out?' The man looked deep into Saleha's eyes. He went on to state that he had lived in a city for three of his seven decades, far from his home, his living and his dead. Yet, the city never became his home, a diabolical stepmother at best.

'Home is the shelter you run to in a crisis, not the one you run away from, or the one that drives you out,' the old man added. 'It is where every night finds a morning. It is a haven in storms and a beacon on dark nights. It is where you're headed now, and I'll pray that you find its warmth soon.'

We left the village, and after three hours of walking through the woods, the sun began to touch the horizon, its fading light blanketing the sky with tangerine hues. We decided to keep walking because, according to Baba's math, we could take the highway in a few hours. Soon, however, dusk fell like a satin curtain and then sprinted away, surrounding us with the eerie gloom of a rayless night. The world became a silhouette, and we turned to the flashlights of our phones, but their beams could not obliterate the fears in our minds.

As the night darkened, our feet hurried and the rustling foliage got louder with their hysteria. The wind howled like an animal in pain, trees swaying to its tune. Squirrels raised an alarm as we walked past, and their squeaks rang through the forest. Then, as a punchline to the jungle limerick, monkeys began to hoot, indicating the threat of a predator, perhaps a leopard. The apes sought shelter on treetops as we spotted the carcass of a newly mauled animal, likely killed by the wild cat. Call me crazy, ma'am, but I think I also smelt leopard spray.

'Run, run,' said one in our group, said all. 'Don't stop, don't stop, don't you stop.'

We rushed through the swaying vegetation, kicking the dislodged stones, as the sounds of animal movement accelerated our steps. We dashed with our unvoiced screeches gnawing at our throats until we spotted an abandoned bungalow. We hurried in and blocked the open door with a pile of our luggage. We fell to the floor and we breathed, only to fight rats the size of small felines. Filled with darkness, as if the night detained in an old trunk, the bungalow's wooden floor grumbled at the slightest movement. The wind tapped its windows, like a ghost knocking at the door, playing a background score for the obscene dance of the wild.

We rested for a few minutes before the men got busy making a fire torch. They broke a walking stick into a two-foot baton. To create a wick, they tore a cotton shirt into strips and wrapped the strips around one edge of the stick. Then, they soaked the wick in kerosene and lit it. Since the torch would not last for more than an hour, they took turns renewing the light source until they all fell sleep. I, meanwhile, stayed awake, writing to you…

In the jungle, the mighty jungle…

Yours,
Meher
About to leave the wildwood, phew

9

Coal and Crystal

19 April 2020
Dear Ms Farah,

How do you feel about bread? If you ask me, I do not think much of it, ma'am. I'm one of those who grumble if it isn't baked right, if its crust isn't crispy and crackly enough. I know it tops the list of five basic human needs, and I understand that its absence could steal lives. I, however, am the rich kind of poor, one who has never had to face chronic hunger, not yet. Of course, I've had my stomach growl, my head fill with a fog, and my abdomen turn into a jar of vacuum. Of course, there have been moments when I found myself standing at the edge of my consciousness, hunger trying to push me off it. But even in the direst of those sinking seconds, I've had a rescue crew of bananas available, or spoonfuls of sugar. Even in the vilest of those pangs, I've never thought of eating from a dead dog—like that man on the highway, squatting next to the carcass in the middle of the thoroughfare, scavenging.

His mouth was covered in the roadkill's blood, his red fingers were busy separating bones from the meat, and his eyes, like his stomach, appeared empty. His hunger had diminished him to a carrion thief, and the way he chewed, he made me look at bread as I never had before. Bread was god to him, Ms Farah; bread was gold. Bread was his greatest foe, and bread, the one true friend. Bread was his master and bread, his freedom. Bread was his journey, and bread, the destination.

'Don't look.' Ma covered Happy's eyes, and asked us to walk faster. 'Must be a madman.'

'No, he's just hungry,' said Baba. Father then crossed the road, handed the man a bottle of water and a few berries we had picked up from the forest. The scavenger did not speak, only a tear rolled down his cheek, salting his palate.

As my eyes stayed glued to the human vulture, Saleha tried to calm my disconcerted bones. 'He's part of the social lattice, which in our country is essentially a grid of diamond and coal,' she said. 'More black, though.'

'What?' I did not understand her.

'Diamond and coal, they're both made of carbon,' she explained. 'It's the chemical bonds of society that turn humans like these, even us, into coal, and others into uncut, sparkling stones.'

'We're all destined for ashes then, being coal.'

Two hours had passed since we left the woods. I believed Baba's math was sound when we spotted a billboard inscribed in Gujarati: 'After whisky, driving risky.' Saleha, a native of Gujarat, had translated the hand-painted sign for us, and although it was only a traffic warning, a warm relief had washed over our bodies. The language of the inscription meant that we had crossed the interstate border into Gujarat without an encounter with the Mad Bull. The threat of leopards, sloth bears, wolves and snakes, yes, but thanks be to the wild, not the deadlier, khaki-clad predator.

We walked by the villages of Gujarat, their narrow roads and monochromatic settlements. I wondered about the people who called them home, and how the novel pathogen might have affected their lives. According to news reports before we left Mumbai, the virus was yet to reach the countryside, and once it did, everyone knew that chaos would reign. Rural India, including Balhaar, does not have enough medical amenities for a regular rainy day, and this seemed dead set on being a thunderous year. Of course, sadhu babas in the villages would prosper, as sales of their jiggery-pokery medicines would rocket. Hooch sellers would profit and so would shrines, and the greatest casualties, as in any man-made or natural disaster in the Indian hinterland, would be women and girls. Drunk men will first beat their wives in frustration over their lost livelihoods, and then sell their young girls into matrimony.

'Gandhiji once said that India's soul resides in its villages,' I told Saleha as we walked past a hamlet. 'If so, it's a wretched soul, a malnourished soul, a soul desperate to break free.'

'It's still beautiful, though,' she replied. 'Like a black rose.'

Rubbish, I did not say. Although Saleha appears worldly and aware, she's ignorant to the fact that her own beauty corrupts her perspective. Beautiful people find everything beautiful, as if these genetic lottery-winners are also born with a high-definition filter on their eyes, seeing the splendour of details that remain hidden to others.

After walking for about three hours on the highway, we spotted a long queue along the side of the road—men, women and children; young, old and rapidly ageing. The chain of human rust culminated into a distant truck, about a kilometre away. Curious, we approached the man closest to us, who informed that the wayfarers had lined up for food. A local charity, he said, was offering hot meals to sad stomachs. We decided to join the chain. Our middles were gloomy too, as our last two meals were forest fruits. I was expecting Baba to protest: 'I'm too proud for handouts; I won't pose for pictures with the free food; I won't become the poster boy of Hungry India, Poor India.' To my surprise, however, he listened to his fragile belly and asked his dear dignity to visit another day.

'Do you want to go see how long the queue is?' Saleha asked me.

I checked with Baba and he agreed. 'Take my phone with you,' he said. 'And do not use it to call your friends. It's low on battery and only has twenty rupees worth of talk-time left.'

As we walked by the travellers, I wondered if the novel coronavirus had vacated the world. The migrants stood close to each other and most of their mouths showed, their masks missing along with their fear of the contagion. They were faces hardened to stone, I noticed, and their feet spoke more than their eyes—naked feet, muddy feet, plastered feet, blistered feet, bruised feet and bleeding feet. They had thrown their luggage and their children to the ground, and every time the line moved, they'd nudge them ahead with their limbs.

As the queue progressed, so did the maladies. Some migrants had fashioned plastic bottles and bags into footwear, some had strips of towels and torn cement sacks fastened around their feet, some had used leaves to fill the holes in their tattered slippers, while one had 'mended' his torn shoes with safety pins, the pins giving away, tearing into his skin. A few shoeless children stood on their toes to keep off the searing earth, while a few others lay on the road, their little, fatigued bodies rolling to keep up with the queue. They belonged to all castes, creeds and sects, those children. The traditional divisions, the great fault lines of our country, seemed to have disappeared. All that remained was misery.

'Please give me food,' cried a middle-aged man, the whites of his eyes yellow, the tears on his cheeks, brown. The blisters on his swollen feet had burst, and a piece of plastic foam, which he probably found by the roadside, soaked the seeping pus. 'I cannot stand in this heat any more. My feet are scabbed. My urine has turned red. Please, give me some food.'

Another man blew air on his son's face, trying to soothe the sun's scars. The boy looked younger than Happy, but his parched lips appeared older. 'We'll get water soon, beta,' the man told his thirsty child. 'Just swallow your saliva until then.'

The boy's cooked face was still tormenting my mind when Saleha pointed to a man a little ahead in the line—a human ox yoked to a bullock cart. He balanced the wooden yoke on his shoulder with a white ox on the other end, while his family—a woman and an infant—sat on the wagon with their meagre belongings. I reckoned that the migrant might have morphed into a draft animal because he did not want his wife, a new mother, to walk in that heat with their child.

'Where is the other ox?' Saleha asked the man.

'I'm the other ox,' he barked. 'Are you blind?'

'No, sorry, I mean, why are you pulling the cart? Where's the second animal?'

'Sold it to buy food,' said the migrant. 'For five thousand rupees. Could have fetched me fifteen.'

'How long have you been walking like this?'

'Twenty kilometres.'

'How far do you have to go?'

'Another fifty.'

The man's answer brought relief. The distance wasn't too daunting and there was a thick chance that the beast of burden would make it home alive. We did not want to eat into his energy, so we left him alone. As we walked further, portraits of our migrant exodus kept emerging, some distressed, some determined, some desolate, and some dying. A child, too tired to walk, lay asleep on a trolley suitcase pulled by his mother, his cheek resting on its handle, his hands dangling on the rectangular case, and his feet dragging along the road. One migrant had fashioned wooden logs and sticks into a makeshift handcart for his pregnant wife and little daughter. He said he had been wheeling the cart for 500 kilometres over seventeen days. As I looked at those people and their tribulations, the highway appeared like an open book to me, with black pages that only seemed to get darker.

'You, how much for a night?' A pervert in a passing car slowed down near Saleha and me.

'Nah, mangoes too raw,' said the man in the passenger seat before the car sped away.

I wanted to hurl my shoe at those men's faces and I would have, had I not just learnt how invaluable footwear was. Like bread, like diamonds.

When we neared the food truck, I could feel its appetizing flavours flirt with my senses, and my mouth was the first to respond to the raunchy display, filling itself with saliva. The volunteers, I noticed, were handing out two packets to every migrant—one for the journey, which included a bottle of water, an energy bar, biscuits and peanut crackers, and another, a freshly cooked meal of dal, rice, chapatti, curry and onions. Every migrant thanked the donors with words, tears, or a talkative silence, while some insisted on physical contact. 'I know I must keep distance,' an old woman touched a volunteer's forehead. 'But I must bless you.'

'Why are the volunteers charging these people for the food?' I asked Saleha. 'One rupee per person.'

'Because the most important thing you can give someone is dignity,' she answered. 'If the beneficiaries pay a rupee, they feel they've earned the meal. Plus, it helps with bookkeeping.'

Although the charity seemed generous, I could tell that the truck did not contain enough food for every hopeful in that queue of about 800 migrants. I was certain they'd run out of packets before our turn, and Saleha and I decided to inform our families about the futile wait. As we began to return, some migrants, as if hearing us, charged at the truck, and started looting the food packets. The hungry travellers pushed, kicked and punched each other, as the volunteers tried to calm them. The decorum of the queue evaporated and people from the far end of the line started rushing towards the truck. A few parents crouched on the floor, covering their children with their bodies, as the starved humans raced against civility for food.

'I haven't eaten in days,' pleaded an old man, too frail for a fight as well as flight. 'Spare some for me, please.'

Hunger, however, begged louder. The migrants overturned the food cartons and ransacked the truck. They snatched the leftovers from each other, as if a pack of food-aggressive dogs fighting over meat, on the offence and the defence, growling, lunging and biting. I turned to look at the volunteers, most of whom were now standing by the roadside, watching helplessly. One, however, appeared to be talking to the police, pleading with them to arrive and restore order. That was our prompt. Saleha and I started running, and we phoned our families, asking them to run too. We could not afford another confrontation with the police.

'I told you,' said Saleha as we rushed towards home. 'We're all coal.'

Coughing and panting after escaping the food truck, I waited with Saleha for our families to reach us. We discussed our options for the journey ahead—trucks too pricey, roads too risky and woods too woody. I looked around, asking the world for an answer, and it pointed me to an idle train, revealing our new backdoor. The forested highway had given way to civilization, and one of its tarry arms led to a small railway station. An unemployed train stood on one of its four tracks, while the three others bore the red wrath of the dry Gujarat sun.

'Let's take the tracks,' I told Baba once he arrived.

'Great idea,' he agreed after mulling over the suggestion. 'Trains aren't running during the lockdown, their routes are shorter than highways, and no cops or railway personnel are patrolling the tracks. It might be the safest, fastest way home.'

'But there will be officials at railway stations, at least the major ones,' said Proton Uncle, defying his gung-ho ethos. Unlike his wife, he still wasn't a gloom-monger, just a classic specimen of a burnt child dreading fire, a baton-charged man dreading magic wands. 'We should check with Om before we start.'

I wondered if Candy Kaka had reached home. We'd spoken to him over thirty-six hours ago, and the way his ambulance was zipping past bulls and batons, his vagrancy should have ended by now. Baba called him, and while still on the phone, he stuck his thumb out and waggled his head up and down, telling us that Kaka was home. In seconds, however, father's head went amok, waggled side to side in brisk motions, while the tip of his thumb stared at the ground. Something was wrong. Everything was wrong.

After the call, Baba informed us that Candy Kaka and his six migrant friends reached their village last evening, and discovered fifteen-foot trenches dug around it. Kaka called his family and learnt that the pits were corona kavach or corona armour to protect the village from the virus by preventing migrant returnees from entering it. The panchayat believes that the wayfarers are Covid-19 carriers and virus vectors, and the furrows were a spectacle of their fear, ploughed with their lack of access to credible information about the contagion.

'Forget civilians, the village council also kept an army man from meeting his family,' Kaka told Baba. The soldier, who had returned to visit his wife and three-year-old son, had to live in a hut he built outside the village and died an inglorious death while setting up an electricity connection.

Candy Kaka and his friends were also treated like criminals, lower-caste ones. Villagers hurled shoes at them when they tried to fill the troughs with mud and forced them into a two-week quarantine in a public urinal on the outskirts of the village. Hills of garbage lie outside the toilet, as Kaka and six other labourers wait inside. They are exhausted from the journey. They have no food or potable water, and they have just lost a friend.

'But why are the villagers treating them like this?' I asked Baba, agitated.

'Stigma of the disease,' he said. 'In Om's village, every person with a cold, cough or fever has their home marked with a DANGER sign. A mob also attacked a health worker, who was trying to educate the villagers about Covid-19 symptoms and precautions. They spat on the frontline worker first, then threw hot water on her, and then pelted her with stones.'

Upon hearing about the madness in Kaka's village, I wondered if Balhaar had gone nuts too. From our grandparents, we knew that the virus had divided the village into two halves—one that believed in the contagion and another that did not. The believers of Group A were cautious. They stood in distanced circles drawn around community handpumps, created wall paintings with precautionary messages, avoided the smoking assemblies in the village square, and refrained from picking lice from each other's heads. They also used homemade masks, and some even tied them around their cows, goats and buffaloes. The sceptics of Group B, meanwhile, were busy wiping out the circles and paintings, inscribing the walls with the word 'Bhookh' instead. The sceptics, said Dadoo, believe that the disease, essentially a hunger crisis, is the government's alibi for population control.

'This coronavirus is a weapon of mass murder and mass profit,' say Balhaar's cynics. 'You get a cold, and they say you have the virus. Garbage. They're murdering healthy people, selling off their kidneys on the black market, and adding their bodies to the corona count. This way, they're making money and reducing the population. Why else won't they return the corpses to their families? Why else would they build those hasty, backhoe graves?'

Scepticism aside, some in Group B believe that the virus could be real, but insist that the government has unleashed it. Like the locust invasion in the past few months, when swirling swarms of the deadly grasshopper damaged crops across lakhs of hectares in Rajasthan. Some villagers, at the time, argued that the state had released the locusts, and now, the state has let loose the virus. 'They want us dead,' they say. 'There is no evidence to prove otherwise.'

About a week after the lockdown, Balhaar's gram panchayat recognized the need to arrange ration for the poorest families in the village. They offered a few groceries to them, and many were living off boiled rice and water or flatbread and chilli paste. Now, the food has run out in several homes, and entire families, including children, are skipping meals, their daily bread contingent on the charity of neighbours. Some have managed loans from private lenders at interest rates as exorbitant as 30 per cent per month, while others are relying on barter—rice for vegetables, and wheat for milk. When the situation worsens, many unmarried girls will get pregnant, bartering sex for spices.

You would think pre-marital sex, even discussions around it, might be considered blasphemous in rural dialect, but I must tell you that isn't the case, ma'am. Quite the opposite, in fact. Poverty often finds answers in sex, ensuring heightened libidos in the hinterlands. A teenaged girl from our village, for instance, went to bed with a boy only because he bought her a new pair of salwar-kamiz. She got pregnant, and the boy snipped all ties. She took another suitor then, one who agreed to pay ₹1200 for her abortion in exchange for carnal compliance. I thought of this exploitative man as the villain, but when I spoke to the girl, I realized that the antihero wasn't just him, but a seamless blend of penury and illiteracy.

'He has a flat-screen television at home, two camels, even a tractor,' the dreamy-eyed girl told me about the new man in her life. 'He also gave me a phone, so we can talk every day. Now, I just hope he takes me as his wife someday.'

As I stood wondering if the stars ever granted the girl's wishes, Baba called our grandparents to check if Balhaar, too, was persecuting its returning children. We hadn't told Dadi-Dadoo of our journey yet, but Baba was compelled to confess now. My grandparents had many apprehensions, but Father convinced them that we were safe and that we would be home in ten days. As for Balhaar, it seemed sane so far. It was housing its returnees in my former school, which was safe for the villagers, as the institution, a thirty-minute walk from my home, was a planet away from the hamlet.

'How will we make it in ten days?' I asked Baba as we walked towards the parked train at Bhilad railway station amid padlocked shops and fettered mannequins. Candy Kaka had confirmed that the retired, lonely tracks were a good alternative to the exposed, telltale highways.

'Easy,' Neutron Sameer spoke out of turn. 'I just checked Google Maps. We're almost seven hundred kilometres away from home. If we walk seventy kilometres over twelve to fourteen hours every day, we'd be home in ten days.'

'It's not easy,' I said. 'The first two hundred kilometres of our journey were anything but easy, and the remaining seven hundred won't be any different.'

'Let's take the tracks,' answered Sameer. 'No cops, no leopards. It's a great idea.'

'It's *my* great idea,' I asserted.

We walked on the tracks in two lines, surrounded by serried slums and desolate farmlands. It wasn't too challenging. All we had to do was take long strides like a marching platoon, aim our feet on the concrete crossties, and avoid stepping on the stone-covered track-bed. The novel pathway extended a rhythm to our insipid walk, and Happy spent the first few minutes jumping between the railroad ties. He declared fatigue soon, soon after Sameer announced that the goal for the day was to walk sixty-six kilometres and reach the Bilimora railway station, where we could rest for the night.

'All we have to do is walk six kilometres an hour,' he proclaimed. 'We have almost thirteen hours until midnight.'

'I don't know, Buchu,' said Electron Aunty, calling Sameer by his nickname, which means nothing. 'That's a lot of walking. Years have come over me in these few days, and I'd be a much older woman by midnight.'

'We have to do it, Ma,' Sameer tried to motivate her. 'We could smile while we do it, or we could brood while we do it. But we have to do it. There's no getting away.'

'Yes,' exclaimed Saleha's grandfather, the length of his strides increasing. 'All hardship is transitory, especially this one. We're losing to win here, surrendering to triumph. Once we get home, we may even laugh over this. God knows this is already the most memorable journey of my seventy-five years.'

Electron Aunty grimaced, but the old man's fervour worked like a trumpet call for the rest of us, an adrenaline-shooting battle cry.

'Come on!' A labourer was enthused. 'We're going home!'

Have you ever had a conversation that carried currents of change, Ms Farah—talks that transcended words into silences, and ones that lingered even when the voices faded? I've had these with Miss Amber and Master Happy. Of course, the natures of these exchanges were different. While the teacher would enthral me with her understanding of the world, pushing me to turn the bad over its head, my brother, still uncorrupted by age and experience, has always pointed me to the good in humankind, unable to acknowledge its dark side. Then, I met Saleha, a cross between the two.

Saleha has experienced the world, even its unpalatable wings, yet adores it. She knows injustice like a close kin, yet refuses to give up on the family. She's aware that the sun may never shine for some on the planet, but won't quit faith in mornings. My discovery of the friend in her commenced with a conversation about someone as inane as Sameer, but by the end of it, it had left me with a confidant, my alter ego.

'That Sameer's plan is unsustainable, so is his zeal,' said Saleha as our feet dodged the puddles of stones on the railway tracks. 'We're far from home, only have a few fruits, little water, and none of us, especially my grandparents, can walk that much. We'll have to figure another way.'

'Don't pay attention to him,' I retorted. 'He's a little over-smart.'

'Yes, he appears to be,' she said. 'Did you notice the blue goggles tucked at the back of his collar? He thinks he's the police inspector from that super-hit Salman Khan film *Dabbang*, waiting to break into an inappropriate dance number any moment.'

I laughed. I like jokes on Sameer.

'He's good-looking, though,' she added, stealing away from my mounting affection for her.

'Who, Sameer?' I asked, my eyes glued to the tracks. 'Yuck.'

'Yes, who else? He's lanky but has a good personality. Don't you think?'

'You can have him,' I said, genuinely uninterested in Neutron. 'I'll be happy to introduce you to him.'

'You like him, don't you?' She chuckled and wiped the mirth off her face after noticing my displeased air. Then, she rerouted her words: 'He's too young for me. Besides, I already have a boyfriend.'

'What? Who? Where? How? When?' I listed most of the fundamental questions of journalism in excitement. Saleha shushed me and asked me to follow her to the end of the group. This was no conversation for grown-up ears.

'Well, his name is Virat,' she said as we trailed the others. 'He's also a volunteer with my NGO, a year older than I am. We met at the organization, and we've been dating for two years now.'

'What's he like?'

'Mostly nice, but too nice at times, which ticks me off.'

'Meaning?'

'For instance, once we saw a woman at a traffic signal, begging for alms barefoot. I thought I'd buy her a pair, but Virat made me give her mine. Apart from the fact that they were my favourite slip-ons, I was shoeless now. I told him, "Darling, I get the kicks out of your big fat heart. I even aspire to your big fat heart. But please don't give away my flip-flops when I've to survey a hundred homes in this searing heat." He laughed and took me to buy a new pair.'

'Is he still in Mumbai?'

'No, even he's walking to his village. His family is from Uttar Pradesh and his father worked as a tailor in a leather workshop near our slum. The same story as everyone else—lockdown enforced, lost livelihood, waited for restrictions to ease, lockdown extended, ran out of money, feared starving to death, packed their world in two bags, and started walking home.'

'So, what about you and Virat? Will you see him again?'

'We hoped to get married in a few years, but I don't know any more. They say hearts that dance to the tune of love always find their music. I'm hoping that's true, or we'll have to find the melody on our own, which will be messy.'

'Doesn't that worry you?' I asked.

In response, Saleha went quiet for a few moments, as if searching her head for the right words. '*Aur bhi gham hai zamaane mein mohabbat ke siwa*,' she said thereafter, '*Rahatein aur bhi hai vasl ki rahat ke siwa.*'

'What does that mean?'

'It translates to: "There are many other agonies in the world, besides the agony of love. Many other joys, too, besides the union of lovers." It's from a poem by the immortal Pakistani poet Faiz Ahmed Faiz.'

'Wow,' I said. 'Do you understand Urdu?'

'No, I look up the translations,' she said, and quickly drifted, 'What about you? Do you have a boyfriend?'

'No. In fact, I do not have many friends either,' I blurted, and as the embarrassment over my dull social life crept in, I went on to justify my statement. 'I mean, there's my best friend, Ira, and a few other girls I talk to in our slum, but no one else. The problem is that I moved to the city only four years ago, and my schoolmates still see me as an outsider. Many of them belong to migrant families too, but they've been in Mumbai longer, so they think they have more right over the city and its classrooms. Apparently, Mumbai isn't as mine as it is theirs. Also, I always rank first, second or third in class. Scorer plus outsider is a bad combination if you're looking for friends.'

'It's strange, isn't it?' said Saleha. 'I moved to Mumbai when I was little, and now, thirteen years later, the city still isn't mine.'

'I think I feel the same way,' I said, discovering a disappointment I did not know I harboured. 'I, too, surrendered to Mumbai, every bit of me, and yet, it didn't become mine. When this Covid-19 crisis struck, it abandoned me.'

'That wasn't Mumbai.' Saleha corrected me. 'That was India.'

About three hours into our walk, we reached a railway bridge that snaked over an oily river. I turned apprehensive, aware that once we were on the bridge, we'd have nowhere to escape, except for jumping into the brown waters, in case a train arrived. As we walked onto the passage, Happy climbed onto Baba's shoulders, while I grabbed the iron side-rails. I also pressed my mask closer to my nose to evade the stench of the industrial waste that leisured on the waters. The multi-lane highway ran parallel to our railway bridge, surrounded by natural drains and domestic sewers that looked like tributaries of the river. The putrid wind ran through our hair, soothing our melting bodies.

'Not to worry, no train coming by.' A labourer turned around. 'But walk carefully, you don't want to trip and fall into that filthy water.'

Once we were off the bridge, Saleha and I resumed our conversation.

'Are you worried you'd never return to Mumbai?' I asked her. 'I mean, I know it's an unrequited love, but I'd still want to return to her.'

'I'd love to go back, but it's okay if I don't,' she said. 'My village needs a lot of work too. Even without the coronavirus, it's a socially distant land. Now, with the virus, it might have turned into a paradise for biases. Also, I'm excited about seeing my brother. It has been two years, and Sourav, like your Happy, is the best little brother a girl could ask for. He is nineteen but has a much older soul. He enjoys poetry, couriers me my favourite sweets every birthday, and has been handling our family's grocery store while in college.'

'Is he good at studies?'

'Oh, he's good at everything,' she said, her smile audible in her words. 'Studies, sports, work, everything. He even offers free tuitions to a few kids in our village every Sunday.'

'How did you join the NGO?' I asked her.

'You're so curious.' She laughed. 'You've got the right germs for a journalist.'

'I don't know about that,' I said, expressing another fear for the first time. 'I don't know if I can become a journalist.'

'Why?'

'Three reasons,' I said. 'One: My parents did not even finish school. My aspirations could be impractical. Two: Baba's hopes stand on the shoulders of my dreams. If my dreams fall flat, so will my father. Three: It's a universal rule—only a king's son inherits his throne. I'm no son, let alone a royal heir.'

'Those are three excuses, I'd say,' she replied. 'Let me give you three reasons why it's possible: One, dreams won't be dreams if they were realistic. Two, your father will feel worse if you never tried. Three, there are queens in the world, too.'

Saleha's words reminded me of Ms Amber and how she, too, believed that I could become a journalist someday. Ms Amber's logic was simple. She said that in this entire infinite universe, with its billions of galaxies and quintillions of planets, with all its darkness and all its emptiness, scientists have found evidence of life only on earth so far. And what diversity of life! Plants, animals, fungi, microorganizms, each sustaining the other in a perfect food web, as if the synchronized beats in a melody. This, she said, means that earth is the universe's favourite child, the only one blessed with a breath, and each of us earthlings, hence, has the unparalleled power to do, be and have anything we desire. 'That's how people emerge from the shadows and brighten the globe with their lights,' she had said. 'Some of the world's greatest leaders, artists, teachers, businessmen and sportspersons have built their legacies this way. Stuff your eyes with dreams, Meher, and leave magic to the universe.'

Even as I thought about Ms Amber's infectious hope, a fatalism had come to dwell inside me, clouding my view of tomorrows. It was perhaps this journey. As I stayed lost, thinking whether the road had altered me, Saleha pulled me close.

'Can I let you in on a secret?' she asked.

'Yes, of course. Anything.'

'And you promise you won't tell anyone?'

'No, I won't,' I swore, pinching my neck.

'Okay,' she said. 'We're Muslims. Your father caught me when I mentioned my name, which sounded Muslim to him, but I could not retreat then, so I said it was Sanskrit. That's why I was careful when I spoke to you, saying Virat, not Arif, is my boyfriend, and Sourav, not Salim, is my brother. We've all taken Hindu names for this journey, Father and Grandpa shaved off their beards before we left, and Mother, Grandma and I have tucked our burqas into our bags. We're posing as Hindus.'

'But why?'

'Because of the whole Corona Jihad fracas.'

'After that Muslim congregation in Delhi?' I asked, remembering the scores of news reports that marked their stories about the religious meet with the trending hashtag: Corona Jihad.

'Yes,' she said. 'The meet was organized by the Delhi chapter of this Islamic missionary movement called Tablighi Jamaat. The congregation took place much before the lockdown, and by the end of March, it emerged as a coronavirus hotspot, turning the virus communal. Everyone, including those among the press, politicians and the public, accused Muslims of bioterrorism, claimed that we were weaponizing the virus to wage a holy war.'

Saleha was right, I thought. News channels at the time were teeming with demonizing reports about the community. The hostility had also led to an assault on Jamaat volunteers, the cops had booked one of their leaders on charges of culpable homicide, and a government official had suggested that Muslims, who gather at mosques, must be shot.

'Mobs targeted members of our community in many towns and cities,' said Saleha, a sadness—no, disappointment—colouring her eyes. 'Some were beaten up with fists and cricket bats; others were refused medical help at hospitals, while many others faced verbal abuse and discrimination. With this climate in the country, it was safer for us to lie about our faith on this already perilous journey.'

'Good decision,' I said. 'And don't worry; your secret is safe with me. I'm sorry for it has to be a secret at all.'

'That's no problem.' She smiled. 'I'm sure you and I, and more like us, will turn all coals into crystals one day.'

We walked in silence thereafter, watching the night take over the day. Although we had covered only forty-five of our sixty-six kilometre target, our zest had lost steam, and most of us were willing to retire. My footwear—brown canvas shoes that I wore to school—was beginning to give away. The forest fruits were over, and with no proper meal in the past one and a half days, hunger had begun to torture our bodies. Some migrant workers smoked every bidi they possessed, hoping to trick their rumbling stomachs, but the pangs persisted.

To compound the trouble, there was fatigue. We had been taking ten-minute breathers every two hours, sitting on the tracks and stretching our legs. Saleha's parents would massage her grandparents' feet during these breaks, but as the night progressed, their legs refused to cooperate. We decided to halt for a longer time, and most of us lay down on the tracks, our heads resting on the iron rails. About half an hour later, the old couple was willing to walk again, but gave up in minutes.

'You go ahead,' said Saleha's father. 'We'll rest some more and join you in a bit. I have your phone numbers.'

'Are you sure?' asked Baba.

Uncle nodded, and Saleha whispered, 'Khuda hafiz' in my ear.

'What does it mean?' I asked her. 'I've heard that parting phrase many a time, but never checked what it meant.'

'It's a religion-neutral greeting,' she said, putting on her radiant smile. 'Khuda is the Urdu and Persian word for God, and the phrase translates to "May God be your Guardian."'

'Oh, fantastic,' I exclaimed, and added foolishly, 'may khuda hafiz to you, too.'

After a few minutes into our walk, Saleha's father called Baba to inform us that her family was going to rest for the night. We decided to stop too and got off the tracks, weary and starved. Hunger beats fatigue, I realized, as although exhausted to the bone, many in our group had difficulty sleeping. They watched the stars, lying on a pile of stones off the tracks, praying for sleep to feed their hunger. I, meanwhile, sat writing to you, making words feed mine.

Although I've wanted to post these letters for four days now, I haven't had a chance yet, ma'am. The highway has no letterboxes, nor do I have stamps. But now that you're completely updated on our journey so far, I'm planning to tell Baba about these letters tomorrow. I'm sure he'll courier them to you as soon as he finds an opportunity. With the lockdown in place, I do not know how soon my story will reach you, but the very hope of it has made this expedition easier, the very act of narrating its travails has diluted its insanity, and the very possibility of your support has built courage. It's like you're here, ma'am—walking, laughing, crying, despairing and hoping with me, just like Saleha, just like the rest of our group. I wonder if this is what camaraderie feels like, and for this feeling, Madam Journalist, I shall always be grateful. To you, to Saleha, and this journey.

Yours,
Meher
Somewhere in southern Gujarat

10

Gibberish

20 April 2020

Saleha is dead, Ms Farah. Dead. Her family, dead. Her heart, like a mother's, dead. The lives she would alter, dead. No fault of hers, no crime. No note, no goodbye. Ebbed away in seconds. Dead. 'Khuda hafiz,' she said as we parted. 'Khuda hafiz,' I told her too. Then, where was god as she withered? Where was his virtue? When that train milled her body, did he look away too?

I'm sorry for the gibberish, ma'am. I do not know how else to outlive this moment. I'm sitting near the Gujarat–Rajasthan interstate border, three-quarters of our journey through, and yet my spirit hasn't moved past those railway tracks. I'm safe, and yet I've never felt this afraid. Does grief feel like fear, ma'am—or remorse, or anger, or some acrid concoction of all three? Am I even feeling grief? I could not be. I barely knew Saleha. Then why does my heart knell with the damp echo of her voice? Why does my mind keep darting to those tracks, pulling her off them? Why does my conscience shame me for letting her go? Am I culpable, madam? Or is it her? Or is it him? Or is it those who shan't be named, those who dare not be named?

Bloodstained currency, mutilated bottles of water, splintered cell phones, mangled footwear, lacerated luggage, flattened coins—my eyes kept rummaging through the debris that lay strewn around the felonious railway tracks. Those things belonged to Saleha and her family once, only a few hours ago, when they still belonged to the present.

As I stood staring at those bloodied tracks on her deathbed, I spotted Saleha's earring, a silver teardrop, now red, fractured. I picked it up and locked it in my fist. I made sure the cops were not looking. Then, I tried to force tears out of my eyes. They refused to budge, stayed anchored at the bottom of my throat, crowding my breath. They sought a stream to flow with, of emotion I did not feel. Only shock, only a void inside my body, something dry, an emptiness, a ravine.

It was 5 a.m. We were asleep in an open space off the tracks, when two railway guards joggled us awake. 'Get up,' they screamed, 'get up and get out now.' We sprung to our feet, all fifteen of us, like that jack-in-the-box, and we stood staring, confused, like that jack-in-the-box.

'What happened?' we screamed back.

'Go, go at once,' they said.

'But why?' we demanded.

'Five people sleeping on the tracks, killed under a goods train.'

'When?'

'An hour ago.'

'How, oh how?'

'Driver honked, could not stop the train in time. Limbs all over. Blood all over. Go, go now.'

We picked up our belongings and began to leave, questions pacing with us. Was it Saleha? Was it her family of five? It could not be. But what if it was? Why did they sleep on the tracks? Why not anywhere else? Questions. Questions. Questions.

Soon, a police officer rushed towards us, grabbed one of our men by his collar and started dragging him away. He ordered the railway guards to bring us too, and we walked like living bodies with dead eyes, imagining the worst, aware of the worst.

I took Baba's phone and dialled Saleha's father. 'The person you're trying to reach is currently unavailable,' said a plain, automated voice. 'The person you're trying to reach…' I tried to look for the murderous train, but it was absent. I remembered it passing by. The iron rails had trembled, the stones on the track-bed had jumped. I had turned around and slept again, oblivious to the blood that jacketed its criminal wheels.

'Sir, do you know who they were?' I asked one of the guards.

'Mangled bodies,' he said. 'All we know is that they were five people—two men, three women.'

I heard, and I ran. I kept running until I tripped over a few rocks hidden by that stale night, fell to the ground, and tore my lip. Baba helped me up with a warning. 'Even if they were Saleha and her family,' he whispered, grabbing my arm, 'the cops must not know that we knew them. Gather yourself, or we'll be in trouble.'

I did as I was told. I held on to my falling pieces, and walked in silence, even as the clangour inside my head was beginning to knock me out. We reached the accident spot, and there, I saw what remained of Saleha and her family, their belongings and their blood. The cops had vacated their bodies, but I knew it was she. It was her ragged bags, her tattered shoes, her injured earring. I obeyed Baba and remained quiet, but many, who had gathered around the remnants, spoke. They spoke in murmurs, grey murmurs of pity.

Masked, gloved police officers went about clicking pictures of the tracks, making notes, and questioning locals. Father lifted Happy up in his arms and turned his face away from the debris. The boy fell asleep in seconds, but I looked and I listened. I kept looking and I kept listening. To believe. To let my senses convince my heart of the truth. Of the gibberish of fate. Of the gibberish of life. Of death.

'I live just across the fields,' a man, who first informed the police about the deaths, recorded his testimony. 'It was around four in the morning when I woke up after hearing the train come to a screeching halt. I rushed to the tracks and saw the driver standing next to them. He pointed to the disfigured, maimed bodies lying under the train. Five corpses and the world splattered with blood. I threw up, and dialled the police.'

'Must have slept on the tracks, assuming the trains aren't working during the lockdown,' the police officer, who was noting the testament, shut his diary. 'But only passenger trains aren't working. Freight and maintenance trains are still in motion across the country.'

'Unfortunate, very unfortunate,' replied his colleague. 'Is the media coming?'

As the cops discussed the press circus that was to ensue, I declared myself guilty. I should have known about the goods trains. I watch a hundred hours of news every day. How did I not know? Why did I let them leave us? I even thought about stopping them. I thought about it, but I did not say it. Why didn't I utter those words? Had I said them, they, too, would have slept off the tracks. Had I said them, they, too, would have been breathing.

As the guilt leisured on my skin, my head throbbed, my muscles felt heavy, and the world became hotter than ever before. My chest would implode, I felt, as my mouth went dry, and every cell inside me trembled. The sun rose, and I shifted the blame on god. 'You are responsible for this.' I stared at the marmalade sky. 'You fix this. You fix this now.'

The skies did not answer, and all the pain in my body coalesced into a ball, started hiking up my throat.

'Not one tear, Meher.' Baba gripped my wrist, his voice as icy as his touch. 'If the cops ask you anything, you'll say you did not know them. Or else, they will never let us get home. Look up now. Look at me. Are you listening, child? Can you hear me?'

I could hear him. I could also hear every question the cops bombarded us with—Did you know the deceased? Do not lie; you were sleeping only a kilometre away. What were their names? Where had they come from? Where were they going? Where were they working? We know they were migrants walking home. Why were they sleeping on the tracks? Were they tired? How long had they been walking for? Where is their home? Do you know their kin? Do you have their phone numbers?

Our group pleaded with the cops, reiterating that we did not know the dead migrants, begging them to let us go. The officers, although exasperated with our unhelpful answers, did not resort to violence, perhaps softened by the stolen lives. They let us leave in a few minutes, once their colleague arrived, announcing that he had found IDs on one of the bodies.

'It was one Ashraf Ansari and his family,' the officer informed. 'Once their post-mortems are done, we'll send their bodies home. We must make sure they reach home.'

Allowed to leave and live, we walked away from the tracks, into the fields, towards the highway. Each of us remained silent, not crying, packing our messy emotions in neat packages, as if we really did not know the people behind those mutilated bodies. Those mutilated bodies. I think I saw a finger on those tracks, or was it a piece of rock? Tears rushed back to my eyes, gathered in pools around my bottom lids, and clouded my pupils.

'Take heart now, Gudiya.' Baba held me. 'The dead weren't our people. They were Muslims, some Ansaris. Saleha and her family are such saints, all five of them. They would never meet this fate.'

'They met exactly this fate, Baba,' I cried. 'And they were Muslims.'

As we walked on the highway, I kept thinking about Saleha, her life and her death. I wondered what death was, if she were in heaven, if there were a heaven. That's when Dadoo's words rushed to me: There is no heaven or hell outside of this earth, he'd told me once. It was a few years ago, after Dadi discovered one of my mischiefs—I'd soaked my palms and fingers in henna and left multiple hand imprints on her white cow. Enraged, she threatened me with one of the most popular deterrents for Indian children: Do not do this-and-that, or the rakshasa will take you to hell and fry you in a cauldron full of hot oil. I sat scared, already having done this-and-that, when Dadoo sat down next to me.

'There are no rakshasas, and even if they do exist, I'm sure their job isn't to deep-fry children,' he said. 'As for hell, we create our own hell and our own heaven while we're alive, and we do it with our karma. Good deeds, benevolence lead to heaven on earth, and evil turns life into hell.'

'No, Dadoo. You're wrong,' I said. 'If you do good things, you go to heaven after you die. If you do bad things, you go to hell.'

'They say that only to scare you into doing good things.' He smiled. 'There is no heaven or hell outside of this earth. Not even after death.'

'What is death?'

'It's when your soul leaves your old body and moves on to a new one, like we shed old clothes and wear new ones.'

'Meaning rebirth?'

'Yes, rebirth.'

'As in that prime-time sitcom? Murdered woman returns as a venomous snake, avenges her death by biting all those who killed her.'

'Yes, something like that,' he said. 'But not exactly.'

'Then how exactly?'

'You're too young for this conversation, child.'

'I'm not young,' I told him. 'You know that. Everyone says that I have an old, rather cheeky, woman living inside of me.'

He laughed. 'Yes, you are my wise child,' he said. 'I'll try to explain. Our souls, they're stuck in a cycle of rebirths and re-deaths. They keep moving through bodies. The tiring loop ends only when they achieve moksha. Now, you'll ask me what's moksha. It's when the soul is released from this eternal cycle of birth, life and death, and the temporary, gender-linked bodies. It's when all of its suffering ends, and it becomes free, *truly* liberated.'

'So do we have to die to become free?'

'No, you can attain moksha while you're alive.'

'How?'

'By becoming aware of the self and the universe. By fulfilling the aim you have for your life, the purpose that you think you were born to fulfil. By serving others. By detaching yourself from your ignorance, angers, fears, expectations and frustrations, and those of the world. By becoming free of desire, even the desire to become free of desire.'

'Desire like milk cakes and satin frocks and big, big TVs?'

'Yes. And pride, recognition, lust, even love.'

'Understood. So do you have moksha, Dadoo?'

'Not yet, but I'm trying.'

'When will you get it?'

'Perhaps after I die.'

'But isn't death the end?'

'No,' said Dadoo. 'It's a new beginning. Life did not come from a void, and death does not mean disappearing into nothing. The soul isn't born and death isn't its end. In fact, birth, life and death are of no significance to the soul, only small parts of its journey towards moksha. I'd be the happiest man the day I die.'

'I have to go wash the cow,' I said, too proud to admit that I did not understand him. 'Or Dadi will dial a rakshasa.'

As I thought about Grandpa's words on that highway, I wondered what he would say about Saleha's death. 'You should be happy for your friend,' he would have said. 'Her soul has passed another cycle of birth and death and is now closer to the ultimate liberation.'

'Nonsense,' I screamed aloud. 'That's ideological gibberish, Dadoo. I want her death undone. I just want it undone.'

I realized I had uttered the words and startled everyone only when Ma rushed to me, and put her arm around my shoulder. 'It happens, child,' she said. 'Such is life. It isn't always fair, but we'd go mad if we kept questioning it.'

'I'd rather go mad every once in a while, Ma,' I wanted to say, 'than lose my sanity forever.'

'You're a practical girl,' Ma went on. 'You keep telling us about the migrants who are dying on their way home, then why are you so surprised? Many have died on the road already, and many others will perish. Some lives are just that cheap. All we can do is pray for the departed, and be grateful that it wasn't us on those tracks.'

I did not answer. She does not get me.

We kept walking, and my thoughts wandered to Saleha's brother. I wondered if Salim knew about the deaths. The accident had destroyed the family's cell phones, so how would the cops reach him? Or will their bodies reach him first? How would he react? How does anyone react when they've lost all? When the discourteous death slyly invades your world, robs you of everything without offering a chance to fight for your family. So arrogant, death. So hoity-toity.

'Are we anywhere close to home?' Happy held my hand as I wondered if I should find a way to speak to Salim. No, I did not have the courage.

'We're getting close,' I answered. 'Why, are you hungry?'

'Yes, so hungry and so tired that I can eat most of the mud on this road, and then sleep on the remaining,' he said. 'Why don't they find a cure for this stupid-idiot virus? You know I don't like injections, but I'll take one in the eye if I could just stop walking. Also, I was thinking, didi, why can't we tell Dadi-Dadoo and our dog, Mirchi, to walk the remaining distance? We could meet them halfway, you know.'

'They'd be happy to come, but what about our home?'

'I don't remember most of it,' he said. 'I remember the dunes, but they're not why I'm taking all this trouble. I'm walking because ... you cannot tell anyone ... Baba has promised to buy me a bicycle once we reach home.'

'Wow,' I said, pulling my brother close, kissing his tousled hair. 'A new one?'

'Yes, full-fresh, first-hand, new.' His eyes gleamed. 'With gears and all, and no side pedals.'

Baba had told him a lie, but I let the boy live it. He was too young for truth. As minutes passed, I realized that I felt better with Happy's palm cupped around my hand. Children, I've noticed, can say enough to dissolve gloom, despite their limited vocabularies. Of course, my brother did not know about Saleha and her family, and I thought it was better that way. I did not need comfort from him, only his presence, his silence. He did probe later, once he had eaten and rested, surprised that my new friend was missing, but I told him that the family had split from our group. As I said, too young for truth.

After a few minutes, Happy threw himself to the ground, declaring that he was too tired to walk. Sameer crouched next to him and then walked with the boy on his shoulders. Spotting me alone, Baba approached me. He started with a story from his childhood, but I refused to listen. He insisted on it, saying it was to do with Proton Uncle, and I gave up on my protest. I, too, was tired, as tired as justice.

'We were sixteen when Jairaj fell in love with Saira,' Baba started. 'His mother, as you know, does hand embroidery on blankets and pillow covers, and Jairaj would sell them in city markets and at fairs across the district. At one such carnival, Saira, a fifteen-year-old then, stopped at Jairaj's stall, spent half an hour discussing bedclothes with him, and left with two pairs of pillow covers after our man offered her an exclusive two-for-one. His eyes kept following her through the crowd, and when she queued up for a ride on the giant wheel, he rushed after her. Of course, they sat in different carts, but he kept staring at the back of her head, smiling at her long braid, as the wheel went round, round and up and down. When he returned, I told him he was foolish, that this wasn't love, but mirages of love—the forlorn winter, the funfair, and its ferry lights. He, however, kept smiling like a happy piglet, oinking and squeaking that he'd marry that girl someday.'

Every few days thereafter, Proton Uncle would rent a bicycle and take Baba to Saira's village, about thirty kilometres away from Balhaar. They would stroll by her home, waiting to catch a glimpse of her in her courtyard. One such evening, Saira caught them. She rushed out fuming but broke into a smile when Proton Uncle offered her a desert melon flower, also called Blind Love in local parlance. Saira accepted the orange-yellow flower and whispered her friend's phone number in return, assigning him a time slot—2 p.m. to 3 p.m. on Wednesdays. Proton Uncle would then walk to the public payphone every Wednesday afternoon, his pockets jingling with coins, echoing the tickle of his teenage love.

'It went on for four years,' said Baba. 'They spoke over the phone, wrote dozens of letters, met at fairs, and promised forever. Then, Saira's older brother discovered one of those letters, and her family barged into Jairaj's home. They screamed and they abused, and Jairaj's family screamed and abused too. Words were about to turn into weapons, but the villagers intervened in time. They promised that Jairaj would never contact Saira again, but the piglet had gone bonkers by now. He was a lunatic in love, a lover turned lunatic. He refused to accept that their stars were crossed, that their union was impossible, and that he was a Hindu, and she, a Muslim.'

'Is that why you hate Muslims?' I asked Baba, now certain about his irrationality.

'Partly, yes, because that relationship almost killed my friend,' he said. 'But more because of the nonsense we've been fed since we were children. India was reeling with communal hatred when we were growing up, and with that blood-covered, divisive narrative all around me, the loathing became a part of me, like an organ with tissues full of spite.'

The first time Baba was acquainted with religious antagonism was as a seven-year-old, after the Bhagalpur riots of 1989. Built on the Ganges in the eastern Indian state of Bihar, Bhagalpur had a history of communal violence. Then, in 1989, rumours of 200 Hindu bodies dumped in a well started doing the rounds, sowing the first seed of violence that would march on to claim 1000 lives. Riots raged across the district, said Baba—the army was called in, and the region's cauliflower fields turned into mass graves. The dead included Hindus as well as Muslims.

The flame of Bhagalpur turned into a fire in 1992 when Baba was ten. The location, this time, was the northern Indian town of Ayodhya, where a mob of 150,000 Hindu nationalists razed the 430-year-old Babri mosque, believing that it was the birthplace of Lord Ram. The demolition was discussed in every home, at every city corner and every village square across the country, including ours. Communal riots swept India, shedding the blood of both faiths, killing 2000. The worst-hit was Mumbai, where nearly 900 died, Hindus as well as Muslims.

'We grew up chanting slogans like "*Bachcha bachcha Ram ka, baaki sab haraam ka*,"' said Baba (We are all children of Ram, the rest are illegitimate). 'We hated even when we did not understand hatred, and with time, the abhorrence became so integral to our skins that we missed questioning it. It's easy to do what everyone does, that's what they call herd mentality. At its worst, it's mob mentality. I'm realizing now that over the years, this campaign of hate, which has been fed to both Hindu as well as Muslim children, has only shortened lives, killed more Indians than any terrorist attack on our country.'

When Proton Uncle and Saira were trying to get married, religious violence had morphed into a wildfire again. It was 2002 and the Godhra riots in Gujarat had killed over a thousand people. Children were slaughtered, women were raped, men were torched, and entire neighbourhoods were gutted. Hatred ruled the day, green and saffron, saffron and green, both colours of the Indian flag, bleeding.

Realizing that their families would never agree to their union, Proton Uncle and Saira eloped one night. Their kin searched railway stations and highways, lodges and hotels, and apprehended them within hours, as they waited at a bus stop, hoping to get married after escaping Rajasthan. Blood did trickle this time, and their families locked them up in their respective homes. Within a week, Saira was married to another man.

Proton Uncle took to the bottle thereafter, drank and drowned, and drowned and drank. It got worse when Saira, unable to tolerate another man in her bed, hung herself by the ceiling fan above that bed. When Proton Uncle heard of her death, he got inebriated, walked to the village bhopa or medicine man, and consumed a bottle of rat poison. The bhopa alerted the villagers, and Baba rushed his friend to a hospital, carrying his fading body in his arms, nudging his disappearing senses, and struggling to keep him awake.

'He survived,' said Baba. 'And he promised to live after his father, a useless drunk who never said a word of affection to him, hugged him and cried, thanked the gods for keeping his son alive. Thereafter, Jairaj began to cloak his tears with a phoney joy and turned into the merry man you see today, the one you've dubbed Proton Uncle. He overcompensates with his cheer and optimism, but deep within him, in a place where he allows no one, not even his wife, he still aches.'

'How did he agree to get married?' I asked.

'It was within a month of his suicide attempt. He did it for his family, and your aunty did it because her parents were poor, and Jairaj's kin agreed to take her without a dowry. She knew about Saira, and she married the half-dead man anyway, hoping that he would learn to love her. Jairaj, however, replaced the love in their relationship with respect. He respects her, he cares about her, he's kind to her, but those cannot be substitutes for love. Your aunty is still waiting for him to come around, and that exasperating wait, at times, shows in her pessimistic temper.'

'So Sameer?'

'He was born many years after their marriage, mostly because Jairaj's mother wouldn't shut up about dying without seeing her grandchild.'

'Why don't you talk to Uncle about all this?' I asked Baba. 'Two decades have passed since Saira's death.'

'I've tried, but he walks away the moment I mention her. That's why I'm telling you this story, Gudiya. Some wounds take time to heal, and some never do. If so, all we can do is bandage our broken hearts and learn to live with them. With Saleha, it's too soon and you must grieve, but I need you to come around eventually, learn to live with loss.'

Baba was still talking when I turned around after hearing the soft sobs of a woman. It was Electron Aunty. Her husband was walking next to her, and as he put his arm around her shoulder, she rested her head on his chest and wept.

A narrow road branched off the highway, leading to a small village. The concrete path, an inheritance from the immaculate national highway, soon gave way to paver blocks and tar roads, eroded, eroding. Women collected water in steel pots from a handpump, while some stood in a queue with their naked children to bathe them.

Goats, cows, buffaloes and dogs strolled about, creepers grew as creepers grow, mindlessly, and the ground appeared littered with assorted varieties of cattle waste. Homes, meanwhile, stood semi-naked, their boundaries asserted by unpainted, brown-brick walls. Kids roamed on bicycles, and upon spotting our cluster of strangers, they pedalled faster.

'*Corona aaya, corona aaya*,' the children broadcasted through the village. (Corona has come. Corona has come.)

We waited for their alarm to draw villagers. Six hours had passed since we left the railway tracks and two days since we ate anything other than fruits. Hunger had eluded us after we lost five from our group this morning, but the exhaustion had compounded, eating into the will that remained. At least two of our men had developed blisters on their feet, which were now oozing blood. The noon sun, however, showed no heart, and the mercury was about to hit forty degrees Celsius. At this temperature, the roads in Gujarat had melted a few years ago, the molten tar turning the streets into wet, adhesive sheets.

Our group discussed that we must rest and eat before we proceed. Hunger, heat and fatigue had also emerged as assassins of late, attacking and killing migrants on their way home. Hence, we decided on entering this village. We hoped to buy groceries from its local store—wheat, rice, potatoes, chillies and salt, and we hoped that the villagers would lend us their utensils, so we could cook ourselves a meal. It was unreasonable, the expectation, but reason, at that moment, was hardly a priority.

'Welcome, welcome.' The village head with a sizeable smile and joined palms approached us as we squatted on the ground. 'I gather you're migrants walking home. How may we serve you?'

'We've been walking for four and a half days now, and we've run out of food,' said Baba. 'We were hoping to borrow your utensils and cook something.'

'We cannot let you cook,' said the sarpanch, maintaining a safe distance. 'We'll cook for you. Let me escort you to the village square. Rest for a while before the food gets ready.'

The aged man, tall and burly with a salt-coloured moustache and a yellow kurta-pyjama, appeared suspicious to me. Why was he welcoming us? Why did he want to serve us? Was he crazy? Was this a trap? Maybe he was planning to call the police while we waited in the square. Maybe he wanted to lock us up in one of those corona camps. No, he could not be just a nice man. Who is? No human, teaches this journey, no celestial being.

'A young man from our village, who was on his way home from Delhi, was killed in a road accident recently,' said the village head, walking us to the square. 'He left Delhi with his brother after purchasing two second-hand bicycles. Five days into the journey, their knees gave up, but they kept pedalling. They'd covered almost six hundred kilometres, and were halfway from home when the accident occurred.'

The sarpanch informed that the brothers had not had a proper meal in days. Hence, as soon as they availed hot, fresh food from a charity, the famished duo sat down on a road divider to eat. It was a quiet street, but within moments, a car appeared, hit the barrier, and left the brothers with grievous injuries. One of the two died in a hospital a few hours later. His parents survive him, also his wife and a five-year-old daughter.

'He died hungry,' said the village head. 'Since then, we've been offering food to migrants. As much as we can afford.'

Sitting under the shade of a bearded banyan tree, the village square was a 200-square-foot platform with three stone benches and a signboard that said nothing. As we placed our luggage on the ground, more villagers arrived. Smiling and greeting, they placed an earthen pot filled with water at one end of the square. After a few minutes, they kept another clay pot next to it, containing buttermilk to aid rehydration in our parched bodies. They also offered to charge our phones, and Sameer gave them our handsets and chargers. My suspicion, which had subsided after hearing about the migrant's death, returned with the lost phones, but no one in my group seemed to share my concern. As soon as the villagers left, they turned their bags into pillows and lay down on the platform. Happy, I noticed, fell asleep in moments, as I lay awake, thinking, avoiding thinking.

The villagers and the sarpanch returned in an hour, carrying steel bowls filled with food—khichri, pickles, and a salad of onions, tomatoes, cucumbers and lemons. They brought piles of newspapers with them, which served as our dishes. They asked us to eat, and eat some more, as if our ingestion was killing their hunger. Our group was pleased, chewing like a groom's guests at a wedding party, but I could not bear to swallow. My intestines felt like they were knotted up, as if caught in a vortex inside my stomach, the one trying to suck in my organs, my bones and my veins. It was Saleha, the typhoon.

'Eat.' Ma stared at me. 'You need the energy to walk.'

I ate and I wept, a pang of strange guilt cursing me for swallowing. Saleha, too, died hungry. How could I eat? How could anyone in the world eat? I stopped and I looked around, and that's when I saw how starved everyone was. Pouncing on the khichri, hasty bites, overloading their fingers with giant portions, swallowing most of their food, asking for more, then some more, licking their papers clean, still looking hungry. My eyes kept observing them, and for the first time in my fifteen years, I felt poor. Their hair and bodies, like mine, had turned into a mixture of sand and sweat, their clothes were torn in places, their feet were injured and swollen, and their breaths reeked of the foul journey. Then, I looked at myself, and I felt poorest of all. I had doubted the villagers, their show of humanity. Others, meanwhile, had trusted. Others, meanwhile, could still trust.

The realization and my tears brought about a coughing fit, and in seconds, I was breathless again. The muscles of my chest pulled in, my heart shuddered inside, and I knew I had to stop crying.

The grief, however, refused to cooperate, and I wept and coughed, and coughed and wept, until my lips turned blue, my body turned warm, and the cough triumphed, stealing away my consciousness. My parents revived me with a few drops of water, and then, as I sat up, I looked around—at the day, the sun, the life, and all their regularity—and I cried without tears.

'You cannot do this to yourself, Gudiya.' Ma embraced me. 'I need you to stay strong. And I know you're stronger than this.' After a moment of thought, she added, 'Why don't you write in your diary? It makes you happy, doesn't it?'

'Not now,' I told her.

As Ma comforted me, Baba called Candy Kaka to check on him, but he did not answer his phone. Within moments thereafter, a middle-aged woman arrived at the village square. Dressed in a wine-red cotton sari with matching lipstick, she wore an urban look and had tied her hair up in a high pony. A golden lanyard encircled her neck, attached to a pair of golden spectacles.

'Madam here is a social activist,' the sarpanch informed us. 'She's here to help you.'

I could not tell if the woman's eyes reflected concern, but they looked, they observed, and they lingered. She enquired about our destination, and most, with little thought, said 'home' before naming various villages and districts of Rajasthan. The woman left the square to make some phone calls, and upon returning, she announced that she had arranged a truck for us.

'But I'm afraid the driver will have to drop you at the Gujarat–Rajasthan border,' she added. 'That's four hundred and fifty kilometres from here, and the journey will take about eight hours.'

'How much will it cost us?' asked a migrant from our group.

'Not one paisa,' she said. 'I'll manage it.'

'Why?' asked the man, now suspicious.

'Because that's my job,' she answered. 'I run an NGO in the city of Surat, not far from here.'

'So why can't you drop us home?' The migrant's desperation pushed him further from faith, even courtesy.

'Because I'm not doing this in an official capacity,' she said. 'Getting travel permissions is tricky during the lockdown, and it would be days before we avail them. Had it been official, the driver would have crossed the border without trouble, dropped you at your doorstep.'

As we waited for the truck, our group thanked the sarpanch and the activist, touching their feet and wishing them long lives, fortunes and hundreds of grandsons each. My father also shared details of our journey with them, including the deaths this morning.

'They were good people,' Baba told them. 'Ashraf was an auto-rickshaw driver, and he had promised to teach me driving and find related work if we returned to Mumbai. His only concern was his septuagenarian parents. He was worried they would succumb to exhaustion on the way. He cursed himself, saying that the journey was a mistake, and that he should have stayed in Mumbai. Now, he's dead. They're all dead. All that remains is… a what-if...'

'You remain too,' said the activist. 'And they remain through you.'

More gibberish, I mused, indulging the sin of ingratitude.

As we sat in the truck facing each other, Neutron Sameer offered me a geography lesson from our Class Nine textbook. Grief works like a hurricane, he said; probably why they name tropical storms after people. As hurricanes draw their strength from warm oceanic waters, grief originates from the waters of our hearts, the ones boiling with agony, which then form dark, thunderous clouds of despair. The clouds swirl with the winds of memory, rotating at a menacing pace, until the pain is enough to create a hurricane.

'The hurricane's only fuel is the heat of our hearts, and if we starve the storm of it, it would never turn into a monster. But if we keep feeding it, it becomes bigger, makes landfall, floods the most vulnerable parts of our beings, and destroys them,' said Sameer. 'In that case, there is no way to stop a hurricane from hitting the coast. All we can do is hold tight, try to survive and, once the storm dies, rebuild our lives.'

'Geography textbook. Chapter Five. Title: Precipitation. Sub-head: Cyclonic rainfall,' I replied.

'Yes,' he answered, looking away.

I did not want to talk to Sameer about Saleha. I did not know if he was right, if he was even making sense, simply because I do not know grief. I've never experienced it before. But today, after my first encounter with it, I could tell it felt more like lightning—a hovering thundercloud that breaks into flashes of electric currents, then dies out, and then, when you least expect it, hits you with another bolt from the sky. There were moments all day when I had held my own, and there were also moments when the lightning struck me with its billions of joules of energy, paralysing my body, and cooking my brain. Tears poured down like torrential rain when that happened, and every part of me thundered in pain.

We had been sitting in the truck for about an hour when Sameer attempted to talk to me. The activist had ensured we did not feel like cattle, having arranged a bedsheet to cover the truck's hard floor and a vehicle big enough for the fifteen of us to lie down. She gave us some fruits, bottles of water and handmade masks before we left and she helped nurse the blisters on the two migrants' feet.

Most in our group slept within minutes of boarding the truck, relieved, even elated at the fast-tracked journey. I, meanwhile, sat next to the vehicle's shutter, peeping from a small gap between the tailgate and the overhead tarpaulin, watching the landscapes shrink to distant dots.

'She was a tremendous girl, you know,' I said to Sameer after snubbing him the first time. 'A real human, a friend of the world.'

'I'm sorry it happened,' he replied, Electron Aunty snoring on his shoulder. 'If you ever want to talk to someone, know I'm here.'

'It's not only about Saleha and her family,' I said, voicing a discontent that had just started sprouting in me, and yet, had overpowered my being. 'It's about this whole exodus. When did we become so vulnerable? I never felt it my whole life. But now, it's like they're grabbing me by my neck, telling me that my life is insignificant, that I could die any moment, and that my death, too, would be as insignificant. Hundreds like us have died on their way home. Hundreds. Women turned widows, children turned orphans, fathers turned pallbearers, and mothers turned to stone. Why did they have to die? They were only trying to get home. We're only trying to get home. That's what the whole world said, right, when this virus emerged? Stay home; do not leave home. Then why is it so difficult for us to get home? Did we do something to deserve this?'

'Nothing,' said Sameer, his eyes glued to mine. 'We did nothing. It's just that every tragedy has its martyrs, and usually, they're found at the bottom-most rung of the pyramid. People like you, me, Saleha—the world does not even know we exist. Hundreds of millions like our fathers work in India's informal workforce. They constitute the backbone of our economy. Yet, they have no legal safeguards. They work in dehumanizing conditions, and they die in dehumanizing conditions, all for humiliating wages. The world does not see them. It's like a selective blindfold. It's like we speak a different language, and what we say is gibberish to them. Then, how would they help someone they can't see or understand? Why will they care about Saleha's life or death if she's invisible and unintelligible to them?'

'It's time they saw,' I looked away, a little uncomfortable with Sameer's soft gaze. 'It's time they understood.'

'That time was decades ago,' he replied, 'But yes, the second-best time would be now.'

'How do you know so much about grief?' I asked him after the words birthed silence.

'I don't,' he answered. 'I just know that it turns into a hurricane only if I feed it with painful thoughts.'

'What pain do you have?'

Sameer looked around to confirm his parents were asleep and then leaned in. 'I'm not sure if it's pain,' he whispered. 'I suspect it is.'

'Tell me more.'

'It's my parents. I'm fortunate to have both my parents, but somehow, they've never loved me together…' He was still hesitant. 'I wish I could explain...'

'You don't have to,' I hurried. 'And I promise you won't have to worry about this any more.'

Eight hours into the drive, around midnight, the truck driver dropped us a kilometre before the interstate border between Gujarat and Rajasthan. I was surprised at how easy the 450-kilometre journey had been, how easy the first few hundred kilometres could also have been. We thanked the driver and walked towards the check post. As we neared it, we saw hundreds of migrants waiting at the border, convincing the authorities to let them pass. With so many like us around, we felt safe and decided to wait with them. I took to writing to you because I felt Saleha's lightning strike again, the thermal burns torching my heart, and the cough sucking my organs in. I feel better now, ma'am, and I'm going to put my notebook away, also because I think I just heard a gunshot.

Meher
The Gujarat–Rajasthan interstate border

11

Home

22 April 2020

> *Following a violent clash between migrant workers and the police at the Gujarat–Rajasthan interstate border early yesterday, officials have detained over a hundred workers for rioting. The migrants, who were waiting to cross the border into Rajasthan, rampaged through the highway after the police refused to let them pass. Many, including police officials and workers, sustained injuries in the skirmish.*
>
> *Officers allege that the irate men ransacked the border, attacked on-duty personnel, pelted stones, vandalized vehicles and hurled abuses. The police said 'reasonable force' was used to control the unruly mob, adding that 'strict action' is now being initiated against the accused.*
>
> —a television news report from earlier today

Thirty-six hours have passed since Baba and Proton Uncle went missing, Ms Farah, and this is all I know about their disappearance. This and the visuals that accompanied the journalist's voiceover—masked-gloved police officers tugging detainees by their hair and shirts, herding them to the corridor of a police station, as the accused flocked, exhibiting no pain, as if a congress of stubborn stoics. Their mouths obscured with masks and handkerchiefs, torn, wrinkled clothes on their begrimed bodies, some only had one shoe on their feet, and their wrists, their wrists were gummed together with ropes, knotted and knotted over again. I tried looking for Baba in those insensate faces. I could not spot my father, lost among men that all looked the same, but I did notice their gaze. None confronted the camera as it panned over their bodies. Most outstared the floor, a few, the concrete sky above.

We had been waiting for nearly five hours at the border when mayhem annexed the night. The six-lane highway was an ocean abuzz with hundreds of migrant workers and their families, waiting to cross into Rajasthan. They stood crowding the border, some sat on walkways along the road, some lay on the edges of forested hills that fenced the highway, and some moved about, questing after food, water and medicines. Their fatigue had inflamed the air, their anguish had enveloped the wind, and their ire had darkened the land. Their negotiations with the police had failed, and their tearful pleas were steadily evolving into discord. Baba went close to the barricaded border, hoping to gather intelligence on our fate. He returned with nothing.

'There's a route via the Mahi River,' a man had propositioned him. 'I can help you cross into Rajasthan through it. No border control, no police problem, no deep shit, only sweet air, so sweet, the air, like jaggery.'

'How much for seven people?' Baba asked.

'Three thousand per person,' the contrabandist stated, 'including the boat ride and the cost of transport to the river.'

'Okay, okay, twenty-five hundred,' he cawed as Baba walked away. 'Okay, okay, two thousand now, full and final, done deal.'

Father did not heed. We had a total of ₹1600, and the finest negotiators in the world could not charter that boat for us. We would have to wait, continue waiting for a breed of clement magic to swoop in, part the barricades, and walk us into our home state. As we sat by the highway, the crowd bourgeoned in numbers and fury. The first sign of rage was the verbal abuses that the migrants hurled at the cops, expletives alluding to the officers' mothers, sisters, daughters and wives, and all the women in their lives. A cop took to the microphone.

'The virus spreads with touch. We request you to maintain one-metre distance between each other, or legal action will be initiated against you,' the officer announced.

'We want to go home,' rang a collective cry in response.

'We cannot let you pass, brothers and sisters,' the cop answered, his voice like a prayer. 'The country is still under lockdown, and we are not authorized to allow your movement. It's my sincere request that you return to where you've come from. The only other option is that you cross the border, and stay in the relief camps that we've set up for you, as long as the lockdown is in place. Please, my brothers and sisters, I speak out of wholehearted concern for you.'

A pensive silence took over the throng. The first option was no option. The second, a devious stratagem. Everyone had heard about those prison-like camps, the airless, waterless, foodless, hygiene-less and doctor-less hellholes. The human grime of the country was rounded up in those camps, forced to breathe only because their deaths would raise eyebrows. Yet, many had managed death, told on life inside those shelters. Some succumbed to medical negligence, lack of basic amenities, and contaminated food and water inside the quarantine centres, while a few others were found dead in mysterious circumstances. One was discovered hanging from a tree inside a shelter, a second died after a snake entered a quarantine centre, a third after he fell from a staircase and another who is said to have set himself ablaze. No one wanted to be in those camps. Like everybody else on the planet, we wanted to be home.

'If we agree on the camps, what's the guarantee that you will not arrest us?' a migrant worker probed the entreating voice behind the microphone.

'There is none, and I will arrest you right now if you don't vacate the highway, or queue up,' came the reply. The voice over the loudspeaker had changed, the soft diction replaced by a brassy monotone.

'What's the guarantee that you won't shoot us if we lined up?'

'That I can promise,' said the new officer. 'As long as you're quick about it.'

A wave of murmurs passed through the assemblage. Although the shelters were no option, rebellion and anarchy were. The workers started inching close to the border, chanting, 'Home! Home! We want to go home!' as if an army of mollycoddled children, stomping their feet, wanting what they want when they want. The slogan was garnished with swear words, and upon noticing the mounting tension, the unsmiling voice returned to the loudspeaker, steelier this time. It dangled the two unsavoury carrots again and someone pelted a stone at the microphone. It could be anyone.

'Maderchod!' the cop exclaimed, the profanity reverberating through the hills. 'Now, I will show you.'

Before the police could act, the migrants reacted, showering stones at the barricades. The few cops rushed at the crowd with their lathis, but the mob had outnumbered them by unjust margins. The workers charged towards the border, overthrew the barricades, and streamed into Rajasthan. The cops, meanwhile, chased after them, grabbing their bodies, beating them with batons and bare hands, and pushing them back into Gujarat. The migrants shoved too, kicking, running, and not looking back. The flinty voice kept blaring over the loudspeaker, its decibels lost to the crowd's clamour.

'Run,' said Baba, as we sat off the carriageway, watching the night of disarray. 'This is our window. If we do not cross the border now, we will never make it home.'

We lifted our belongings and ran towards the interstate partition, which stood 300 metres away. Soon, we heard a blast. We ducked and covered our heads with our hands. Our bodies still crouched and frozen, we saw another golden-white explosion amid the crowd, then another, and then dozens of times over. What the police lacked in human resources, they were making up with their favourite non-lethal projectile, tear-gas shells. From my near-miss with the gas bombs early in the journey, I knew those were tear-gas shells. No atom bomb, no raging fire, a miniature explosion, a thick, translucent smoke and fire in our eyes.

Men, women and children ran away from the bombs, and we ran with them, as if a wild, headlong rush of frightened animals, sharing a common impulse. The smoke smelt acidic, a little like vinegar, and it had turned the air turgid. Our eyes burning, watering and blinking, we kept bumping into each other, kept falling to the ground. Since Ma was holding my hand and Happy was in Baba's arms, we were still together, but we'd lost Proton Uncle and his family to the misty stampede.

The shelling continued, our eyes and throats itched, but Baba insisted on crossing the border. We ran towards the partition, and as we neared it, we saw that the cops had now barricaded it with their vehicles. Three officers, armed with long rifles, stood guarding it, and we could hear the sirens of more police vans approaching us. The cops had called for backup. We turned around and started running towards Mumbai, as our ears rang with a multitude of sounds—some like explosions, some like gunshots, some like shattering glass, some wails, some curses and some prayers. Sounds, but no sight. A lathi landed on my back, and then on Ma's, and we ran into the white smoke until we had outrun the batons. We jumped onto a hill and kept climbing until the noises turned distant. Then, we turned around and saw bundles of clouds crowding the earth, Baba and Happy lost in one of them.

Ma and I sat on the hill, coughing and sneezing, our noses secreting profuse, uncontrollable amounts of mucus. We tried to look for familiar faces in the warring throng and I felt the coughing fit return. The spasm passed in a few minutes, but it left a tightness in my chest, which seemed to grow stronger every second. Ma made me double over, and with that nauseating ache near my heart, I thought I would die. The pain left on its own after a few minutes, as abruptly as it had arrived, and my eyes started scanning the melting clouds, looking for Baba in those hand-to-baton combats. Gunshots had swallowed the conundrum by now, and tens of police officers had joined the riot, overpowering the migrants that remained.

As the police lined up the workers in a queue, Ma and I descended the hill. The highway lay littered with breathless canisters, tired stones, stranded luggage and martyred footwear. We picked up what belonged to us and walked around, looking for our family, when we spotted Sameer and Electron Aunty. They had lost Proton Uncle to the stampede, they said, their bodies covered with bruises. Then, near the divider of the highway, we spotted Happy. His forehead was bleeding, and he sat staring at the border, his eyes silent, the trail of old tears frozen on his muddy cheeks.

'They took Baba away,' he said as his innocence fled him. 'They took my father away.'

It's a museum of the forlorn, this migrant camp. It isn't about air, water, food, shelter, excretion, sleep, or security any more. Through this centre, we've chanced upon those essentials, levelled up on the needs pyramid. We're fed, rested, nursed and safe, and yet, the faces in this camp have a funereal pallor, the eyes seem damp, the shoulders droop, the lips tend to tremble, and the heads hang low. Despite all the food, the sturdy roof and the enclosed washrooms, residents of this centre keep thinking about their homes, their ailing parents and worried wives. Some do not even know if their families have had enough to eat of late, if their children have fallen hostage to hunger already. They imagine the worst, Ms Farah, judging the present by the past.

After we found Happy, we walked towards the barricaded border and approached a police officer. She promised that Baba and Proton Uncle were in a migrant camp nearby. She promised we would meet them as soon as we reached the shelter. Our smoke-filled instincts whimpered, alerting us of the trap, but we were no land's children now. We had nowhere to return to in Mumbai, and the home we were chasing, although only 150 kilometres away, seemed further than the stars. With reluctant feet, we followed the uniformed woman, praying she wasn't venturing too far from the truth. We joined that queue of the powerless, waited with the other nowhere people, and as the sun invaded the morning sky, we closed our eyes and we hoped.

Five police officers monitored our walk on the four-lane serpentine highway as it cut and cut through the hills to satiate man's need to move. We saw a beer bar, and a few workers scooped up some mud from its ground, and rubbed it on their foreheads. They were paying homage to our home state, the tavern indicating that we were now in Rajasthan, officially past the alcohol-prohibiting land of Gujarat.

After a twenty-minute walk from the border, the hills on our side parted again, making way for a narrow grassy path. The macadam road led to a school, its walls painted with moralistic say-sos—the image of a toilet with a hoarding saying, 'Dignity House,' dissuading pooping in the wild; a picture of a pony-tailed schoolgirl with a caption probing, 'Men want mothers, sisters and wives, why not daughters?' and another of Mickey Mouse waving rainbow-coloured balloons, each inscribed with an abstract noun—Patriotism, Secularism, Equality, Liberty, Fraternity.

The cops instructed about 120 migrants from our assembly to queue up outside the school and began to escort the others to another camp. I rushed to the policewoman and asked her if Baba was brought to this shelter. 'Yes,' she lied. 'Where else?'

Encircled by the shade of ancient trees, seven classrooms—rectangular non-sturdy porta-cabins—stood glued together, a barren playground in front of them, where a woman in a protective suit sat behind a wooden table. She seemed busy with a foolscap notebook, as if marking pupil attendance on the school register. When we queued up before her, she asked us to maintain a two-foot distance from her and each other, and she ordered us not to worry.

'We're here to help,' she said, introducing herself as Ela, a public health worker. 'We shall serve you three hot meals a day, clean water to drink and bathe, and ensure that you have enough room to rest.'

'But, madamji, we're not homeless,' said one of the migrants. 'You're confusing us with the homeless.'

'Yes,' said another. 'You're reducing our problems to food and shelter. You're getting it wrong. You're all getting it wrong. We're stranded and hungry, yes, but we're not homeless. Our needs, aspirations and vulnerabilities are different from those of the homeless. Our need is to be with our families. Our aspiration is to earn our living, and our vulnerability, it wouldn't feature if you left us alone.'

'Yes, my point exactly,' screamed a third. 'We're migrants, migrant *workers*.'

'Workers, not beggars,' growled a fourth. 'Respect the difference. Respect us. We're grateful that your cities employed us, paying us five hundred rupees for a job that would only fetch us hundred in our villages. We're indebted, we do not deny that. But now, amid this global crisis, we want to go home, and instead of sending us home, you're locking us up in these strange places.'

'We're the ones who built the cities you pride yourselves in,' roared a fifth. 'It's our blood, sweat and tears that uphold your world-class metros and your hundred-proof skyscrapers. And now, you're penalizing that same blood, at a time when we need you the most. Show some grace, some character, and let us go home. Don't worry, we'll go walking.'

More such words led to chants, and echoes of 'home' rang all around us. The police officers intervened, charging at men with batons, prompting Ms Ela to rise from her chair. 'No need for assault,' she admonished the cops. 'Put those sticks away.'

The health worker then turned to us, appealing for peace. I decided to like her. She persuaded more and rebuked less, explained more and insulted less. She stated that with the pandemic and the lockdown, we would be safest in the camp until the restrictions eased, and it was legal for us to travel again. By returning home, we could also infect our families, in case we were infected. Some migrants argued, insisting they were healthy, but she stood her patient ground and explained how the disease worked. She said that the pathogen was like a cunning trespasser at times, one that sneaks into bodies so slyly that no one can notice the squatter's presence for days. 'Aye-sim-toh-mat-eek,' she said. 'Many remain asymptomatic.'

'With the ongoing exodus, the state is now thinking about opening up borders for migrants,' Ms Ela added. 'As soon as that happens, perhaps in a week or two, you'll be on your way home. Till then, please allow us to take care of you.'

Most of us conceded, and those still hesitant, their protests perished after a man, who tried to flee the queue, was beaten back to it. We waited in line, as Ms Ela noted our names, ages, addresses and phone numbers. As she scribbled in the register, her subordinate, Ms Mira, went about the queue, pointing a pistol-shaped thermometer at our fists, separating those with body temperatures above ninety-nine degrees Fahrenheit. At least six persons before our turn, and Happy, the seventh one. 'The gun said a hundred point six degrees.' Ms Mira asked the boy to step away from us.

'You can see, madamji, he has an injury on his forehead,' Ma told the woman, wrapping her arms around Happy. 'The bleeding has stopped, as I've tied a cloth around the wound, but I'm sure he's got a fever because of that. He doesn't have corona-forona, I swear to every god.'

'You needn't worry.' Ms Ela looked up from her register. 'We're only being cautious. We'll test him for the virus, and he'll be back with you as soon as his reports prove that he's healthy.'

For the first time since we left Mumbai, I saw Happy cry, wail and then shatter. A police officer tried to pull him from Ma, and the boy pushed the cop away. His tiny palms placed on the officer's thighs, he kept pushing until the man was metres away from his mother. I was surprised at Happy's livid grunts, his strength, even his courage. Perhaps, they lay rooted in the knowledge that it was a cop, who distanced him from his father a few hours ago, and it's a cop, who is now pulling him away from his mother. I wondered what the treacherous journey had meant to my little brother. I wondered if he'd ever outgrow its memory. I wondered if he'd lose his father to the follies of power. Our father. Our all.

'Can you check your register for Gopal Balhaari and Jairaj Balhaari, please?' I requested Ms Ela as Ma went after Happy. 'They were brought here earlier today.'

The woman sifted through the pages and replied in the negative. I tried to look for the police officer with the false promises but realized that she had already left with the other migrants, walking them to a different camp.

'Can you check again, ma'am?' I appealed. 'Please.'

'They're not here, child,' said Ms Ela. 'But let me get done with these registrations, and I promise I'll help you find them. In exchange, please convince your brother to isolate himself. He could be infected, and if that's the case, all of you are at risk.'

Ms Ela was right. Happy could be infected. Any of the millions of migrants who had fled India's cities in the past month could be infected. The dictatorial quest for home had overpowered each of our journeys, leaving little room for fear of the virus. Social distancing was lost to the chock-full trucks and milk containers that we travelled in. With little water to drink, washing hands was irrational. Hygiene was an unrealistic fancy on the journey, and our masks were dirty, dead and decaying from days of usage. And that instruction about staying home, well, we were still in the midst of that rigmarole, finding home.

Happy agreed to the isolation, once he learnt that the health workers would help us find our father. He walked with Ms Mira as she escorted him to a classroom on the furthest end of the school, housing other migrants with a fever. Then, she showed us to our room, one next to Happy's—a 400-square-foot space, twenty-four single-bed mattresses on its floor, separated by a foot's distance. The classroom had a grumbly ceiling fan, moody tube lights, and a cupboard where two lizards felt at home. Colourful images of birds, animals, fruits and vegetables crowded three of its four walls, while a blackboard was affixed on the fourth one. The door, meanwhile, had the image of a short, semi-naked boy, sharp arrows emanating from his body, identifying his various parts—head, hair, chest, waist, knee, nose, finger, foot. Happy's old syllabus, I found myself thinking.

As we placed our luggage on the mattresses, the healthcare workers handed out plastic kits, each containing biscuits, mosquito-repellent cream, soap, towel, glass, plate, toothpaste, masks and water. They offered balms and pain relief sprays, nursed wounded feet with bandages, and arranged doctors for those in need. They also brought dozens of lemon wedges to help us clear our airways after the tear-gas shelling. As I sucked on one of the wedges, I felt a sense of relief. Our migrant camp wasn't a franchise of hell.

'The police picked up some men from the border after the brawl this morning,' Ms Ela spoke before I approached her. 'Your father and uncle could be in their custody.'

'How do we find them?' I asked.

'It's too soon,' she said. 'They haven't announced the arrests yet, so we don't know where they're holding them. From the families here, we know that at least six other men went missing this morning.'

'Would they have beaten up my husband?' Ma asked as Electron Aunty echoed her query.

'No, of course not,' said Ms Ela, turning her gaze to the floor. The mediocre liar.

'Who sleeps on a railway track?'

'Such reckless behaviour.'

'Sad, but if you sleep on the tracks, you die on the tracks.'

'So, like, none of them heard the train coming? Fishy.'

'Either they were stupid or suicidal.'

A television news journalist highlighted these statements, reporting reactions of social media users to the deaths of Saleha and her family. He said that the accident had alarmed several, including some grade-A politicians and Bollywood celebrities, but many others had called the deceased 'negligent' and 'irresponsible' for their act of lying on the tracks. It's a punishable offence, they asserted, a conspiracy to malign the state, and that the dead migrants, who 'could not have been in their right minds,' had only themselves to blame.

I sat aghast at the blunders of opinion. Sameer offered to change the channel, but I insisted on watching, listening, seething. They were not wrong, Ms Farah, those sanctimonious observers, typing away on their smartphones, tucked in their leather couches, inside the cocoons of their concrete homes. They were right. Saleha and her family were stupid, stupid for they set out on this precarious journey despite the instruction to die in place, stupid for they fell for the hope of life. They were reckless, yes. They were reckless for they believed that they would live even after they lost their jobs, even after starvation threatened to gag them, and even after their city tossed them out like old bread. Negligent. Yes, they were negligent, for they believed that trains weren't running during the lockdown, for they reasoned that millions of migrants wouldn't be walking home if trains were in motion. They were irresponsible. Irresponsible, for they lost their judgement to law-enforcers and their batons, for they allowed their instincts to get so impaired that they did not think for one second that maybe, just maybe, the tracks could turn into their deathbed. No, they were not in their right minds, so exhausted from the journey that none of them, not one of them, could hear the heavy rumbling of that train. They were all those things, Ms Farah, but let me tell you this: they were not suicidal. They wanted to live. They had chosen to walk because they had wanted to live. Death would have come easy; all they had to do was stay back in Mumbai. Living, on the other hand, took work, and when they chose this journey, they consented to live.

After that blathery bulletin about social media prattle, the newscaster switched the screen to another journalist, who was also reporting on the massacre. This one was in a torpid little village near the Gujarat–Rajasthan border, only a few kilometres from our camp, Saleha's home. The frame included a journalist seated next to a boy, his head buried between his arms, his legs drawn to his chest, and his body pulled in tight, as if a frightened snail. He was sitting outside a hut, men mourning next to him, and women wailing inside. He was Salim, said the journalist, Saleha's brother.

'When did you last speak to your family?' the journalist asked him.

The nineteen-year-old did not acknowledge her query, not even when she nudged him with her microphone.

'What were their last words to you?' the reporter made a fresh attempt. 'You've lost your entire family. How do you feel?'

Salim stayed mum.

'How do you feel?' the journalist persisted.

'How do you think he feels?' an old woman rushed out of the hut, and answered for the boy, placing her scaly hand on his bowed head. 'He feels lonely, like an alone child in a dark, sealed room, aware that this is eternity. He feels lost, with everyone in his family dumped in his past. He feels afraid, dreading the days he'd have to breathe. He feels angry about the punishment without crime. That's how he feels. Go now, leave at once, and come back when you have sensible questions to ask. How he feels, she's asking.'

Thereafter, the old woman returned to beating her breasts in the hut. The journalist restrained herself for a few seconds, but once the camera had captured a 360-degree view of the village around Salim, she returned to him, hoping to add words to the silent visuals. 'You will soon receive five lakh rupees as compensation. How do you feel about that?'

Salim did not look up.

'How do you feel about the compensation?'

'Tell them to use it to help other migrants,' he answered, now staring at the camera lens, his eyes red from the onslaught of reality. 'Use it to save other children from getting orphaned.'

As Salim stood up and walked away, the journalist concluded her piece-to-camera. 'As you can see, dear viewers, the entire family has been wiped out. Salim, the only living member, is bereaved. The village is bereaved. The government has been quick to announce compensation, but the question remains: why were the migrants sleeping on railway tracks?'

I felt disgusted with the journalist and asked Sameer to change the channel. It was our second day at the migrant camp, and we had been watching the news for several hours, hoping to get some information on where the police had taken Baba and Proton Uncle. They could not contact us, as both their cell phones were now switched off. Sameer suggested that we call our grandparents through Ms Ela's phone, but all that call did was plunge the elders into a panic. Our fathers had not contacted them either.

I knew Baba was in trouble. If he were safe, he would have done everything in the world to send us a message, to check if we were safe too. I thought of calling Candy Kaka, but we did not have his number, and the last few times Baba dialled him, he did not answer his phone. Ms Ela suggested that we keep checking the news for updates, and showed us to an office at the far end of the playground—a staff room with a dining table, six chairs, and an elderly television set seated atop a stool.

While Sameer and I remained glued to the television, Ma and Electron Aunty prayed and then stopped praying, disillusioned with prayers. Uncertainty over our missing family tore each of us, and we wondered if they were together, if they were safe, even alive. The one relief was that Happy's fever had subsided. We spoke to him through a window in his room and he appeared comfortable on his mattress. To test him for Covid-19, a doctor put something in his nose, he said, something tickly.

'Has Baba returned?' he enquired. 'And Uncle?'

'They'll be here soon,' Electron Aunty told him. 'I'm positive.'

While Happy is feeling much better now, my coughing pangs have grown more frequent, running into several minutes, wilder than ever before. Since I do not have a fever, Ms Ela said that I needn't be checked for the virus, but she, too, was shaken by the barking sound of my struggle for breath. She started a round of antibiotics soon after, and said that the medicines will not work if I did not stop crying. She thinks tears are optional.

As Sameer sifted through the channels, I noticed that most of them were reporting on Saleha until a headline leapt out at us. 'Migrants turned Murderers,' it proclaimed. Two men stood outside a police station, with handcuffed wrists and faces garbed with black veils. Despite the purdah, I could tell that the criminals felt bare, as their necks hung low in a spectacle of shame. In the foreground, a police officer with three silver stars on his khaki shoulders was addressing a press conference:

'We've arrested these two men while they were trying to flee to Delhi after murdering a man from their village. The accused, both daily-wage migrant labourers in Mumbai, had returned to Rajasthan three days ago, walking and illegally hiring an ambulance with five other migrants. When they went to their village, the villagers refused to take them in, and sent them to quarantine in a facility outside the village. However, on their first night here, the men escaped the centre, filled the trenches around their village with mud, and visited their families.

'When the news reached the village council, they pelted stones at the seven men until they returned to the centre. The panchayat also announced a social boycott on their families, inscribing their homes with the words, 'Corona inside. Enter at your own risk.' This enraged the accused. Their families could not fetch water from the handpump any more, or leave home to buy groceries, medicines, or any other essentials. Within a day, most of their kin had run out of food and water. This fuelled the migrants' rage.

'The morning after the men barged into the village, a member of the panchayat, the victim in this case, informed the police about the incident. Soon, officers reached the quarantine centre with healthcare professionals to test the men for Covid-19. The seven returnees resisted, and then attacked the officials. Our men left, returned with more staff, pinned the migrants' down, and collected their nasal swabs. Thereafter, five of the seven workers stayed in the facility without creating trouble, but these two accused went rogue.

'The duo sneaked into the village that night, gagged the thirty-three-year-old who had called the police and dragged him outside his house, beating him with sticks and blows. The victim's wife and children tried to push the assailants away, but these migrants were like men possessed. They kept thrashing the man until he lost consciousness and stopped fighting back. Villagers witnessed the assault, but they did not intervene, as they were afraid of contracting the virus if they touched the migrants, both suspected coronavirus carriers. Even after the accused fled, the villagers did not help the victim, as the workers had touched him. When the police reached the spot, the victim had lost a lot of blood and succumbed in a hospital soon after. We've sent his body for an autopsy. Further investigation is in progress.'

As soon as the officer concluded his speech, journalists, who stood surrounding him, raised their hands with queries, leading to a question-and-answer round that went thus:

Q. *The motive does not sound convincing, sir. Why were the accused so angry?*

A. *They had had an arduous journey home, and they'd also lost a friend to dehydration on the road. They were angry before they reached the village.*

Q. *Have their Covid-19 reports arrived?*

A. *Yes, they've tested negative.*

Q. *Sources inform that the men were quarantined in a public urinal. Is that right?*

A. *No. They were put up in a facility near the toilet.*

Q. *We have pictures of them living in the toilet.*

A. *They got drunk and sneaked into the toilet.*

Q. *Why would they do that?*

A. *To drink their hooch in peace, I think.*

Q. *How did they acquire alcohol? Wine shops are shut during the lockdown.*

A. *We're investigating.*

Q. *We've heard that police officers beat the men up before collecting their nasal swabs. They also wrote, 'I have violated the lockdown. Stay away from me,' on their foreheads.*

A. *It's a rumour.*

Q. *It cannot be. A video has gone viral, showing an officer scribbling on one of the men's foreheads.*

A. *If that's true, necessary action will be initiated against the concerned officer.*

Q. *Are the accused habitual offenders?*

A. *No. This is their first offence.*

Q. *Don't you think this murder is a fallout of the punitive journey?*

A. *A murder is a murder, nothing else.*

Q. *Don't you think this crime is a result of the stigma that accompanies Covid-19 due to insufficient outreach in rural India?*

A. *A murder is a murder, nothing else.*

Q. *Please share the names of the accused.*

The cop answered, and Sameer and I looked at each other. We knew that name. After watching the officer's press briefing, we were even expecting that name, and yet, when he uttered it, the world dissolved and hell came alive. It was Om Uncle, our darling Candy Kaka, a murderer.

I am tired, Ms Farah. I'm tired of this endless journey, this unidimensional expedition like time, both inevitable and irreversible. I'm tired of the infinite nature of its finite roads. I'm tired of the patient sufferance and I'm tired of the fight. I'm tired of suffering fools, ma'am. I'm tired of the past, the present, and I'm already tired of the future. I'm tired of the memories I'm yet to make and I'm just tired of staying awake. I was a daughter and they took my father away. I was a student and I might never go to school again. I was a dreamer and they've shown me my place. Well done, world. Brava.

As I wait in this migrant camp, the phantom of hope dances before my eyes, singing songs of the sun, trying to lure me with its promise of light. Away with the fake fairies, I tell the ghost, shoo, shoo away. How do I indulge the moron? How do I hope in a world built with the fabric of night? How do I hope after watching the fear in my parents' eyes, after having my friend die? How do I hope when I've heard the cries, seen pleading hands being walked upon, and enduring feet broken with violence? How do I hope when I've been spurned by the foot of the world, when humanity itself is fettered, and when justice itself has surrendered? There is no room for hope, ma'am. No crack big enough for light.

Today, more than thirty hours after we reached the camp, we learnt from television news reports about the migrant workers whom the border police detained after the tear-gas shelling. We suspect that Baba and Proton Uncle were among them, but how do we confirm the premonition? Whom do we call? No one would tell us if they were beaten, if they bled, and if the bleeding ever stopped. Where do we go looking for them? The police station, the prison, the hospital, or the morgue?

Ever since I watched the news reports today, I've been putting words together, weaving arguments that would bring my father back to me. I cannot comprehend what to say. What do I say that hasn't been said before? What words do I engage? How much dignity do I throw at their feet that they haven't trampled upon before? Baba did not hurl those stones at the police. He did not vandalize their cars, hurl abuses, or wound their pride. Who would believe me, though? They run the world, not me. The justice, the liberty, the equality, the fraternity, the prosperity, the independence, the democracy—it's their inheritance, not mine. The sun that warms up their world, it burns my skin. The wind that tickles their bodies, it uproots my home. The rain that delights them with its earthy fragrance, it leaves me shivering. It's vanity, their obscene dance of freedom. It's bombast, their ugly boast of progress. It's a fraud, their greatness.

Everyone talks about human rights. They say such rights are inherent to all human beings, from birth until death, not granted by individual states, but protected by universal laws. These include the right to work in just and favourable conditions. The right to social protection. The right to an adequate standard of living. The right to physical and mental well-being. Also the right to equality before the law and protection from torture. They say dignity, fairness and respect are the values that form the basis of these rights, and you earn them the day you're born human. Then, Madam Journalist, why did we not inherit these rights? Why do they elude us even today? Must we undertake to prove we're human?

Must we prove that the men, women and children who toil in the heat, rain and sun, who build your homes, offices and schools, construct your cities, shrines and multiplexes, erect your hospitals and hotels, assemble your ships and bridges, unclog your drains and dispose your shit, who work as factory hands, loaders, painters, welders, barbers, carpenters, waiters, gem polishers, cobblers, sweepers, drivers and rickshaw pullers, who stand by the side of the road selling fruits, vegetables, newspapers and tea, who knock at your car windows at traffic signals, hawking flags, flowers and trinkets, who mop your homes and scrub your toilets, who bathe your children and walk them to school, who bathe your dogs and walk them to poop, who cook your meals and massage your feet, who polish your cars and tow them when stranded, who guard your buildings while you're asleep, who labour in furnaces, mines and kilns, who work with metals, chemicals, fire and rusted machines, who skin cattle and dispose animal carcasses, who often double as mules, while also living as sons and daughters, husbands and wives, and mothers and fathers, who are found in every nook of the country, as boatmen in Kanyakumari, as corpse-burners in Varanasi, as leather tanners in Kanpur, as light technicians on the film sets in Mumbai, who extend the pace and rhythm to all your cities, who also breathe, sense and feel, who also hope, dream and think—must I endeavour to prove that they're all human? I will not do that, ma'am.

Then what would the world have me argue? On what part of our lives or these homebound journeys do they need light? Must I argue that it's incorrect to rob workers of their wages, drive them out of their homes, and plunge them into the bladed hands of starvation? Must I argue that it's unjust to beat humans with lathis, fog their senses with gases, pack their children in airless containers, and leave them to suffocate and die? Must I argue that amid a global crisis, when billions have sought the refuge of their homes, indulging this human instinct is not a crime? Must I argue that no such seeker deserves to die? Or that no boy, no girl, no child deserves to be orphaned? Must I argue that these workers are as crucial to our nation's progress as its doctors, engineers, economists and scientists, and that none of these white-collared mavens would have a home or office if it weren't for the sweat of these workers? I will not make these arguments, ma'am. If I did, it would be an insult to you and us.

Since we embarked on this journey a week ago, I've been trying to understand the idea of home, what it means to me, and why humans are willing to lose all for a few walls. I peeked inside me for answers, but I found them in those around me, in their resolutions, and in their defeats. Home is where fear dies, ma'am, where solidarity dwells, and where love begets love. It's where your smiles remain honest, where you're mothered and you're nurtured, and where you cannot bear to see the ache of others. It's where the feelings of the mind are not blunted, and where interest does not draw a film across the eyes. It's where mercy does not veil her face, and no heart is dead to warmth. It's where all journeys begin and end, where we all belong, where we can leave and know that we shall still belong. It gives you wings to fly, the home, and room to fall flat. It's a winter hearth, the home, a summer stream. And if that is what home means, ma'am, I wonder if this country, this world, is my home. They could not be.

Meher

Afterword

In the early hours of 27 April 2020, five days after Meher wrote the last of her eleven letters to a journalist, she was still at the quarantine centre when she suffered a coughing spasm, lost consciousness, and never woke up. Doctors tested her body for Covid-19, and although she had been asymptomatic, she tested positive for the virus. Owing to the infection, medical officials could not conduct a post-mortem on her corpse, but concluded that her co-morbidity, an undetected lung condition, could have aggravated the impact of the pathogen and stole her life. Her body was buried in a mass grave dug for coronavirus-infected persons in Rajasthan, her home state.

Over a month after the first national lockdown in India, on 29 April 2020, the government sanctioned interstate movement of stranded migrant workers. Meher's mother and brother returned to their village thereafter. Her father, Gopal, and his friend, Jairaj, are still lodged in Gujarat's Modasa sub-jail, held as undertrials on charges of rioting. Gopal is unaware of his daughter's death. He is awaiting bail, and is eager to return to his family.

Meher's notebook, where she wrote her eleven letters, was buried with her. Her mother believes it's what she would have wanted.

Author's Note

17 May 2020

Surrounded by a sea of migrant workers like himself, Gaurav, whose name I've changed to prevent further persecution, stood in the blistering heat of Gujarat, awaiting a bus that the state had promised would take him home. The agonizing delay coalesced into anger, and the migrants clashed with the police, hurling abuses, brawling with on-duty officers, and vandalising public property. Gaurav could not be seen in the video that the police produced as evidence against him and dozens of other migrants. He even tried to escape the chaos, and yet, he found himself in a prison, crushed by the heavy hands of despotic bureaucrats.

'They stood us in queues, and beat us with plastic rods,' Gaurav told me. 'The migrants in the video, they met a much worse fate. The police poured sanitizers down some of their throats and administered electric shocks to their genitals. Despite the beatings and the torture, none of us received medical help.'

Gaurav lived in a Gujarat-based prison thereafter, looking at the sun and the moon that peeped in through the window of his barrack, praying for his innocence to be rewarded. He knew it was impossible. The cops had slapped him with a host of charges, including the attempt to murder policemen, and if convicted, he'd serve time for up to ten years, away from his wife and his soon-to-be-born child, paying for his desire to be with them amidst a global crisis.

In July 2020, nearly two months after his arrest, the Gujarat High Court granted bail to Gaurav and most other accused in the case. The court, apart from its own observations, was obeying a Supreme Court order, which had asked states to consider withdrawing the offences lodged against migrant labourers during the lockdown. The relief was nothing short of a miracle, the man told me. 'I walked out of that prison, elated that I was free, only to learn that I'd lost all,' said Gaurav. 'My pregnant wife, who did not know about my arrest, lost our child to her anxiety over my disappearance, while my mother now lived on the cot.'

Gaurav is one of the many migrant workers I interviewed during the course of my research for this book. Of course, not all of them were locked up in jails or awarded charges that would have them imprisoned for a decade, but each one of them had their stories, stories that illuminated their Homeric journeys, and ones that spotlighted their resilience, their courage, and their sobering hope.

Like most others, I first watched the jarring images of migrants walking home on television. Then, I started visiting the highways in and around Mumbai, witnessing the migrant exodus for myself, the colossal humanitarian crisis that had come to engulf us. Migrant workers, I saw, were fleeing the cities they built, trudging hundreds of kilometres to their rural homes, walking under the stars and the sun, in a trickle, in a flood, in the dead of the world.

'Are you comfortable walking, Dadi?' I asked an elderly woman, who leaned on a walking stick and did not look younger than ninety.

'Yes,' she answered without slowing her decisive steps. 'I only have to go four hundred kilometres.'

I watched the woman disappear into the horizon, and I wondered if she understood the magnitude of the task that lay ahead of her. There were no trains, cars or buses on her way home. There were endless roads on foot, livid authorities and dangers unknown. There was heat, fatigue and a fatal pathogen on the loose. Many had died on the road already; many others left for the dead. What made her think she'd be an exception? What made her believe she'd survive? I wondered and I looked around. Then, I saw her tenacity in each of those migrants on the highway, young and old, brawny and frail, healthy and ailing. Each of them appeared fearless, neither disappointed nor in mourning over their fate, just determined to find home, to survive.

The men and women on that road, they were among the 450 million internal migrants in India, humans who form the bulwark of our economy, while living in Dickensian tenements, mostly working as daily-wage labourers without safety gear, written contracts, job security, paid leaves, health care benefits, social security, or fair wages. Plunged into survival anxiety after the state announced the lockdown, these workers set out on foot for their villages. Half a million had fled the cities by the end of the first week, and according to urban geographers, as many as three crores by June 2020.

Their journeys were hardly easy, accompanied by death, an infallible species of evidence that kept testifying to their travails. An unofficial documentation, for instance, recorded 991 lockdown-related, non-Covid deaths until 30 July 2020, most of them migrants and their families. These included 209 deaths in accidents due to walking or during migration, forty-seven due to exhaustion, 224 due to starvation and financial distress, twelve due to police brutality or state violence, ninety-six deaths in Shramik trains, and forty-nine in quarantine centres. 991 or almost six times the casualties in the 26/11 Mumbai terror attacks, dead.

As weeks passed and the troubles of India's migrant workers persisted, even compounded, I began to believe that their exodus belonged to history, with the great journeys triggered by wars, conflicts and natural calamities. As a journalist, who has reported on India's informal economy and the workers who pillar it, I knew that their plight was to be blamed on the systemic, structural decay that has spanned decades. Exploited and abused since time immemorial, their mass departure had lent them sudden visibility in the national discourse, and now that their obscurity was beginning to dissolve, I wanted to seal their cold realities in ink, ensure that we never drown them into oblivion again. This book, thus, is my attempt at documenting their story. To forget them again would be treason.

Writing *Homebound* came with its challenges. As the author of two non-fiction books, my first instinct was to write a true account, relaying the journeys of a few migrant workers as they marched home. Considering the topicality, I had to write the book soon, and with the restrictions on public movement, I knew that wouldn't be possible. Being an independent journalist, I do not have a press card, and could not travel to villages to meet the characters of my story. The lockdown, thus, turned me to fiction, and filled with doubt, I embraced the risk of failure.

As I went about creating Meher's world, I realized that, as a writer, I can manage non-fiction, relying on facts for rescue. Fiction, however, challenged me. Fiction despises the creative censorship that walks in with truth, yet demands its reason. It compelled me to peep within, and it exposed parts of my being that I did not know existed. It turned my family and friends into raw material, and it made me feel vulnerable and free, dubious and determined, all at once.

As I rode this rollercoaster of ironies, I found myself struggling at every step—the plot, the structure, the conflicts, the characterisations, and the internal journeys of my characters. Then there was the expectation of literature, of language, of my own. All I felt sure about was the foundation, the facts behind the story I wanted to tell, and that's when I made a rule: Stay true to the narrative and to the humans who inspired it. No imagined atrocities, no made-up brutalities, no fictional victories, just what happened, just what *really* happened.

That rule, in turn, has dictated the architecture of this book. It's a fact that migrants were fogged with tear gas as they rushed towards their homes. They did endure lathis and the downpour of blows. They were drenched with chemicals. They did die on railway tracks. They did succumb to dehydration and exhaustion. They were locked up in prisons and airless, milk containers. They did give birth on highways. They were at the risk of getting raped by motorists who trailed them. They did swim through rivers, walked through forests, and burned in forest fires. They did pretend to be madmen, talking to themselves and flinging stones, so cops won't stop them. They were locked up inside warehouses without food and water. They were looking for edibles in garbage heaps. They did scoop up milk from overturned carriers. They did eat from a dead dog. Their foreheads were stamped with messages like, 'Stay away from me.' They did find trenches dug around villages, their homes that refused to shelter them. They were sent to quarantine in public toilets. They did turn into human mules, into uncivilized beasts, and one, into a murderer.

To understand my characters, these birds of passage, I knew I had to visit the villages they called home. Hence, in October 2020, I set out on a research trip, visiting villages in Maharashtra, Gujarat and Rajasthan, sauntering along the road that Meher and her family trudged, and interviewing migrants like her. I spoke to NGOs along the way, the families of these returnees, and villagers, who saw them as a threat. And the more migrants I spoke to, I realized that the long walk home was hardly a defining moment for them.

'Yes, I walked for about eight hundred kilometres,' a man from a village in southern Rajasthan told me. 'It was difficult. We did not have food, the cops beat us up a few times, but we got home eventually. It's like ... how do they say in films? Happy ending.'

I realized that this narrative was true for many migrants, who were not enraged that their cities had abandoned them, that their employers had robbed them of their wages, that their labour contractors had fled without notice, that they were beaten along their journeys home, and that no one had rushed to their rescue. Like the brick-kiln labourer in the book, their saga of resilience was not polluted with grief, despair, or self-pity. To them, walking home was just a part of the hand they'd been dealt, simply because they did not expect more. From fate, from god, from the government, from their cities, or any of us.

While many migrants seemed indifferent to the hardships they had endured, many others sobbed as they spoke, recounting those days and nights, their horrors, wondering if they'd ever be able to forget them. These were the angry ones, the ones who still seethed, still hoped, still expected, and the ones who still hadn't given up on the world. And from these men and women, Meher was born. Her outlook also sprung from the many girls I'd met in Mumbai's slums, girls as young as her, girls with the same dreams, same ambitions as her, despite their dilapidated homes. They speak better English than you and I do, these girls, and they walk the planet with fires within them. They destroy our classist views, these girls, and they make us wonder what builds them. I wanted Meher to be that girl too, to have their dreams and their vocabularies, their idealism and their courage to seek.

I created Meher with all the love I have in me, and I did not want her to die. I wanted her to live, flourish, become the journalist she wanted to become. But letting her live, I'm afraid, would have defied the cardinal rule I set for this book. It would have meant being dishonest to her story, and to the truth.

Puja Changoiwala
20 August 2021, Mumbai

Acknowledgements

Homebound would have been impossible without the many migrant workers, who shared their stories with me, and offered a generous peek into their lives. Although I've promised not to name them, I'd like to thank each one of them for their time, their patience, and their recollections, which weren't always easy.

I would also like to acknowledge the enormous help offered to me by NGOs, migration specialists and other experts, who introduced me to the various troubles the workers faced during their journeys, the nuances of their lives and their homes, and the structural issues that mar India's informal workforce. I would particularly like to thank Rajiv Khandelwal at the Aaajevika Bureau in Udaipur, Kriti Joshi and Gagan Sethi at Janvikas in Ahmedabad, Bharat Shah and his colleagues at Chhanyado in Surat, Shrey Parikh and Madhish Parikh at Elixir Foundation, Parashram Lohar in Salumbar, Menka Damor in Banswara, Dr Vipul Mudgal at Common Cause, Nandu

Menat at Jana Gana Mana Yana, activist Ramkrishna Mistry, and advocates Anand Yagnik and Pratik Rupala.

My sincerest gratitude to the residents of the villages I visited, who let me into their hamlets and their homes. Many thanks also to the journalists, who documented the exodus as it unfolded.

My gratitude to Anushree Sawalka, who helped me transcribe the days of interviews.

Countless thanks to my literary guide, David Godwin, for his tireless faith in this book, for believing in it even when I didn't, and for fighting for it.

Immense gratitude to Prerna Gill at HarperCollins for being the editor and friend she is, for rescuing me from my moments of doubt, and for keeping me sane through the publishing process.

Much love and gratitude to my family and friends. You're the wind beneath my wings.

About the Author

Puja Changoiwala is an award-winning journalist and author of two non-fiction books – *Gangster on the Run* and *The Front Page Murders*. As a journalist, she writes about the intersections of gender, crime, social justice, human rights and technology in India. Her work has been featured across news networks, publications and more, including BBC, CNN, *The Hindu*, the *Guardian*, *National Geographic* and Al Jazeera.

Previously a senior correspondent with *Hindustan Times*, Puja is a recipient of the International Centre for Journalists' Covid-19 Reporting Award, the Laadli Media Award for Gender Sensitivity, Red Ink Award for Excellence in Indian Journalism and the Iceland Writers Award among others.